Praise for The Belvedere Club

"Snappy and full of sass, Briana Kaleigh fields the punches in *The Belvedere Club*, the evocative debut by Nicola Trwst. A girl with attitude who you want on your side when it comes to murder. I loved it."

—*Cara Black, author of the Aimée Leduc Investigations, set in Paris.*

Advance Praise for Bolinas Bongo

"Nicola Trwst has created a quirky, fun character who thinks outside of the box when it comes to solving crimes:
Murderers beware.
We look forward to seeing more of this offbeat character."

—*J. J. & Bette Golden Lamb authors of the Gina Mazzio RN -- medical thriller series.*

"Briana Kaleigh, the audacious journalist and accidental sleuth from *The Belvedere Club* is back with a vengeance in *Bolinas Bongo*. The story zips through Marin County to its secret beaches in a wave of snappy dialogue, outrageous humor, and murder. I can't wait to see what kind of mayhem she'll be up to next."

—*Cynthia Greenberg, author of Burmese Jade.*

Also by Nicola Trwst
Bayou Nights (2013)

Briana Kaleigh Mysteries
The Belvedere Club (2012)
Bolinas Bongo (2013)

Bolinas Bongo
By
Nicola Trwst

NgH Press
San Francisco, CA

Many people are to thank for helping me bring *Bolinas Bongo* to press.

For sharing their professional knowledge:
Marin County Coroner: Kenneth Holmes
Marin County Sheriff's Department: Sergeant Crain & Sergeant Fruy
Kathleen Foote
D. P. Lyle, M.D.

For sharing their critiques, ideas, and patience:
Margaret Lucke, Bette and J.J. Lamb, Shelley Singer, Judith Yamamoto, Enrico Antiporda

My Editors:
Cynthia Greenberg, Debbie Blasco, Kim Richard

Many Thanks to you all.

CONTENTS

THE MOVE...1

THE SURFER 7

THE BEACH 13

THE BODY..24

THE CLIFF 29

THE FEDS...39

THE CALL...48

THE FILE...55

THE FRIEND 63

THE DROP...70

THE BRUNCH 75

THE CONNECTION..84

THE VOICE...91

THE DOG..96

THE REPORTS... 103

THE ROSE 111

THE WATCHMAN.. 119

THE CAR 126

THE BOX 133

THE BLUFF 140

THE CONFUSION.. 145

THE LIE 156

THE STORY.. 163

THE ESCAPE.. 169

THE HIDEOUT... 176

THE EDITOR.. 184

THE TOILET 190

THE GETAWAY 197

THE PRISON 204

THE HOTEL 214

THE RANCH 220

THE STALL 225

THE PRAYER 230

THE ARGUMENT 239

THE KISS 244

Bongo:

An African antelope with a reddish-brown coat, and the only type of antelope where both female and male have horns.

The Move

This cross-country move to California was supposed to be my epic second act in the tragedy called *My Life*, but this apartment looked more like a toxic wasteland than a promising new future.

The walls were pumpkin orange, the baseboards a dark yellow-brown. The forest green rug, once plush, was trampled as flat as a football field. A sofa covered in psychedelic fabric that had seen better days was pushed against the far wall. A blue and white print of a rowboat hung askew above it. White vertical blinds, at least they had been white about fifty years ago, covered a picture window that faced west.

"It's sorta dark," I said.

Dusty—my latest buddy and Marin County Sheriff's Detective—bounded to the window like a six-foot-two, two-hundred-pound five-year-old. "Look, Briana." He yanked the blinds open. "You'll get plenty of light in the afternoons. Come through here and look at the bedrooms."

I followed him to a corridor that split left and right. He went into the room at the right, I headed left. The empty bedroom was pale blue and smelled like cat piss.

Dusty pulled up behind me, excitement radiating off him in waves. "This is the guestroom. You can use it as an office or rent it out for some extra cash. Come see your bedroom."

The larger bedroom was also pale blue, a respite from the multicolored main room. A mattress/box spring set was shoved into one corner, the mattress stained and sunken in the middle.

Longfellow once wrote: *Into each life a little rain must fall.* My poor, pitiful life had been stuck under a deluge for far too long.

I'd quit my D.C. job at the *District Dispatch*, or maybe I was fired; through all the shouting it was unclear who had the upper hand, me or my ex-editor, Terrance. I sold all my earthly belongings: a Honda Civic, a Salvation Army sofa, a large-screen T.V., and an air mattress. And I flew across the U.S. to start over with the only friend I had left in the world.

Friend might be a strong definition for my relationship with Dusty. We'd met a little more than two months before when I'd wormed my way into his murder investigation of my best friend, Haylee's, death. That trip to California had just about been the end of me, emotionally and physically. I still had awful nightmares, and, from time to time, I heard Haylee's voice speaking to me. One of the reasons for this cross-country move was to remove the familiar from my sight and, hopefully from my hearing.

"Not bad for two thousand a month," Dusty said, rubbing his hands together. "It's a steal in Marin, believe me. The landlord is also throwing in the heating."

"How cold does it get?"

"It's June. In another month it'll be pretty cold."

Did that make sense?

I walked back into the main room and might have burst into tears except that I'd been raised with six brothers and learned pretty early on that tears from a female reduced most men to blithering idiots. Dusty didn't deserve that. Not yet.

I headed to the narrow kitchen. The linoleum floor was a green and grayish white checkerboard. "I thought you said it was furnished."

Dusty shoved past me to open a cabinet. The shelves were full of chipped plates and fogged glasses. "See! All your cooking needs."

What I saw was the fat cockroach, slinking across the stovetop. Two thousand a month, furnished, and heated had sounded too good to be true. Now I knew it was, but I was unemployed and my savings were meager. At the moment, I couldn't afford better, especially here. Marin County has the fifth largest income per capita in the country. It makes the middleclass neighborhood where I grew up in Boston look like a ghetto.

Dusty continued, unfazed by my lack of interest. "There's the sofa and the bed...you said you had sheets, and we'll get you a table and chairs from my friend Bob, who recycles."

He was so energized, so thrilled at his precious find that I couldn't break his heart by telling him that I'd have to be dead and four days buried before I'd lie on that bed.

Before leaving my East Coast life, I'd gone to Boston to say goodbye to the four of my six brothers who were still speaking to me and to visit my adopted family, the Macklins. The Macklins were Haylee's parents, and no matter how hard the visit was, I owed it to Haylee to look out for them.

"Yer know, they call dat place Sodom and Gomorrah," Mrs. Macklin had said in her heavy Irish brogue. "Waaat will yer do in de land of sin? They'll eat a grand lassy loike ye for breakfast."

Lassie? I was thirty-two.

"Detective Arkansas has some contacts in San Francisco. He'll help me get a few investigative stories written that, hopefully, I can sell freelance. Otherwise, I always have my camera."

Mrs. Macklin crossed herself with the sign of the Trinity. "De one with idols on 'is desk?"

"Buddha."

"That's waaat oi said, idols."

She, like I, had distrusted Detective Arkansas—Dusty—from the first meeting. The size of a bear, Dusty was a Buddhist monk in the making. He shaved his head before a full moon, chanted, did yoga, and kept Buddha statues all over his office. But the big fellow had a way of growing on a person. Okay, that's not really true. He'd grown on me, but most of his fellow officers considered him too weird for words.

Afraid of catching botulism or picking up some flesh-eating bacteria in the apartment, I walked back to my three large suitcases and flipped one on its side. I sat on top. "I'll need to install a cable connection for my computer."

Dusty dropped down on the sofa and the cushions on each side rose up around him. "All you need is wi-fi. The guy next door has a router and it's not password protected."

Did a sheriff's detective just tell me to steal bandwidth from my neighbor?

Dusty's cell phone chirped. He pulled it from his shirt pocket and looked at the faceplate. "I have to take it. I'm on call."

I stood and peered out the front window. My rent-a-wreck was the only car in the asphalt parking lot. A green Ford Focus with a cellulite-pocked body and a black hood. Rent-a-wreck was too kind. Rent-a-disaster. Rent-a-joke. But at ten dollars a day, the price was right.

"Fish and Game," Dusty said, shoving his cell back in his pocket. "There's been a shark attack out in Bolinas. I have to go."

"I'll go with you."

"You just arrived. Don't you want to settle in?"

I watched the sun-splashed dust particles rise from the sofa as Dusty stood. "I'm more interested in earning some cash," I said. "Maybe this is the story that'll introduce me to the local market."

He shrugged. "Suit yourself. It won't be pretty." He paused, running his eyes down my tan Tahari pants. "Besides, shark attacks are way too common. Sort of like jumpers. Neither story will draw much interest."

I figured his reluctance had something to do with my mini freak-out over Haylee's death. That was personal, this wasn't. I grabbed my camera bag. "Maybe I can sell it as a human interest piece."

He scrunched up his nose. "Do you, at least, have sandals or tennis shoes?" He asked, looking at my ankle boots. "Sand will be involved."

I dumped out one suitcase on the rug and grabbed my running shoes as Dusty hovered in the doorway. "I'll change in the car."

I locked the apartment and followed Dusty down the stairs and up the road to where his black Sentra was parked in Lowrie's parking lot. Since his divorce, he'd been living on a boat in Lowrie's Yacht Harbor. Another way to live within your means in Marin County.

After I switched shoes and we settled in for the drive across sunny San Rafael, I thought about the Golden Gate Bridge, which was farther south and majestically linked Marin County to San Francisco. Dusty's earlier remark about jumpers referred to the dozens of people each year who turn up from all over the country to fling themselves off the famous landmark. The jumpers hit the water at about seventy-five mph. Like hitting a cement sidewalk. Most died on impact. Not fun.

I'd lost my mother to childbirth, my baby girl to SIDS, and my best friend to a psychopath. No one knew better than I the weight of sorrow, but I'd never once considered suicide as a solution. For a while, I'd lost myself inside a bottle of Irish whiskey, which some considered a sideways attempt to end it all. I don't think I'm that complicated. If I'd wanted to off myself, I'd have offed myself.

No matter how bad things got (and some say I was comatose after I lost my daughter), there was always a pinprick of something, call it hope—but that seems too strong an emotion; call it faith—but I'm not sure what I believe anymore; or call it simply a wish. A minuscule golden nugget at the back of my mind that made me know I'd survive.

Just as my thoughts had crossed to the dark side, so had the sun. We were speeding down a narrow incline, driving through a thick gray cloud. "What's going on? I'm getting cold."

"Coastal fog," Dusty said, and reached across the console to switch on the heater. His windbreaker crackled. "Wait till next month when all this moves inland."

"That's why I'll need heat in July?"

He nodded. "Welcome to California."

The Surfer

The residential street dead-ended at the beachfront. In front of us the ocean disappeared into a wall of fog. We parked between an abandoned Fish and Game SUV and an ambulance where two men in matching jackets were loading an empty stretcher with equipment.

"We won't have to walk as far as I'd thought," Dusty said, nodding to a crowd near the water's edge. He got out of the car. He cupped his hands around his mouth like a megaphone. "Hang back until I see if it's okay for you to join in," he called over the roaring wind, blowing in from the ocean. "These F and G guys are usually pretty cool. Shouldn't be a problem, but we have to follow protocol."

He dropped his hands and went to the back of the ambulance. "Alive?" he yelled to the men.

"We haven't been down yet," the shorter man called back. "Tommy's taking a look. He's with the Fish and Game guys." At that moment the man's walky-talky squawked.

Dusty took off down the concrete steps and across the beach before I could ask if he had an extra coat in his trunk. My jacket was of the business suit variety with only three buttons. Shivering, I pulled up the collar around my neck and folded the lapels over my chest to cut the chill. I jogged to the steps and waited for his signal, the wind whipping my face. My hair was usually long enough not to fly, but that wasn't the case today. Strands kept finding a way into my mouth.

The fog amplified the sound of breaking waves. Close to shore, a Coast Guard boat bobbed on the waves rolling into the sandy beach. The two ambulance men started down the steps, the stretcher loaded with boxes and bags and towels.

"Hey, are you that actress," the shorter one asked. "The one that was in that movie, oh, what's it called?"

"No," I said. "Not even related."

"Told you," the taller guy said to his partner. "Now, move it."

If I had a dollar for every time someone asked me if I was Julianne Moore, I'd be richer than Bill Gates. Honestly, besides the hair color I didn't see the resemblance.

Behind me a second ambulance, siren wailing, raced down the street, too late for the party. I took out a cigarette. The trick would be to light it in this wind. I was trying to quit because it bothered Dusty, but who quits during a shark attack? I'd quit tomorrow.

I stepped to the opposite side of the ambulance and took out my lighter.

Off to the left of the emergency personnel, a small group of bystanders had gathered. Several had dogs in their arms or held close on leashes. One man held a metal detector. They were closer to the action and in a better place for me to await Dusty's signal. I started across the sand. Before I reached the dog walkers, Dusty's summons sliced through the wind.

I took one more drag and put out the cigarette in the sand. I shoved what was left into my pocket and jogged over to where all three ambulance guys were on their knees. A strange smell caught my attention, not the metallic scent of fresh blood, which I'd expected, but more an odor of rot.

The stretcher blocked my view of the injured surfer's body, all but his two thin legs, wet and sand covered.

"He's alive," Dusty said, pulling me away from the group. "Probably will lose the arm. It's a straight attack, one witness." He tossed his head in the direction of a man wrapped in a Coast Guard blanket. "You want to take some pictures for us?"

The three ambulance guys lifted the injured surfer onto the stretcher. I didn't see the injury, but clumps of red sand were everywhere. "Will I get paid?"

"I don't have a budget for that. It's either you or my cell phone. I figured yours would be more professional and you'd be eager to earn favor with the department."

Favor won't buy a new sofa. "Fine." I pulled out my Nikon and dropped the bag behind me on the sand.

"I warn you, it's pretty gross."

"Once I'm behind the lens, it's only shapes and colors." That was true; the lens gave me the distance I needed to look at anything, but eventually I'd see the photos in their entirety, probably when I downloaded them to my laptop.

"Make room," Dusty said to the others, and the all-male group broke apart.

Flies were already aiming for the flesh. The shark's bite had severed the bone below the elbow. A tourniquet was tied above the elbow, but the hand below was already looking dead.

Shoot, don't look, I reminded myself and raised the viewfinder to my eye. I shot from several different angles. I'd worked with enough police to know what they wanted.

"Done," I said to Dusty. "Anything else?"

"Yeah, over here." He pointed to what was left of the surfboard. The bite had taken a huge chunk off the board.

"Wow." I shot the picture.

"Might as well get one of the witness." He pulled me by the arm around behind the Fish and Game guys.

The man wrapped in the Coast Guard blanket lifted his head.

A surfer. A bonafide, California, sun-kissed surfer with wild sun-bleached curls and a spray of freckles across his nose and cheeks. "Oh, he's adorable."

Oops. Did I say that aloud?

From the smile that spread into the surfer's bloodshot eyes, I judged that I had. I raised the camera and framed those perfect teeth in the viewfinder. My heart was racing, I was having a hard time holding the camera steady. I zoomed in on his face and took a second shot. For my eyes only. Something to warm a lonely night.

"Great. Now, out of the way. Go stand over there with Mr. Adorable," Dusty said. Aloud.

The Fish and Game guys chuckled and gave me a smirk. But the surfer "dude"—I guess I could say "dude" since I was officially living in California—was still smiling and I wanted a piece of that.

Embarrassing myself was a moot point, so I walked up to him and said, "Hi."

"Hey."

"Sorry about your friend."

"He's a newbie. I've seen him a couple of times, but I don't really know him."

The V of his exposed, hairless chest was pebbled with goose bumps. I should have walked off then, because I couldn't see torturing him further with inane conversation just so I could look at his chiseled features and dream about what might be. "What's your name?"

"TJ."

Short…and sweet enough to lick.

Dusty was helping the ambulance guys get the insulated blanket over the injury. From the raised voices, I gathered the wind was the problem. "TJ, could I write down your information in case there's a way for me to turn this into a news article?"

"Sure, we can go back to my place and I can put some clothes on," he said, and then, as if reading my lustful thoughts, "or take them off."

He'd just watched a guy get mauled by a shark and he was hitting on me?

Yes! I still had it.

Okay that was tactless, even for me, but the last man who'd shown me any interest had turned out to be married. I felt the need to soak up every second of this ego-inflating moment, Lord knew it wouldn't last. "My camera bag's over here." I picked up the bag and shook it free of sand before putting my camera back. I took out a pad and wrote TJ on a clean sheet. "Last name?"

"Taylor."

"Address?"

I wrote Taylor next to TJ and scribbled his address below. "Is that in this town?"

"Yeah. Down the street and to the left."

"What is this town?"

He cocked his head as if he hadn't gotten the joke.

"I just moved to California...like a few hours ago."

"Bolinas. It's a great place. Let me show you around."

Before I accepted his invitation, Dusty stopped beside us. "Ready to go?" He took my pad and read what I'd written, then he turned to TJ. "You're local?"

TJ nodded. He took a step back from Dusty.

"All year round?" Dusty asked.

"For another month. My mom's sick."

"I've read your statement," Dusty said. "I don't think I'll need anything else, except maybe a phone number."

TJ recited his number and Dusty wrote it on my pad. He tore the page off and handed the empty pad back to me. "Thanks," he said to TJ. "You can go. You must be freezing."

Dusty turned to me. "Let's go. I have to get an I.D., contact the family, and then write this mess up."

"You took my information."

"I'll give it back after I copy the number onto his statement."

The ambulance's siren screamed to life and the ambulance backed away from the curb and took off down the road. Everyone on the beach scattered. I looked at TJ. "Nice meeting you," was all I could think to say.

My spirits soared when his tanned features fell with a look of disappointment, but then they crash landed when he set off across the sand.

"See you around," he said out of the side of his mouth.

My chest deflated. I threw the strap of my camera bag over my shoulder and hustled after Dusty, my ride home.

The Beach

Dusty, complaining about the mountain of paperwork the attacked surfer had left him with, had dropped me at the apartment. He'd said I could stop by the department later and we could grab dinner at the shopping mall across the street. I'd pictured greasy, carb-laden foods and told him I'd rather settle in. It had been a long day since I was still on East Coast time.

But standing in the middle of the stinky apartment with all the windows open, I couldn't figure out what to do first. Mist, seeping in off the bay, swirled around the room, chilling me, but also invigorating me. I stared into the overturned suitcase at my feet. Shoes, sheets, towels, and a few winter sweaters littered the squished carpet. Among the clutter was a gold and silver framed photo of me and Haylee at our college graduation. I squatted and picked up the photo. I blew some white dust from the glass.

There wasn't a table or flat surface anywhere. I walked into the kitchen. The windowsill was too narrow, the stovetop too dangerous. The kitchen counter would have to do. I set the frame next to a stained coffeemaker that I planned to soak in bleach for a week.

We looked so young, so carefree, so ready to conquer the world.

God, I'd like a drink.

My eyelids stretched wide open. Where had that thought come from? But I knew. I also knew that inactivity wasn't an option. Not tonight. I ran to my other two suitcases and unzipped them. One was chock full of summer clothes. The other was a mishmash of toiletries, electronics, and memorabilia. I started with the clothes, pulling the folded stacks out and carrying them to the bedroom.

Inside the closet, I ran my hand over the shelf of raw, unpainted wood. It needed protective paper, which I didn't have. Carefully, I centered the first stack of pants and then went back to the main room for more. Between trips, my mind wandered to TJ and his golden skin. It was a pleasant image, one that relaxed me. I wondered what the surfer dude was doing?

"Surfer dude," I said aloud.

It sounded better aloud. It sounded oh, so, Californian. I was really here.

"Surfer dude." I figured I could say it a few more times before the fun wore off, but then what was I going to do?

My camera case was on the psychedelic sofa. I dug through it until I found the pad where I'd written all of TJ's information. When I opened it, I saw the ragged edge of the page that Dusty had torn off. Did I really want to call Dusty for TJ's phone number? His ridicule was already ringing in my ears, but that wasn't all that bothered me. It was too soon for him to learn how afraid I was of my own company. The last thing I wanted was for Dusty to see me as needy or desperate.

Hell, I wasn't desperate. I was in a strange, new land that smelled a lot like cat piss and a little like settled-in marijuana fumes. But I didn't want to be alone. Not tonight. I wanted company, frivolous company.

I tilted the pad to see if the writing had left indentations. A few. I glanced around at what was left on the carpet. I'd shipped a few boxes with writing tools, books and general stuff I didn't need right away or couldn't carry on an airplane. They were due to arrive in a few days.

I'd seen a pencil somewhere, but for the life of me couldn't remember where. If I ran the page over the kitchen floor, the dirt might show the impressions, but I might lose the texture of the paper. What else? Lipstick? Too heavy. Oh!

I dove for the shoebox with my cosmetics and fingernail polishes, banging my knees on the not-so-soft carpet. At the bottom corner, a black eyeliner pencil was hidden under brushes. The soft pigment wouldn't damage the paper. I scribbled lightly across the empty page and watched TJ's address and phone number appear like buried relics.

I found my cell phone and tapped in his number. His voice rose higher when he recognized who I was. My heart soared. This was the ego boost I needed.

"I'd like to drive back out and talk to you about the shark attack, if you aren't busy," I said. Actually, what I wanted with him was a bit more X-rated.

"Cool," he said.

"I'm new to the area. It may take me awhile to find Bolinas." I mentally slapped myself for not paying attention on the drive back. All I remembered was that I had gone over a mountain.

"You'll never find Bolinas. It's tucked away and there aren't any signs. Why don't I meet you in Stinson Beach? Lots of signs to Stinson and I'll ride with you back to Bolinas. There's an indie band tonight at Smiley's."

"Sounds good."

He rattled off directions to the Sand Dollar Restaurant in Stinson Beach and told me he'd be outside in one of the rocking chairs. After disconnecting, I went to my laptop and pulled up my own directions. I didn't have any printer paper yet so I printed the map on photographic paper. While it was printing, I took my shoebox of cosmetics to the bathroom and spruced myself up.

Luckily, I'd brought a few winter sweaters because if this afternoon was an indication, it was going to be cold. "Surfer dude," I said as I changed clothes.

* * *

TJ's directions were perfect. Despite the blinding fog, I found the restaurant as soon as I hit town. TJ was seated in one of the six rockers on the broad porch. He'd discarded the blanket (darn), but he looked almost as cute in a red fleece jacket that made the yellow of his curls pop.

"Sorry about the car, it's a temporary rental," I said as he ran his hand over the dull black hood.

"I love it. It has personality."

I scanned the dimpled metal, trying to see what he saw. Maybe the personality of an eighty-year-old stripper.

He climbed in the passenger side and I got back in, out of the cold.

"Continue north," he said, pointing up the road. "I'll let you know when we're close."

"What about your car?"

"I hitched in."

I pulled out onto the empty road. "How come there're no signs? Town too poor?"

"Oh, no. It's more nefarious than that."

TJ looked way too young to use a word like "nefarious."

"Since the sixties the town has been fighting an epic war against the Department of Transportation. The highway engineers put up signs and they disappear in the night."

"Why?"

"To keep out tourists. Tourists bring development and the locals are afraid some developer will turn the town into a weekend paradise. No one wants that."

"So they steal the road signs."

"My mom had one turned into a coffee table. Years ago each new sign was built with stronger and stronger material. Still, it would disappear. Once, the department painted *Bolinas* in white on the road and it got painted over later the same night by, what we call, the Bolinas Border Patrol."

"That's crazy."

"Back in the late eighties, the town actually voted three-to-one against putting up any signs. That kept the highway engineers away for awhile, but every now and then, a new sign appears in cheaper material to discourage the sign collectors."

"Like your mom."

"Yeah. We're getting close. Slow down. There." He pointed to a narrow road on the left.

I turned off Highway 1 and a short way down stopped at the stop sign. "Will you be giving away town secrets if you tell me left or right?"

"Probably." He grinned. "But go left all the way into town. We can grab a bite at the café, and then go listen to the music at Smiley's."

Smiley's, a white clapboard building that looked like something out of a Wild West movie, was on the left. I found parking almost in front. I guessed the locals walked to town.

We headed across the street to a rustic-looking café. A small lamp over the door lit the rough wooden exterior. As I went through the door I expected to see cowboys. Instead, the smell of fresh baked bread greeted us and I felt my hips expanding with each breath.

TJ lead me to a table by the windows. We were two of seven diners. An older couple at the back and three men seated next to the wall. No cowboys.

"Food's good here. Get what you want, it's on me."

A date. I hoped my smile wasn't too goofy.

I picked up the paper menu and read through a list of comfort foods like mac and cheese and fully loaded nachos. In the hopes that I might end up naked later, I flipped to the salad section.

We gave the young waitress our order and TJ surprised me by asking for a Coke. If I'd just watched a guy's arm turned into chum, I think I'd be ordering something harder. A lot harder. I figured he was a few years younger than I was, twenty-seven or eight, but I hoped not younger than that. I thought about asking, but decided I didn't really want to know. I didn't want anything to mar my "surfer dude" fantasy.

"Do you like living here?" I asked. "It seems so remote."

"It beats some of the places I've lived."

"Like where?"

"Houston. My dad moved there and I lived with him for a while. Surf's better here. So's the company." He nodded to the waitress as she placed our food. Her long sun-streaked hair was pulled back in an elastic band. A sweet smile passed through her large brown eyes.

I picked up my fork and flipped around the lettuce of my Caesar Salad. His nod to the pretty waitress had been full of secret words, full of a language not spoken. If he was going to hit on her, I was out of here.

I ate in silence for awhile. When the silence became uncomfortable, I thought about asking what he did, but he was a surfer and surfers didn't really work, did they? "How long have you been surfing?"

"Since I was a kid."

"Is it dangerous? I mean, you hear a lot about these shark attacks. Doesn't that frighten you?" It frightened me. I'd seen that guy's arm when I'd downloaded and forwarded the images to Dusty. I put my fork down. Suddenly, this afternoon was more real than it had been hours ago.

TJ pushed a lock of hair behind his ear. "Surfing is frightening. When you hear the roar of that wave coming at you and you know it can snap your neck or pull you under until your lungs explode, you learn respect. And yeah, every season a few attacks happen, but you learn to be safe. There're things you can do, like don't surf at dawn or dusk. After a storm is bad, too, but it's also one of the best times to get good swells. The guy today was off surfing alone, another no-no. He was paddling out when I saw his board shoot in the air. If he'd been closer to me and my buddy, we could have gotten him out of the ocean faster." TJ shook his head. "When we pulled him out of the surf, I think he'd fainted or something. There was blood everywhere."

He took his paper napkin from his lap and refolded it on the table. "You have a pen?"

I reached into my bag and handed him a Bic.

"I pulled another guy out a few years ago," he said, sketching an oblong circle that looked like a banana on the napkin. "See, most shark attacks are a case of mistaken identity. This is what a surfboard looks like from beneath the sea."

I looked at the drawing and imagined I was underwater looking upward.

TJ drew an arm off each side of the board. "Now, to a shark, these here looks like the fins of a dolphin or sea lion, when it's just some poor surfer paddling in the wrong place." He added a fin at the end of the circle and it looked like a dolphin. "The shark comes from underneath and takes a bite, thinking it's dinner."

I saw the case for mistaken identity and wondered if I could turn it into an article anyone would want to buy.

Probably not, unless the attacked surfer turned out to be someone important, such as a Silicon Valley whiz kid.

"If you're lucky," TJ continued, "the shark will bump your board first, testing the quality of the meat. Realizing the board isn't food, it might swim off, but at the very least, the bump alerts you and gives you time to move closer to shore."

"Have you ever come in contact with sharks while you were surfing?"

"Sure, we all do sooner or later. Are you going to finish that?" he asked, pointing to the rest of my salad.

His grilled cheese and fries were already gone. I shook my head. Too many flashbacks of the surfer's arm. I wondered if Dusty had an I.D. yet.

When TJ finished my salad, he waved the waitress back over. "Briana, this is my sister, BJ."

His sister! "Nice to meet you." TJ & BJ. Was his mother afraid she couldn't remember their names?

"Welcome to California," she said without a smile.

He'd told her about me. My spirits rose again.

"We good?" he asked her.

"Get out of here," she said, starting to stack our plates.

* * *

Outside, the night rumbled with the sound of the band's bass, drums, and vocals. A large American flag hung from Smiley's balcony.

"You'll like these guys," TJ said. "They're local. From up the street."

We crossed the road and I stopped in front of the entrance. I glanced around at the town. This afternoon I hadn't seen this area. "Where's the beach we were on earlier?"

He pointed back up the road. "If you take the first left, that's Brighton. It dead-ends at the beach." He pointed the opposite way. "This road dead-ends at the beach, too. Want to walk down there?"

Hmm. Tough decision. A loud, raucous bar where I'd have to fight the urge to drink or alone with a cutie on a dark beach?

"Sure."

As we walked, TJ talked about the different wave patterns of Bolinas's different beaches. I feigned interest, but didn't understand much of what he was saying. When we reached the end of the lamp-lined street, he slipped his hand in mine and helped me down to the sand. When we started walking into the dark fog, his warm hand stayed nestled in mine.

With limited vision, about ten feet total, I had the impression the sand stretched to infinity. The wind was gone and the air was oddly warmer than it had been this afternoon, or maybe my hormones were heating me from the inside. My heart was definitely beating faster.

TJ walked on and appeared to have a destination in mind. Off in the darkness, waves roared and broke against an unseen shore. After a while, TJ pointed out a small cove cut into the cliff face.

"Why don't we sit over there?" he said, already walking in that direction.

Tree branches, from the trees growing out of the cliff, crossed above us, sheltering the indented cove. TJ slumped to the sand and pulled me down beside him. A mound of burnt logs from an old fire pit were scattered at our feet.

"Are you cold?" he asked, moving closer to me.

So obvious, I tried not to laugh as his arm went around me.

"This is nice," I said, snuggling nearer to his muscular body.

"You're nice," he said.

When I turned to him, his lips were on mine so quickly that he must have been afraid I'd refuse. I pulled him closer and let my lips part. His mouth was warm; he tasted like the salty air. He relaxed against me, waiting to take as much as I'd give.

We stayed lip-locked long enough for my back to start aching from the awkward position. I inched away and lay back on the sand. My fingers dug into his soft fleece jacket and I pulled him down to me. As I did, a drop of something splashed the center of my forehead.

TJ repositioned himself, sliding up along beside me. Our lips were inches apart when another drop of something hit me square on the forehead. I glanced up into the tree branches above me. A pair of bulging human eyes looked back. Bulging not in a curious way, but in a dead way.

I screamed, shoved TJ off, and wiped my forehead all at the same time. I leaped up, screaming and pointing and wiping.

"Look! Look! Look!" I kept repeating, but TJ slumped in the sand, glowering as if I were a nutcase.

I hopped and shook my finger again at the lifeless face in the branches. This time TJ rolled his head over and looked up into the branches.

"Shit!" he yelled and scrambled to his feet. He kept wiping his hands on his jeans as if he'd touched the body or something. "Oh, man," he said. "Oh, man."

My hopping somehow became walking. Unable to get over the thought that dead body fluid had dripped on me, I jogged circles around TJ, who was oddly static. "Look at me," I said. "Check my forehead. Is there blood on it?" Blood was almost preferable to the bacteria-laden purge fluid.

"I don't see any. Did you see blood?" he asked, sounding almost curious. "Oh, man."

"Ahhhh." The absence of blood meant purge fluid. Uck. I looked at the fingers I'd used to wipe my forehead. I'd have to wash them with some kind of disinfectant. Maybe scouring powder and bleach. I squatted and ran them back and forth over the rough sand.

"What do we do? Who do we call here in Bolinas?" I asked, massaging a handful of sand through my fingertips.

"I dunno."

"Who did you call for the shark attack?"

"I didn't call anyone. People just started coming."

"Great."

I looked around for my handbag. It was still under the tree. Uck. Using my foot, I snagged the strap and pulled it across the sand.

I took out my cell and called Dusty.

The Body

Battery-powered arc lamps, the kind the night crews use for highway repair, lit the beach. The body had been removed from the tree branches and the Scientific Investigations Section (SIS) was going through the area leaf by leaf. Dusty had barely said two words to me other than to stick me and TJ in a deputy's custody. I hated not being part of the action.

TJ's tan was looking paler under the lamps. Two attacked bodies in one day were a bit much for him. He might be thinking Houston wasn't such a bad place after all.

"How are you doing?" I asked him.

"I'm ready to bolt. How much longer will we have to stay?"

"The deputy took our statements and he already has both our addresses. It shouldn't be too long. Want a cigarette?"

"No way."

The look of disgust stretched across his features told me I wasn't having one either.

Dusty had backed away from the cove and was looking up the cliff face. With the fog so thick, it was impossible to see the top. He probably thought the body came down from there. The facedown angle would suggest as much.

He spoke to another deputy and turned to walk in our direction.

"What are you doing out here?" he asked when he reached me.

I looked at TJ. "I came back to have dinner with TJ. You remember him? From this afternoon."

"Hey," TJ said.

Dusty's mouth screwed into a strange expression. He almost looked as if he was preparing to spit. He looked from me to TJ. "How old are you?" he asked TJ.

"Twenty-one."

Gulp.

So much for my secret rendezvous. Why was I so stupid about men? If I could have shrunk into antimatter, I would have. I was worse than pitiful, I was pitiable, and now Dusty knew. "It's getting late and I'm still on East Coast time," I said. "How much longer do we need to hang around?"

Dusty turned to the deputy guarding us. "You have their statements?"

The deputy nodded.

"I guess you can go. I'll want to talk with you both tomorrow after I've reviewed everything." Dusty turned to me. "Don't leave the state."

Funny.

"Great. I'll be at home," TJ said, then to me, "You coming?"

Was that an invitation?

I cut my glance to Dusty. His head was cocked, his eyes wide and kinda wild. "Ah…no. I'll catch you another time," I said.

TJ was already walking away. "Whatever," he said, the end of my surfer wet-dream carried in the tone of his voice.

Dusty turned and walked away also. I scurried after him.

"Not a shark attack, I gather."

"Nope."

"A fallen hiker?"

"With the back of his head bashed in and his genitals cut out, hmm, I'd say no, probably not."

"His…?"

"Everything."

"Ouch."

Dusty stopped. He shook a finger at me. "You're not part of this one. Go home. Or go to that kid's house, but get out of here. Now!"

"I thought he was older."

Dusty shook his head, but his jaw looked tight enough to pop out of joint.

I knew I should walk away, but I cowered instead. "I'm not sure I can find my way back to San Rafael in the dark. I hadn't expected to stay this late." Actually, I'd expected to return with the light of dawn to guide me.

Dusty brought his fingertips together as if he was about to pray. I'd seen him do this before, and the only thing he might be praying for was not to kill me. I kept my mouth shut; oddly, that was something that was harder for me to do when I needed someone's help than when I didn't.

Finally, he spoke. "You've been here less than twenty-four hours and I'm ready to put you on a plane back to Crazyville."

At that moment the same two ambulance guys broke through the fog, carrying the bagged body away on a stretcher. "I hate this job," the shorter one said. "We're supposed to be helping people, not bagging them."

"We're helping these nice policemen clear the beach," the taller one said. "Now shut up and walk faster. I want to get home before my wife does."

It was almost midnight; I wondered where his wife was, but I didn't wonder long. Dusty cut across the sand without another word. I ran after him.

At the bottom of the cliff, orange numbered markers dotted the sand inside the cove. One marker was next to a boarding pass stub that I recognized. It must have fallen out of my pocket while I was jumping around trying to scrub body juice from my forehead. I pointed it out to Dusty. "That might be mine."

"Step back!" he snapped before walking over to the marker. "This belongs to one of the witnesses," he said to the technician who was photographing and noting the markers.

He stood there for the longest time, looking from the overhanging tree, around the cove, and then back up at the branches. He looked straight up a couple of times, maybe looking for broken branches, but the fog was almost opaque.

"Send me the preliminaries," he said to the tech, and then he turned and walked away.

I followed. "I could sell this story. An article like this could get me back on a crime desk."

"Shut up," Dusty said and walked faster.

I sped up, too. "I mean, they cut off his…well, you know. How often does something like that happen in sleepy Marin?"

Dusty didn't answer.

"This might be the story that gets me noticed by the *Chronicle*."

We'd reached the steps that led to the road. Dusty stopped to give instructions to the deputy stationed there. When he was finished he turned to me. "Where's your car?"

"Parked in front of Smiley's."

Dusty stepped over to a sheriff's cruiser and said, "Get in."

Once we were inside the car, Dusty switched on what looked like a GPS map of the area. He followed some lines with his finger, then mumbled to himself.

"I want to drive to the top of the hill and take a look," he said. "Afterwards, I'll drop you at your car and you can follow me back." He didn't wait for me to reply, but started the car to let me know I didn't have a choice.

"How did you end up under the body?" Dusty asked, reversing the car too fast.

I gripped the armrest. "After dinner we decided to walk on the beach."

"That spot! Who chose it? You or him?"

"He did, I guess. Why?"

Dusty didn't answer so I was left to figure out what he was getting at on my own. It took a few minutes because it was so farfetched.

"Are you suspecting TJ?"

Dusty glanced my way as the car climb the steep hill, but he stayed silent.

"I saw his face," I said. "There's no way TJ knew the body was in the tree. He freaked. Screamed like a girl."

Dusty snickered.

"I mean it. Don't even go in that direction. He was as shocked as I was."

The Cliff

Still on East Coast time, I woke up at six a.m. to a room full of sunlight. I kicked the sleeping bag into a lump by the wall and wondered who I could find to haul those toxic mattresses away. Speaking of toxic, last night I'd showered—scrubbed and scrubbed the death from my skin—but I still felt the need to shower again and wash my hair, which was beginning to itch.

If I wanted to be a part of Dusty's investigation, I had some serious groveling to do. After we'd driven the road above the cliff, he'd little more than grunted when he'd dropped me at my car. You'd think he'd be pleased I found the body. Eventually, someone would, and wasn't it better sooner than later when there was more trace evidence to find?

What was his problem?

I picked up a pair of shoes and two books from the living room floor and moved them into the guest bedroom. Renting the room out for extra cash was looking more and more appealing. I stacked two of the three suitcases and slid them over to the sofa. A makeshift coffee table.

Pleased with my cleverness, I headed out to take on Dusty. By eight, I was seated on the pier by his boat. I'd finished my double latte and one of the three buttery croissants I'd bought for Dusty. If he didn't hurry, he was going to miss breakfast.

Inside, his phone rang twice. I'd heard words like "sure" and "weather" and other mumblings I couldn't make out.

30

He stepped out on deck. "What are you doing here?" he asked, a cell phone pressed to his ear. "Hold on," he said into the phone.

I held up the white paper bag and the cup of OJ. "Breakfast."

He shook his head. "You need a hobby." He turned his back to me and continued his call, while walking to the bow.

This was going to be harder than I'd thought. He was really mad. I wondered if his anger might be more about the TJ situation than the dead body hanging in the tree. A few months ago, there might have been a fleeting moment—less than a nanosecond—of attraction between us. But after hundreds of emails and several phone calls, there hadn't been so much as a whisper of that attraction. By the time I decided to move out here, I was sure that I'd imagined it.

Besides, Dusty was training to become a Buddhist monk. Did Buddhist monks even have sex? And he certainly wasn't my type. He was big and confident whereas I leaned more to scrawny and needy types, kind of like my brothers.

Oh. Was that a therapy moment?

"I have to go out to Bolinas," Dusty said, breaking into my thoughts. He was standing on deck right across the water from me. He wore a pair of tan khakis and a Hawaiian shirt that made his skin look tanner than it was. If not for those stupid sandals with the leather straps wrapped around his ankles, he might actually look presentable.

"Can I come?"

"Want to visit your boyfriend?"

"I came to California to get back on a crime desk. Dead man hanging in a tree." I threw my hands in the air, miming surprise. "Crime."

"Sorry. You crossed to the other side when you became a witness."

"Off the record then. I won't write anything that isn't public knowledge."

He paused as if weighing his options. "If you bring your camera, and no, you aren't getting paid." He started to go below deck, but looked over his shoulder. "Move…your …butt. The fogbank is on its way in and I don't have time to go by the department and grab a camera. If you're coming, we have to go while we can still see down the cliff face."

I tossed him the bag of croissants, set the OJ on the dock, and took off at breakneck speed to get my camera. I wouldn't have a second chance.

* * *

The road above the cliff was residential, narrow, and one-way to avoid head-on collisions. We parked several times and hiked through private yards, but always came up short of where the body had probably gone over. When the cliff side grew too narrow for houses, we parked yet again and walked through a copse of trees to where we could look down.

The fogbank hung like a curtain on the horizon, beautiful blue skies ahead of it. Seagulls flew over us and dove down, landing on the beach below. Other birds took flight when we stepped too near the trees where they nested.

I pointed to a cutout in the cliff wall below us and to our right. "That looks like the cove. See the scattered firewood?"

Dusty squatted and scanned the ground beneath us. "I think we're still due east of the drop site, but take a picture and watch where you walk."

He waited for me to get the shot. Then slowly, we hiked west through small trees and scrub until he motioned for me to stop.

"Look here, these branches are broken. We don't want to contaminate the scene until I get some techs out here." He pointed out the edge of the cliff and the broken bushes. "Can you take a shot of this?"

"Do you have time of death yet?"

"Coroner says forty-eight hours give or take. I doubt the drop was made during the day, so I'm thinking sometime Tuesday night. Here…" He slid his hand under my elbow to guide me. "Back out off to the left."

I stiffened at his touch, which felt way too familiar. I glanced downward, my hair falling around my face and hiding my awkwardness. A silent voice screamed inside my head for me to pull my arm away, but before I did, he dropped his hand and we were again walking side by side.

I took a deep breath, wondering where my weirdness had come from.

Dusty pulled out his cell phone and called for the Scientific Investigations Section. "It'll be about an hour before SIS can get here. We'll have to make sure no one comes this way," he said. "Let's head back to the car."

He drove the car up to a piece of road that dead-ended into the last house on the street. For about ten minutes we sat without saying a word. Dusty stared out the windshield at the cliff and I stared out the passenger window at the houses. No one drove by, no one walked by. As dead as a morgue.

The silence inside the car grew increasingly oppressive. I thought this might be a good time to apologize for my stupidity with TJ, but we were getting on so well maybe I should let it drop. The likelihood I'd ever see TJ again after that last memorable kiss was slim and to be honest, it probably bothered me more than Dusty.

"I think we should talk to the neighbors," I blurted without thinking.

"We need to wait for SIS."

"Because we might miss the killer if he strolls by?"

Dusty growled. "We can't let anyone mess up the drop site." He growled softer and a minute later he was out of the car. I followed.

"Off the record," he said, as we walked up the driveway of the first house across from the car.

The red brick, ranch-styled home was trimmed with wood painted yellow-gold. The grass was mowed short and flowers bloomed in all but two of the blocked off gardens that bordered the yard.

A tall, lanky white-haired man came out to greet us. He was dressed in black jeans and a burgundy pullover sweatshirt. A black bandana was tied at his throat. "What's going on down there?" he asked.

Dusty flashed his badge and introduced himself.

"We saw all the lights last night. Got us curious," the man said.

Dusty didn't say a word about the murder, but launched into his questions. "Did you see anyone parked up here Tuesday?"

The man shook his head. "Tuesday? What were we doing Tuesday? Oh! We were at the Giants game. Won tickets."

Dusty reached into his jacket and pulled out his notepad. "Was anyone else at home while you were gone?"

"No, just me and the wife here now. The kids are back East. Have a daughter studying art in Paris."

"You and your wife both went to the game?"

The man nodded. "Had a great time. Giants won."

"Who'd you win the tickets from?" I asked.

Dusty's gaze shifted to me and he gave me a slight nod. Or maybe I imagined it.

The man stiffened and tucked his chin. "Hum. Don't know. I assumed my wife had entered some silly contest. You want me to ask her?"

"Please," Dusty said and wrote something on his pad.

The man disappeared in the house while we waited in the driveway.

"Maybe someone sent them the tickets to get them out of the house for the evening," I said, killing time.

"Sherlock, your powers of deduction never cease to amaze me."

Ah, my Dusty was back.

The man returned with a tall, thin woman who was dressed in the same folksy style as her husband. A knee-length jean skirt with brown wool tights and a gray zipped up sweatshirt. Both tall, both white-haired, they made a handsome couple.

"My wife, Thelma," the man said.

Thelma didn't wait for introductions. "I don't know where the tickets came from. I thought Ed entered some silly contest."

Ed laughed. "And I thought you did."

"Do either of you remember entering any contest? Say at a service station or grocery store?" Dusty asked.

Both appeared to give it serious thought. Then both shook their heads at the same time.

Dusty made a note. "Would you have the envelope they came in or any paper that might have been in the envelope?"

Ed looked to Thelma. "I had the envelope with me at the game. Hold on, it may still be in my purse," she said before turning to rush up the concrete drive.

"Don't touch it," Dusty called after her.

He pulled out a pair of plastic gloves and started stretching them out.

Thelma returned with a black leather handbag that looked more like a backpack than a purse. She pulled the opening as wide as it would stretch and peered inside. "There it is." She offered the opening to Dusty. "The blue envelope."

Dusty slipped on a glove and reached in and pulled out the envelope. *Courtesy of Bank of the West* was stamped across the front next to Thelma and Ed's address.

"That's right," Ed said. "I remember now, they were from the bank."

"Is this your bank?" Dusty asked.

"Sure is," Ed said.

"I banked with them a while back," Dusty said. "This isn't their logo." He looked at me. "Bags are in a tackle box in the back seat."

I scurried down the driveway and out to the car. Inside a paper tube, three plastic bags were rolled together like a cigar. I grabbed the tube and ran back up the driveway.

"How about your neighbors?" Dusty said, dropping the envelope in a bag and sealing it closed. He snapped off the glove. "Did your neighbors win tickets?"

Ed squawked. "That guy," he said, pointing to the next house over. "He doesn't go anywhere. Might be dead for all I know."

Dusty's eyebrows rose and he peeked over the top of his sunglasses at the house next door. "Antisocial?"

"To put it mildly," Ed said.

"Now, be nice," Thelma said to her husband. "Plenty of folks come here to escape society, Officer. Nothing wrong with people keeping to themselves."

Dusty cracked a smile. Now, if I'd said that, he would have snapped my head off with some remark about antisocial behavior being the first marker of the criminally insane. Instead, he asked Thelma and Ed to stop by the Marin Sheriff's Department sometime in the next day or two and give a set of prints that they could match against the envelope.

We left Thelma and Ed behind and walked down the driveway.

Dusty stood in the road, looking both ways before checking his watch.

"Are we going to visit Mr. Psychopath?" I asked, nodding up the neighbor's narrow drive. The yard was thickly planted with bushes and tall trees. The house wasn't visible, but I had the uncomfortable feeling that we were being watched. I glanced over at Ed's house, but he and Thelma were gone.

Dusty shuffled around. "Thelma's right. A lot of these folks like their privacy. I hate to bother them."

"A dead guy. No *cojones*. Fake winning game tickets. Need I say more?"

Dusty looked up the road again. "Okay, but keep your mouth shut."

We had stepped about six feet into the neighbor's drive when we heard the distinct sound of a shotgun being cocked. Once you've heard that sound, you never forget it. The first time I'd heard it was during a bar fight in D.C. I still thank the ancient wooden booths for saving my life.

Dusty's hands went into the air. Mine followed.

"Marin Sheriff," Dusty said. "I have a few questions."

"No answers here. Turn yourselves around and skedaddle," came a voice from the other side of the juniper bush.

"I can do that," Dusty said, "but I'll have to come back with a few armed deputies to ask you what I need to ask. We may have to take you in if that shotgun isn't regulation or registered."

Shit. Was he trying to piss this guy off? My knees started to tremble. My hands were getting heavy.

"You win any Giants tickets?" Dusty asked.

No answer.

"You home Tuesday night?"

Still no answer.

"Okay," Dusty said, "we'll do it your way." He turned away from the house and lowered his hands. He took a few steps back down the drive before the man spoke.

"No, to the first. Yes, to the second."

Dusty stopped. "You see a car pull up here?"

"Didn't see anything. About eleven p.m. a car rolled up. Big trunk."

"Color? Make?" Dusty asked without turning back.

I felt like a hostage at a bank robbery, my hands in the air, my eyes flipping from the back of Dusty's head to the talking juniper bush.

"Heard it, didn't see it," said the bush. "Older model, big trunk. Heard the engine shut off, the trunk slam shut, and a few minutes later the engine restart."

"You weren't curious?" I asked since he'd sure been curious about us.

"None of my business."

"Have you ever *heard* that car up here before?" Dusty asked.

"Not that I remember. Lots of cars come up here at night."

I bet they did. Nice view, great make-out spot, except for Mr. Shotgun here. I wondered if TJ ever brought a girl up here on a warm night.

"How can you be sure the trunk was large?" Dusty asked.

The bush was silent. Maybe growing brain cells. Then it spoke.

"Cutlass Supreme. Maybe an '89."

"What color?"

"Told you, I didn't see it."

"How can you be that specific?"

"My third wife had one. I'd know the sound of that engine anywhere."

"We'll need your wife's current address."

"Dead. Two years ago in Tennessee. Wasn't the same car. Didn't have the rattle, just similar is all. Might be an older year, but I'm sure on the make."

Dusty had that faraway look. "Thanks," he said. "Hope I won't have to bother you again, but if I do, I suggest you hide the shotgun." Dusty started for the road, leaving me behind.

I looked at the bush. Smiled as broadly as I could without hurting myself, and started walking, my hands still above my head.

The Feds

The SIS team unloaded their van. Dusty showed the two techs the path he thought the killer took. I lit a cigarette and waited at the street as far from Mr. Shotgun's house as I could get without contaminating the crime scene.

When Dusty returned, his cell phone was pressed to his ear. "No kidding," he said. He pressed his lips together as if he didn't like what he was hearing.

I listened for a minute, but his conversation sounded as interesting as a dentist visit. I pulled out my cell phone to make my own call, then remembered Haylee was gone. It wasn't the first time. Lately, I'd think of telling her something, run through the conversation in my head before I remembered that I couldn't tell her. There was no one left to tell.

I looked up TJ's number, but that's as far as my thought process went. What would I say? As I put my cell phone back in my bag, Dusty ended his call.

"New development," he said and tilted his head to the car. "Put out the cancer stick and get in. I'll tell the techs we're leaving."

While I waited in the warm car, I took out my camera and thought about grabbing a shot of Mr. Shotgun's house, although the house wasn't visible through the thick growth of bushes and trees. On second thought, I didn't believe Dusty's car had bulletproof glass so I put the camera away. Nothing antisocial people like more than having their pictures taken.

"What's up?" I asked as Dusty dropped into the driver's seat.

"The fire department is sending someone up to keep people away while the tech guys work. As soon as he arrives, we can go."

Before he finished his sentence, a blue Ford truck pulled up and parked in front of us. A woman with short hair and broad shoulders got out.

"Guess he's a she," I said.

I glanced back at Mr. Shotgun's house and wondered if he was still in the juniper or if he'd moved to a higher elevation, like the yucca tree.

"Okay, we can go," Dusty said, slamming the car door shut. He started the engine and made a U-turn.

"My batteries are running low. Can we stop for a latte? I'll buy you a donut."

"Start with the donut jokes and I'll take the mountain road at ninety-five just to hear you scream."

"You'd kill us."

"I'll put on my siren."

My head was starting to throb from a lack of caffeine. If he was serious, I'd surely lose my breakfast croissant down the front of my shirt. I held up my first two fingers. "Peace."

He smirked.

I figured I had a fifty-fifty chance he wouldn't take the road fast. "Are you going to tell me about the new development or is it a three guesses kind of thing?"

"We have a ping on the database," he said. "A big one. Seems the powers that be have been in overdrive since early this morning with no one thinking to put me in the loop."

"Still lost."

Dusty shot me a look of irritation, but I didn't think his annoyance was with me. "This isn't the first case in

California where the victim lost his junk," he said. "In the last ten years, it's the third."

"A serial killer?"

Dusty grunted.

"Cooooool," I said, picturing my name in the byline. "Now you *must* let me work the case. This could pay my rent. I might even get a book deal. Don't worry, when I'm a famous author, I'll still remember that it was you who got me started on my path to greatness."

"The way things are already going today, it won't be my call."

* * *

Back at the Sheriff's Department, the conference room was buzzing with activity. The Sheriff, a tall wiry man of few words, was seated across the table from me and I handed him the crime scene photos as they came off the printer. A corkboard had been placed at the end of the table and Dusty and another deputy were busy pinning the current evidence to it. The Sheriff knew of my previous input with the department, and from all appearances he was okay with it or I wouldn't be sitting here. Rumors were, he was a laid-back kind of guy. He had to be to let a Buddhist monk with a bad sense of style rise through the ranks despite grumblings from his colleagues.

Dusty had changed into a dark blue suit with a pale blue shirt and a yellow tie. The jacket flattered his broad shoulders, and his regrowth of hair, sprouts as I liked to call them, made him look quite handsome. This was a Dusty I'd never seen and if I didn't know him better, I might take a shine to the old boy.

Nah.

A man and woman came in. About the same height, five-seven, both were dressed in dark suits; both had dark short hair, the man's shorter than the woman's, but not much; both waited for the Sheriff to stand and introduce himself before they introduced themselves.

FBI. Special Agent Wagner—the man—and Special Agent Clark—the woman. There really were two. For a moment I thought I was seeing double.

Dusty introduced himself and then me. "Briana was one of two witnesses who found the body. She's worked with us in the past."

Special Agent Wagner glanced across the table to the evidence board then back at me. "If she's working this case, we're out of here."

Dusty's gaze dropped on me. He nodded to the door.

That was my cue to get out. Whether it was the fresh caffeine pulsing through my blood stream or my instant dislike of Agent Wagner, I wanted to say *no*, but I couldn't afford to piss off Dusty again. I wanted in on this case. It had revenue stamped all over it.

"Lieutenant," the Sheriff said to Dusty.

That was my second cue.

Dusty's shoulders went up and his voice went down. "Wait for me in my office."

Without a glance at either agent, I got up and left, gently closing the door behind me.

Dusty's office was at the other end of the hall. He'd left his computer on with Internet access for me to use. There was a cable snaking out of the wall that hooked to the Sheriff's Office's intranet. If I wanted, I figured I could connect the cable to the computer and get in. All I had to do was disarm the Internet and put up the firewall. The two actions had task icons on the desktop to make it easy. The hard part would be guessing Dusty's password. Since he didn't have a dog, he probably used his sister's name, Rocky. Buddha seemed too obvious, even for him.

An eight-inch bronze Buddha sat on the desktop's edge near the wall staring at me with ruby eyes. Several one- and two-inch Buddhas sat around the base. Some had smiling faces; others looked more somber. For a normal person, that should be enough Buddhas, but no, five other statues held court on different spots on the rectangular desktop.

Ignoring them all and with the desire to connect to the Sheriff's Office's intranet, I went to work on the Internet, Google searching dead men in trees.

Forty minutes later, my stimulation level dropped and I grew bored with the computer. I scavenged Dusty's desk drawers for something to occupy me. Nothing. Not even a Hershey bar. How could he live like this?

I glared at the big Buddha and cussed Wagner's name. "Don't look at me like that," I said to the statue. I opened the empty top drawer and swept all the little Buddhas into it. I slammed the drawer shut and cocked my eyebrow at the big Buddha.

I needed another coffee and a cigarette, not in that order. Okay, I was still wired. Maybe I should pull back on the caffeine. I opened the top drawer and took out the little Buddhas. I placed the smiling ones around the desktop and all the others with their disapproving expressions at the bottom of the big Buddha. Maybe he could make sense of them.

"Up," Dusty said, strutting into the office. He motioned me out of his seat with a wave of his fingers.

I scooted around the desk and dropped into the nearest chair, crossing my arms.

He dropped a light blue folder on his desk, then sat. When I reached for the folder, he flicked my hand away.

"Do the Feds know that many native tribes bury their dead in trees?"

Dusty propped his elbows on the desk and clasped his hands together.

"No?" I continued. "Maybe you need a research assistant. The Aborigines of Australia, the Sioux of the Southwest, and even indigenous tribes of British Columbia bury their dead in trees. Maybe the killer wasn't dropping the body off a cliff, but burying it in a tree."

"So our killer is a Canadian Indian?"

"You're messing with me, but my point is a little research goes a long way. Has the victim recently been to Illinois?" I asked. "I can tell by your expression no one has thought to ask that question."

"And it's important...why?"

"Testicle-eating fish."

Dusty threw his head back and howled with laughter.

I raised a finger. "The Pacu, originally from the Amazon and cousin to piranhas, have been fished from a lake in Illinois. Fishermen have spotted others in the same waters."

He chuckled. "Your research skills are proven but—"

"Wait! There's more."

With one hand on his stomach he waved me back. "No, please, no more. You're talking too fast. As it is, I'm only catching every third word. How much coffee did you have?"

"A triple espresso."

He whistled. "I thought you were getting a latte."

"A temporary lapse of judgment." I dropped my hand onto the folder. "Can I look at the photos? Get an idea of the other two crime scenes."

"It's all off the record," he said.

"Of course."

He glanced longingly at the folder as if trying to decide. Finally, he nodded his okay. I snatched up the folder and opened it. It was empty.

Dusty grinned, "got ya" splashed across his face. "What did you think?" he said. "You're a witness. If a good attorney knew how much you already know, he'd find grounds to have you discredited."

"You still have TJ. We saw the same thing."

"Ah yes, the surfer." As if he had a diagram, Dusty slid the small Buddhas into their previous spots on the desktop.

"Does the FBI have any ideas? Are they thinking it's a woman?"

Dusty reared back, his forehead furrowed. "Why a woman?"

"Makes more sense to me. Cutting off the tender parts…that's such a female thing to do."

"Actually, it's not. Look at the data. Women rarely mutilate." He leaned back. "The blunt force trauma would have required an extreme amount of upper body strength—"

"Have you ever played stickball?" I asked, knowing full well how much blunt force trauma I could inflict if I had the right tool, preferably a Louisville Slugger.

"Let me finish. That plus the dissection, plus the strength required to move the dead weight caused them to rule out the possibility of a female perp. Women don't generally move bodies."

"Move the body! Can you say *wheelbarrow*?" I leaned across the desk. "I'm five-seven, one-hundred and thirty-five, thirty-six… Don't lift your eyebrow at me! Okay, one-thirty-nine pounds. You don't think I could toss that guy over the cliff?"

"This perp didn't use a wheelbarrow to throw our victim over a cliff. I saw the ground. That body was dragged. I don't have his exact weight yet, but I find it hard to believe a woman did that. And if two people were involved, only one dumped the body."

"Is it possible there were two killers?"

Dusty went silent. He'd revealed more than he wanted.

"Of course, it's possible," I said. "As possible as a female perp."

Dusty pulled the intranet cable to his laptop and plugged it in. "But our only witness heard one car door open. Did the second person wait in the car? I don't think so. He or *she* would be too visible, especially on a private road."

I jumped up, not sure where I was going, but I needed to move. "What's our next step, finding a link between the victims?" I walked to the doorway and peered out.

From the pause alone, I knew I wasn't going to like what he had to say.

"Briana, you know you can't be anywhere near this case. One, you're a witness. You found the body. It would compromise the case. Two, the Feds have taken the lead on this one. It's not my decision. Three…" Dusty crossed his arms and huffed.

"What's three?"

He shook his head. "I'm tired. That's all I have for now, but give me an hour I'll come up with a three."

"Are you kidding me?" Now I crossed my arms and dropped back into the chair causing it to slide across the smooth floor. "I found the body. That's all my testimony will entail. Nothing I learn can change that."

"Hey, I'm sorry." He typed a few words on the keyboard. "I'll find you something else. Let me see what's going on."

Something else wouldn't be this big. It wouldn't get me noticed by the *Chronicle* and it certainly wouldn't get me a book deal. Okay, a book deal was a long shot in any case, but a serial killer who collects the jewels of his victims. Priceless.

"Deputy Thompson is working on a gang crime in San Rafael," Dusty said. He clicked the mouse button. "Looks interesting. You want to read the info?"

A woman in a floral dress and a fuchsia sweater walked in and handed Dusty some papers. "The autopsy on Dr. Grimes, sir."

Dusty started reading before the woman had left the office. I walked around and tried to read over his shoulder, but he grabbed up the empty folder and shoved the pages inside. "You heard what I said."

"But I know you didn't mean it."

"Sorry, Briana. This time I mean it. You'll compromise the case."

"How did you get an I.D. so quickly?"

"Briana."

"It's not going to compromise anything to tell me."

He huffed. "His wallet was on him. Now, I have to work. I've emailed you the gang info. Go home, read it, and if you want to talk with Thompson, I'll put you in contact."

The Call

Back home, I shoved and banged on the front window frame, trying to open it. I gritted my teeth and shoved again. Paint chips flaked off and drifted to the rug, but the frame didn't budge. "Damn Feds."

If Dusty thought I was going to go quietly, he was sorely mistaken. I wasn't putty in anybody's hands.

I might have tried more, but I heard the excited fiddle and banjo notes of *God Save Ireland* coming from my cell phone. Haylee's mom.

I thought she'd understood that I needed some time and distance. "Hello, Mrs. Macklin."

"Briana, me flower. We may 've a wee problem 'ere."

My shoulder tightened. I started to pace. "What's going on?"

"Fifi. Poor darlin' 'asn't taken a bite since yer left."

I laughed. Fifi was Haylee's high-strung poodle. The dog's dislike of me was a hundred-percent reciprocated. I'd once made a drunken promise to Haylee that if anything happened to her, I'd take care of her beloved Fifi. Did I mention that I'd been drunk?

"Briana!" Mrs. Macklin snapped. Her tone made me feel as if I should salute.

"Yes, ma'am."

"Oi can't just let de precious waste away."

Sure you can. "There must be another reason why the dog isn't eating. Have you changed brands or given her something she doesn't usually eat?" In my short time with the dog, I'd found she ate anything and lots of it.

"She misses yer. She lays by the door every day waitin' for yer ter return."

"She's probably waiting for Haylee to return."

"That's not goin' 'appen, is it?"

The tears in her voice unleashed my Pavlov's response. My eyes began to water. Mrs. Macklin had taken to Fifi as if she were her grandchild. I knew she didn't want to give the dog up. It was a piece of Haylee for her to hold to. "How are you?" I asked, wondering if there was another reason for the call.

"Can't complain. Keepin' busy wi' de twins."

The twins were the sons of Haylee's brother. They were born a few months before their Aunt Haylee's death. If it hadn't been for them, I doubt Mrs. Macklin would have survived her loss.

"Do the twins get along with Fifi?"

"Oh, they just love 'er. Lately, though, probably 'cause she's not eatin', she's gotten grumpy. Snarls when they pull 'er fur."

I stifled a laugh.

When I inherited Fifi, she came with a maintenance stipend, the four thousand dollars left in Haylee's bank account. Mrs. Macklin had insisted I take the money to help me get started in California even though she had wanted to keep Fifi. We'd argued over it. I felt she needed the money to take care of Fifi. She insisted she had enough money and that Haylee would want me to have the inheritance.

In the end, I'd relented, but never felt comfortable about it. I'd used the cash on first and last months' rent for the apartment. I cleared my throat. "What do you want me to do?"

"Oi want yer ter come 'ome."

"We talked about this."

"Well, den." She paused. "Oi only see wan solution if yer are dead-set on staying so bleedin' far away."

"I want to give California a try."

"Yer family is 'ere."

I assumed she included herself as my family, which she certainly was, more so than my blood brothers. "I need a new start. I thought you understood."

After a long pause and deep exhalations she said, "I'll 'ave ter fly Fifi out dare. Ye 'ave a place yet?"

I looked from the orange walls to the ochre baseboards. Home sweet home. "Yes, the address was in the email I sent you."

Her silence told me that she was still upset. "Why don't you give it another day or so? I know Fifi loves you. Everyone loves you."

"Gran, darlin'. Let's do dat, den. We'll give it another day or so."

After I disconnected, I felt like a nap. Life was too heavy to carry today. I needed an assignment, something to keep me busy. But mostly, I needed time to pass faster so I could start accepting the past.

I'd read over Thompson's gang case. It looked about as interesting as a traffic report.

Wondering if the apartment would ever stop stinking, I went to the kitchen and opened the rear window. Below and up the pier to the right, Dusty's boat sat, still locked up tight.

It was almost dinnertime and he was still at the office. Working. Would the Feds be there this late on a Friday? The first order of business was to link the three cases. A serial killer chooses his victims much like a lion stalks the weakest zebra in the herd. What linked these victims? What singled them out?

I had Dr. Grimes's name and felt pretty confident that a quick Internet search would give me all I needed to know about him since he was local. But I still needed to dig up information on the other two victims.

Before taking a deadly, drunken fall off an icy roof, my father, a Boston cop, would gather his buddies around our kitchen table and try to solve some of the most difficult cases of the Boston Police Department. These guys weren't always privy to all the evidence, but gathering what they could was part of the fun. Because this was a parlor game for most of them, I don't know how often they shared their findings or suspicions with the real detectives. My brother Garrett and I spent many hours at those gatherings as go-fers for whatever the men needed: beer, sandwiches, pen and paper. Garrett, who eventually joined the Boston PD, later told me that those cops helped solve a few cases for the detectives.

One thing I remember my father saying about serial killers was that they were a different animal. The only way to find one was to crawl inside his head and think the way the killer thought.

The FBI already knew this. No doubt they'd already drawn up a profile of a personality type that they thought they were looking for. It wouldn't hurt to have a look at that profile. The trick was getting it away from Dusty without his knowing.

* * *

My rental car sounded like a freight train as it rumbled up 101. I needed to trade it in on another wreck before I went deaf. The Sheriff's Office's parking lot was almost empty. Court had ended two hours before and the administration staff was long gone.

The deputy posted in the entrance phoned back to Dusty and he came to meet me.

"Hey dude," I said, "how about dinner?"

He tucked his chin. "What did you call me?"

"Ah, nothing." So much for that Californiaism. "My treat."

"As long as you don't ask me about the case."

"Oh, that makes it your treat."

He grinned. "Come on back while I get stuff together. He led me into the private offices and past the conference room where he'd been working. As we walked by, I caught a glimpse of the corkboard and the posted information. Considerably more than when I'd last seen it.

"Where do you want to go?" he asked when we reached his office. He picked up his black laptop case from a chair and dropped it on the desk.

Because of his Federal visitors, Dusty was still in formal attire. Otherwise, I'd find him in jeans and the laced leather sandals that really annoyed me. "Why don't you change first and then we can decide?"

His hand flew to the yellow tie knotted at his neck. He pulled it loose. "Good idea. My clothes are in the locker room."

I sat in front of his laptop. "Before you go, pull up Thompson's file. I want to read through it again. I have a few questions."

Dusty peered down at me and chuckled. "I haven't logged in anything on the new case if that's what you're up to."

"Love the trust. Just pull up Thompson's file."

"You're taking me for an idiot?" He shoved the laptop shut and unplugged the cables. "Out you go." He swatted with his hand. "Come on, you can wait for me in reception." He put the computer in its case and tucked it under his arm.

I huffed, but snatched up one of his business cards from a card holder on his desk.

I pretended to read it as we walked back down the corridor, then I turned to him. "Mexican would be good. How about that place you took me to on my last visit?"

"Sounds like a plan."

So that he couldn't see, I folded the business card in thirds.

When we reached the short hallway that led to the reception area, I scurried down it quickly so he wouldn't follow. A heavy wooden door cut off the public office from the private ones. I shoved the door open while Dusty waited in the corridor. He stood watching until the door shut so I couldn't sneak back in. I'd hoped he wouldn't, but I let the door fall closed between us while reaching around and shoving the folded card against the lock mechanism. The door closed on top of the card. I waved to Dusty through the small window in the middle of the door.

He flipped me a wave, then turned away and continued to the locker room.

One one-thousand, two one-thousand, three one-thousand... At ten, I was pretty sure Dusty wasn't coming back. I tugged back the door handle and slipped inside. I bent to retrieve the folded card, which had fallen to the floor.

Most of the offices were dark. The only two lit, near the conference room, were in the opposite direction.

I crept down the hall, slowing up as I approached the conference room. It was empty. *Yes.* I rushed to the corkboard. Sure enough, the profile was there, as well as all the victims' photos. I'd grown up with crime scene photos scattered around our kitchen. I'd seen the classic bullet between the eyes. I'd seen stab wounds. I'd seen missing body parts, but I'd never seen a hacked off pecker and I was thrilled that none of these images showed that particular dissection. It wasn't an image I wanted to memorize just as it wasn't an image Dusty wanted to look at while he worked the case.

Dusty's blue folder was on the conference table. The rest of the crime scene photos probably were in there.

When it came to images, I had a pretty good memory so I scoured each posted picture until I had its essence memorized. They were mostly dumpsites and possible evidence. I unpinned the profile and the victims' information. I scanned the board for any other pertinent info. The victims' addresses. I unpinned that, too. I turned to the folder and flipped through it quickly, ignoring the photos and snatching up all the forensic information. I took off down the hall for the photocopier.

The machine was a relic. It hummed and clicked and took almost five minutes to copy everything. I ran back to the conference room, pinned the victims' info and the profile, and jammed the forensic papers into the folder. I didn't have time to place them properly. Dusty would be back any second. I ran to the short hallway and pushed through the wooden door so fast that the deputy at the front desk turned to look. I dropped my head and shoved the copies into my camera bag.

I'd taken four steps toward a chair when I heard Dusty's voice behind me. "You ready?" he asked.

When I turned to greet him coming through the doorway, I was still out of breath. He noticed. The question crossed his features.

"I need a cigarette," I said as way of explanation.

"You're barely breathing now."

"Withdrawal. Let's go. I'll smoke one in the lot."

The File

Saturday morning cigarette smoke swirled around my head as I read over my copies of Dusty's case. But even after two cups of coffee I couldn't find any obvious detail that linked the three victims. If I could, then the FBI wouldn't need me. Oh wait, they didn't need me. Yet.

Information—such as where they shopped, worshipped, ate—had been furnished by the wives of the first two victims. I assumed Dusty was collecting this information today from wife number three. He'd said as much at dinner last night.

What I noted were the similarities. All three victims were men. All three worked in high-paying professions. And all were found with their wallets, at least one of which contained a substantial sum of cash. Robbery, ruled out.

Victim one: Victor Schuss, 51, CEO of Schuss Trucking. Resided with his wife and teenage son in Sacramento, California. Marriage good. Wife unemployed, but a previous employee of Schuss Trucking. Son was B+ student and played on school basketball team. Family attended Saint Marks Lutheran Church where Mr. Schuss was an Elder. Family annual net income $300,000.
Body was found in December 2006 in Old Sacramento. Dumped on the side of the road. Cause of death: asphyxiation. Genitals removed after death.

I stubbed out my cigarette in a small plate I'd found in the cabinets. I thought back to the photo of Mr. Schuss pinned farthest to the left on the crime board. It showed a man with a blue plastic bag tied over his head lying in some leaves. The hacked-out parts weren't visible.

Sacramento was north of Marin County and to the east. Interesting that victim two was down in southern California, far south of Marin County.

Victim two: Stan Henry, 52, corporate lawyer with Landano Systems. Resided with second wife of five years. Marriage good. Amicable divorce. Second wife unemployed. Mr. Henry had no church or club affiliations. Second wife belonged to Bel Air Garden Club. Family annual net income $1,200,000.
Body found March 2010 in Ventura County. Found behind Mobil Gas Station. Cause of death: blunt trauma to the back of the head. Genitals removed after death.

Less info on victim three, but eventually I would have access to more information because of proximity.

Victim three: Dr. Marshall Grimes, 47, heart surgeon. Resided in Ross.
Body found in June in Bolinas. Dumped over cliff, caught in tree. Cause of death: blunt force trauma to the back of the head. Genitals removed before death.

I would never need that photo; Thursday night, I'd mentally taken one myself. The interesting thing here was that the victim was mutilated before death. In serial killer language that meant the killer was escalating. He or *she* had tortured this last victim.

I couldn't stop thinking that the perp was a woman. Cutting off the joystick was personal. I'd thought about doing it to Conor, my ex, when I got my hands on him. Being Haylee's cousin, he'd shown up at her funeral. Nothing brings Irish families together more than an old-fashioned wake.

We'd talked. He was living in Texas. Said he wanted the divorce as much as I, but when the private detective that I'd hired to deliver the papers returned without a signature, I knew I'd been duped. I called his hotel and he'd already checked out. Another year I'd have to cover his ass on my taxes.

After all the time, money, and anxiety I'd wasted over the last year trying to get that signature, yeah, cutting something off seemed only fair.

I reread the forensic information. Victim one had been strangled while victims two and three died by blunt force trauma. It was believed that victim one and victim two's manhood had been removed with the same tool, which linked those murders. Would victim three be linked the same way? Victim three was linked to victim two by the method of death, blunt force trauma. Were they beaten with the same instrument?

How could I get the final forensic file on Dr. Grimes?

Sacramento. LA. And Marin County.

It was almost as if the killer was taking a tour of the Golden State. Could the killer be meeting these men in bars or clubs? They were all married. A woman scorned, and all that. Victim one was found on the side of the road. Dumped. No strength required. Victim two was found behind a service station. Some lifting and dragging required. Victim three…I'll never forget where he was found. All that lifting and dragging. Maybe the female perp was strong.

Okay. I was being sexist. My personal anger shouldn't enter into this case. I reached for the FBI's profile. Male. White. Between 30 and 40 years of age. Homosexual or latent sexuality. I continued reading. The profile made a good argument as to why this was the killer. From articles I'd written in D.C., I knew that these profiles were mostly right. In the information age, profiling had gained respect.

Okay. If the killer was a *man,* could he have met these men in bars or clubs? Absolutely. Maybe somewhere else if the victims were on the down-low. I knew nothing about the down-low lifestyle and realized I should educate myself.

I reread the information furnished by wives one and two. Nothing had been asked about homosexuality. Both said they had good marriages. An oxymoron.

I went to my laptop and read a few articles about living on the down-low. These men didn't consider themselves gay. Then, there was a long history of men marrying women only to come out as gay afterwards. Maybe that was the situation with my victims. One way to find out.

I did a reverse directory look-up for wife number one and up popped a Sacramento phone number. I called, but got an out-of-service message. Back to the computer. Traces are fairly easy to do if you know which services to use. I paid a yearly subscription to one that had earned me my money back two years in a row. A new phone number popped up that was issued only six years ago. I crossed my fingers and dialed.

Wife number one's voice was low and raspy. "I don't go by Schuss any more," she said without offering me her new name.

"This is Special Agent Clark," I said. "As you know, your husband's murder is still an open case and I've been reviewing the information you gave us. Perhaps you've already answered this, but it's not in the file."

"I told you everything I know."

"This is delicate, but I have to ask. Is it possible that your husband had homosexual interests?"

"Anything's possible," she said. "He was a sicko in every sense of the word."

The red lights were flashing. A siren screaming in my head. Lie. Lie. Liar. Over the years she'd forgotten that she told the agents she had a good marriage. Years always changed the facts. But to go from a good marriage to "a sicko."

Too many questions came to me at once, but I, or Agent Clark, had to tread lightly. I didn't want information about this call getting back to the FBI. "Is there any behavior that you recall that might hint at homosexual desires?"

"Like what?"

Oh, hell, I don't know. "I...ah...did your husband have a lot of homosexual friends?"

"He didn't have any friends."

Sociopath? He ran a company. Maybe he was just busy. Before I formulated my next question, the ex-Mrs. Schuss, or whatever she went by, cut me off.

"Listen, I have someone at the door. I gotta go."

"Okay then. Sorry to have bothered you," I said, but the line went dead.

Had she realized her error? Was that why she cut the call? Did it matter? The bigger question was why had she lied in the first place?

She'd been afraid. Of what? Of being a suspect? Of her husband's "sicko" secret being exposed? What was it that made him "a sicko"? Perversions?

A message popped up on my screen. An email from the private detective I'd hired months ago. I'd told him I wasn't paying the other half of his bill if he didn't get an address on my ex. I clicked it open.

He congratulated me on my instincts about Conor. He'd done exactly what I'd said he'd do. He'd driven from the wake in Boston to New York City and from there, flown to Texas. Of course, he had. You didn't live with a man day in and day out, have his child, lose his child, and not know his habits. He had little money so he'd chosen the least expensive way to avoid my tracking him.

I emailed back that I wanted an address, but even as I typed, wife number one's word "sicko" repeated in my mind.

Investigating victim one or two with my limited financial and physical resources would be a waste because of the distance and the lost years. Instead, since he'd practically been a neighbor, I needed to focus on victim three and find out all I could. Then, I'd use what I'd learned as a bargaining chip with Dusty to obtain info on the first two victims. He would be so impressed that he'd beg me to work the case.

I closed my email.

The wife, Mrs. Grimes. I should start with her, but Dusty was visiting her today and it wouldn't be cool to run into him while encroaching on his job.

Start with a Google search. I typed in victim number three's name, Dr. Marshall Grimes. His professional page came up on Linkedin. Nothing remarkable about his photo. Average looking. Steel-colored hair. Sharp jawline. Thin lips. I wouldn't recognize him in a crowd. He was the youngest of the three victims.

I found a couple of articles. He'd done at least one heart valve replacement. A few service reviews. All unremarkable. Average three out of five stars for personable, but he was a surgeon. They aren't known as the huggers of the medical profession. Five out of five stars for office cleanliness and promptness. Good for him.

His address was in Ross. From what little I knew about Marin County, I knew that Ross was one of the more upscale towns. Didn't victim number two live in a chi-chi neighborhood? Bel Air.

Using the map software, I searched for victim number two's address and clicked on satellite view. Wow. The house looked like a sultan's palace. Were those tennis courts? I did the same with Dr. Grimes's address. Smaller than victim number two's place, but bigger than a bowling alley.

Time for a daytrip. I walked to the kitchen window and checked to see if Dusty had returned to his boat. The exterior lock glinted in the sunlight. He might still be in Ross.

I walked back to the laptop and pulled up directions to the house in Ross. Still no printer paper.

* * *

I spent the afternoon buying badly needed items: juice, bread, tuna, laundry soap, bleach, paper, and printer ink. Afterwards, I drove to Ross. Third Street led me west. As I turned left into San Anselmo, a quaint town with lots of antique shops, my cell phone rang. I had to pull to the side of the road because it's illegal to drive and talk in California.

"Where do you think you're going?" Dusty asked.

I glanced around for his Sentra, but knew he often drove a sheriff's mobile when he went out on official business. I didn't see either. "I'm trying to find Office Depot. Where are you?"

"You passed the turn for Office Depot about six miles back."

"Oh."

"Yeah, six miles."

Neither one of us spoke for a minute or two. My mind raced, but I couldn't come up with anything that sounded plausible. "Guess I should turn around."

"Good idea."

"Later."

"Wait. My friend Bob is bringing over some furniture for you. How long you think you'll be at Office Depot?"

"I'll go another time."

"Thought so."

I turned the car around and headed back to the apartment. Halfway down what the locals call "Miracle Mile" I spotted a sheriff's cruiser parallel to me on a service road. It had to be Dusty. I passed him without glancing over.

Now, I'd have time to hide the Office Depot bags from my earlier shopping trip before he got to my place.

The Friend

Bob was shorter than Dusty with more girth. He had hair though, lots and lots of mousy brown waves. He entered the apartment and shook my hand until I thought it might drop off. "It's great to meet you. Dusty's told us, ah, me...told me so much about you." His smile stretched across his face, displaying a beautiful set of teeth. They were so straight and white, I wondered if they were false.

I glanced at Dusty, not sure what to ask first. Who was us? And what had he said?

"Come on, Bob," Dusty said. "Let's bring the table up."

Their footsteps rattled down the iron staircase. I looked around the apartment to see if I needed to move anything, but I had nothing to move. I'd set the printer up on the kitchen counter, and left space for my laptop beside it.

Again their footsteps vibrated the staircase, this time moving more slowly. The table must be giving them trouble. I stepped outside in time to see Dusty hoist the round mahogany tabletop over the last step. They set it down and huffed.

Bob wiped his forehead. "Heavy sucker," he said, "but she's a beaut."

"It is," I said, running my hand over the silky wood. "Where did you get it?"

"Left on the street. People do it all the time. They don't want something and they don't want to pay to haul it away so they put it on the sidewalk with a 'For Free' sign and make my day."

"How much do you want for it?" I asked, hoping it wasn't too much because I was already lusting for the sturdy, smooth top and the single pedestal with four thick masculine paws.

"It's yours."

"Mine?"

"I recycle."

"A little farther," Dusty said, ordering Bob back to work.

They grunted and hoisted and wiggled and shoved until the table was inside. They took another break before carrying it over by the kitchen.

Bob wiped his forehead again. "It probably had leaves that went in here." He pointed to a center seam. "Probably still in their attic or basement. I'll keep an eye out in case they find them one day and put them outside."

"I'll get the chair," Dusty said before rushing to the door.

"Sorry, I only have one," Bob said. "It doesn't exactly match."

"I'm happy for anything and everything. You wouldn't want a mattress/box spring set, would you?"

"People don't really recycle mattresses, but show them to me."

I led Bob into the bedroom.

"They're pretty gross," Bob said. "You should chuck 'em."

"Chuck what?" Dusty asked, filling out the doorway.

Bob pointed and scrunched his face as if to say, *tick, lice, and flea infested.* Okay, maybe those were my words, but his had to be similar.

"What's wrong with them?" Dusty asked.

"I haven't had my black plague vaccination," I said.

"Where are you sleeping?" Dusty asked.

I pointed to the balled-up sleeping bag in the corner.

"Dusty, help me carry them to the truck. I'll take them to the dump on my way home," Bob said, lifting the bottom of the mattress and sliding it forward.

Dusty grabbed the opposite end. "They're perfectly good. Add a mattress pad. Some sheets."

I grabbed my throat with both hands as if I were strangling myself, tongue fully extended and shook my head.

Dusty made a hissing sound, but they lifted the mattress and carried it out.

"They're perfectly good," Dusty said again out on the landing.

I hoisted the lighter box spring up on its side and dragged it across the carpet. Bob and Dusty met me at the front door.

While they carried the box spring down the steps, I checked out my new chair. The tall ladder-back style didn't match the table's clean lines. It wasn't mahogany but pine, painted blue; much of the paint was chipped off, giving it that antique class or maybe that just-been-pulled-from-a-dumpster panache. The seat was made of a woven grass that had seen its share of heavy butts. It sagged well below the frame that held the weave. Slowly, I tested my weight.

It creaked and cracked, but felt sturdy enough. I'd need to add a cushion because my rear was wider than the seat. I didn't sink down onto the weave, but remained painfully perched on the seat frame.

"What do you think?" Bob asked as he and Dusty came through the door.

It took a minute for me to realize he was talking about the chair. Well, the chipped blue paint blended nicely with the orange walls and psychedelic sofa. "Comfy," I said.

"I know. I'll try to find you a second one." He glanced at Dusty. "For when you have company."

"You need to find her another mattress," Dusty said.

"No," I said. "Some things you have to break in new."

"You're going to sleep on the floor until you have enough money for a bed? That's crazy. That mattress was perfectly good."

"If I earned some money writing a good article...say ...about a serial killer."

"Stop right now or I'm out of here."

"How about a beer?" Bob said. "Lifting's heavy work."

Dusty didn't wait for me to answer. "We'll grab a beer later," he said. "Briana hasn't had time to grocery shop. She's been too busy hooking up with surfers."

"I thought he was older!"

Dusty was obviously trying to help me save face in his obnoxious way. "One," I said, lifting my index finger. "I haven't seen surfer dude. Two." I lifted my second finger. "I have groceries—what do you think I did all day since I don't have an article to work on? Three." I stuck out my thumb. "Bob, what Dusty is avoiding saying is that I have a problem with the drink so I don't keep alcohol around."

"Do you care if we drink?" Bob asked.

"Not at all."

He turned to Dusty. "You have beer. Run down to the boat and bring us up a couple," he said.

Dusty glared at him and anyone else might have backed down, but Bob didn't seem to notice the silent lasers firing at him.

"You heard the man," I said. "He needs payment for his grunt work. I'll buy you a six-pack to replace what you drink."

Dusty looked at me, his face full of trouble, but then he started for the door. "I'll go grab the beer, you'll buy nothing. You can repay me by getting off my case about the serial killer." And he disappeared through the open doorway.

"Not going to happen," I called after him.

"Serial killer, sounds exciting," Bob said, slumping down on the sofa.

"I wouldn't know. Dusty's keeping me out of the loop. How do you two know each other?"

"Thursday Nights."

"What do you do Thursday nights?"

"A men's group. A group of…men. We call it Thursday Nights. Dusty joined right after his divorce."

That perked me up. "Oh?" He never talked about his divorce. I only knew that he'd had one. He talked about his growing up in a commune before his parents moved the family to Petaluma to raise chickens. He talked about his sister, Rocky—Rocky Arkansas. Almost as sick as naming a kid Dusty Arkansas. He talked about joining the police force because he was sick of watching people he loved be bullied, but he never mentioned his marriage and I had maybe five minutes to get the whole story. "Does Dusty talk about his marriage in this men's club?"

"Has to. It's one of the conditions."

"Conditions for what?"

"Maybe you've noticed, he has a problem with anger."

"I've noticed, but he handles it well enough, if keeping it bottled is handling it."

"He didn't always…handle it, I mean. He was suspended and the only way he could get back on duty was to join… Maybe I shouldn't talk about this."

"Well, tell me about his wife. Did you know her?"

"No. I met him when he joined the group."

"Right. You must know what went wrong in the marriage."

68

"She left him for another woman. He didn't take it too good. Plus, cops have this weird sense of humor. He got teased a lot."

During our investigation of Haylee's murder, I'd always thought his aversion to gays was strange for a practicing Buddhist. Now I understood that it was personal. "I'm assuming there's a psychologist or psychiatrist linked to this group?"

"Dr. Ford. He's just a psychologist. We're not crazy or anything."

"You seem like a sweetie. You don't have anger issues, do you?"

Dusty came through the door, a dark bottle of beer in each hand. He offered one to Bob. "Why'd it go quiet all of a sudden? What were you talking about?"

"Your men's group."

Dusty's head turned so fast to Bob, I thought I heard a snap. His jaw tightened, his knuckles grew white around the bottleneck. The famous Dusty anger in action.

Static crackled in the air. Who would speak first? Bob looked like he wanted to dig a hole in the sofa and crawl inside. He curled into a ball, his girth encompassing him like the shell of an armadillo.

"Did Bob tell you why he's in the group? Did you, Bob?"

Bob looked like he might cry. I couldn't let Dusty break him like this, not after his generosity.

"We didn't get into specifics. He said that you two met in a group called Thursday Nights," I said. "I'm a little surprised. You don't strike me as the group kind of guy. Is it a Buddhist gathering?"

"Bob's too chatty. We're not supposed to talk about the group. It's a rule. Isn't it, Bob?"

Bob rocked his head, the color returning to his face.

"How about I make you guys some stir-fry? It's the least I can do as payment for all your toting." I didn't wait for an answer, but hopped off the chair and rushed to the kitchen.

If there was going to be a murder, I didn't want to be a witness.

The Drop

The stir-fry didn't sit well with my stomach, or maybe my distress was learning what I already suspected about Dusty. He was a man too close to the edge. One good ignition, one bully too many and... Boom!

On the other hand, he was flawed like the rest of us. He and his Jesus sandals were flawed. Flawed was good. Flawed was character. I hoped Dr. Ford couldn't fix him.

I checked the clock on my phone. 2:26. The floor felt harder tonight. Maybe it was missing the mattress. I wasn't. The room already smelled less humid, but it wouldn't be minty fresh until I replaced the carpet. That was a plan so far in the future, cars would probably fly first.

I crawled out of the sleeping bag and walked to the living room without turning on a light. From his boat, Dusty had a full view of my apartment and could see if any of my rooms were lit. That felt invasive. He'd always know if I was up, or sleeping, or cooking, or working on the laptop, which I'd moved to the beautiful dining table.

But now, since I was hoping to drive out to Ross under the cover of night, his nearness felt particularly invasive. I looked out the front window to the parking lot below. My pitiful car sat alone. No one had dared to park near it. Why? Bad paint wasn't contagious.

Could I even find Ross in the dark? It would be difficult to read my printed map. I had a GPS function on my phone. Now seemed a good time to figure out how it worked.

* * *

Twenty-some minutes shy of four a.m. I reached the residential town of Ross. I passed through the center and a few turns later, the road began to climb. I drove by Dr. Grimes's mini-mansion and followed the road until it dead-ended at the Ross Cathedral. If Ross didn't have a cathedral, this was a mansion built to look like a gray stone cathedral complete with at least one tower. I turned around, passed, and then parked catty-corner from Dr. Grimes's place. Inching around in the seat, I had a clear view up the Grimes' drive and of the left side of the house. This wasn't true for other mini-mansions on the street, most of which were completely hidden behind high hedges or brick walls.

So...

I was Dr. Grimes. I've rewired some guy's cholesterol-clogged heart and I'm headed home. Do I drive up my paved drive into the garage, or do I park in front of the garage door and go in the house by the side door? The side door with the outside lamp that had just popped on as if its sensors picked up on my gaze.

I slid down in the seat. Had the door known I was watching it? Ridiculous. I needed sleep. I raised back up and turned around again. Someone was coming through the door. I slouched down, but was still able to watch as the person came down the drive toward my car.

Was it security?

The footsteps echoed in the stillness. The person passed my car. I peered up and over the dashboard, then pulled myself up. A woman dressed in a dark overcoat was walking down the road, hands in her pockets, hair blowing in the breeze. She wasn't wearing tennis shoes, so she wasn't going for a middle of the night jog.

What was Mrs. Grimes doing out walking at four a.m.? Was it Mrs. Grimes? Probably a neighbor sitting with Mrs.

Grimes until the poor widow could sleep. That made more sense. I wished I'd had the foresight to look up Mrs. Grimes on the laptop, but never in a million years would I have expected to run into someone leaving her house in the middle of the night.

The woman was almost at the end of the street and would be out of view once she turned the corner. I couldn't very well follow her on foot. Two separate women walking at this hour would look more than strange. And the car made so much noise I couldn't follow in it, either.

Quietly, I opened the door. With one foot on the ground, I started to slide out when the woman stopped a few yards past the corner. She stood in front of a public mailbox. I slipped back into the seat but stayed where I could watch. I pulled the door closed, but didn't allow it to click shut. Thanks to a lone streetlamp, I saw her fairly well. She looked my way, then looked to her left up the road. She opened the box and dropped a light-colored, letter-size envelope inside, closed the box, and started walking back my way.

I slipped down in the seat, farther and farther the closer she came. I was unable to see her, but her footsteps passed and turned up the paved driveway. I waited a minute before reaching up for one last look as she disappeared into the Grimes' house.

The light over the door went out.

I didn't see any other lights on in the house. What had she mailed? A letter? A bill? Maybe she couldn't sleep and was doing her bills. Did people still manually mail payments? I didn't. I paid everything online. Did people still mail letters? I didn't. I had email. The more I thought about it, the weirder my responses became. First, I needed to find out if that was Mrs. Grimes. Then, I had to find out if her mailing something in the middle of the night had any significance. How I'd do that was a mystery to me.

* * *

After a few hours sleep I was on the Internet browsing society pages with Mrs. Grimes in the foreground. Long reddish-brown hair, petite stature. She'd been the woman walking to the mailbox last night. No doubt in my mind. Even with my wily imagination, I came up with only two reasons why that might matter. The first was grief and loneliness. Her husband was murdered and she couldn't sleep for emotional reasons. The second possibility was that she knew the murderer and was afraid to close her eyes because that knowledge put her life at risk.

I doubted she would venture into the dead of night if she was afraid of being murdered so I mentally marked off the second reason.

What if she needed to pass on a communication that she didn't want traced? Emails could be traced. Phone calls could be traced. If so, was this communication related to her husband's murder? The spouse was always the first suspect.

Then again, neither of these reasons accounted for the other two murders unless it was a group coup where each wife killed the husband of the other. That sounded like a bad made-for-T.V. movie, but stranger things have happened.

Victim one had a bad marriage. I should find out what kind of marriage victim three had. I could ask Mrs. Grimes, but if she was involved she'd probably lie.

Neighbors.

Dusty's team had probably already questioned the neighbors, so I could be Miss Follow-up. How would I introduce myself? How would I get back to Ross without Dusty following me?

I went to my kitchen window and looked out. Dusty was on his deck, dressed in sweats and exercising. He was poised on the palms of both hands and the tips of his toes. He looked like a table I could set my Diet Pepsi on. As if he sensed me watching, he arched his butt in the air, settling on his feet. Now, he looked like an upside down "V." Even in sweatpants he had a decent-looking tush.

Last night, I'd left my car parked on the street when I'd returned. He might not hear it if I left while he was busy. I grabbed my camera bag, which had my notebook and wallet, and rushed out the door.

The Brunch

My car wouldn't start. The whirr of the starter, the rumble of the motor, then nothing. I tried again, pumping the gas. A roar…then silence. I tried once more as this time might prove I was wrong and this wreck really wasn't a hunk of junk.

No, I was right. I hopped out and kicked the door closed. I may have dented it, but with all the other dents, it was hard to tell.

I walked back to Dusty's boat. He was standing on his head, his hands cradling his skull. His face was the color of a rotten eggplant.

"My car won't start."

"What's wrong with it?"

"Va-rooooom and nothing."

"It's an old car."

"Your face is purple. Looks like it's about to explode."

Dusty brought his knees down first then righted himself. "Good for the skin," he said, standing and straightening his clothes. "Let's go look at your car."

He crossed the plank that led to where I was standing on the pier.

"It's up on the road."

He grunted as if to say something, but didn't. With the planks squeaking beneath us, we followed the pier to the harbor's entrance.

"I was hoping to talk with you before you took off for Ross," he said.

"Why would I go to Ross?"

His lips tightened. "That's how you want to play it?"

We climbed the concrete steps to the sidewalk. Cars loaded with bikes and surf boards whizzed by.

"I was going to do some shopping, but if you're planning on keeping tabs on everything I do, I need to look for another place to live."

His shoulders slumped and he held up a hand. "You're right. And I'm sorry. But I promised to help you find some articles to write and I feel bad the way it's gone so far. I know this case would generate income, maybe enough to pay your rent for a month or two."

"You're not including the runaway bestseller I was planning to write. You did *not* roll your eyes at me!"

"Listen, Briana, I can't let you compromise the investigation."

"If I do my own investigating, it won't compromise anything."

"But if you dig up something, sooner or later you'll have to share it with me or another agent, and that's when the case goes south, legally speaking."

I handed him my keys. He popped the hood and took a step back, waving at the air over the engine. "Whoa, one thing I know, it's flooded. Looks like you have a heavy foot."

"I gave it more gas to keep the engine turning, but it still died."

I watched him fiddle with a few things, his fingers turning blacker and blacker.

"Give her a try," he said. "Just turn the key, don't give her any gas."

I climbed inside and turned the key. Magic. It started, but if I headed out to Ross now I might get a guilt headache. I climbed out of the car and thanked him.

We stood there on the sidewalk, cars whooshing by. If we couldn't talk about the case, there was very little to say. Dusty glanced back over his shoulder.

"What did you want to talk to me about?" I asked.

"Oh, right. I wanted to take you to brunch. There's a place across the way," he said, nodding out toward the bay. "We can sit outside by the water. A formal welcome. We haven't really had time to welcome you, what with the shark attack and then the surfer…I mean, the case. You know. So what do you say? Brunch?"

"Ah, okay. Sure."

"Great. Let me change and we'll go on over."

We were silent as we walked back to his boat; the squeaking planks sounded ominous. Dusty disappeared inside the boat while I waited on the pier. I walked to the end and looked down into the stagnant water. It smelled of algae and seasickness.

After college, my first real job had been photographing regattas for the *Plymouth Review*. As much as I loved the wind in my face, I never learned to like sailing. The tossing motion of the deck below my feet caused a prickling sensation at the back of my neck. My mouth would go dry and my stomach would heave, and eventually, I'd pray for death.

Dusty called to me. He was standing lower than the pier.

When I reached his boat, I saw that he was standing in a small rubber dinghy with a motor at the back. He held his hand out to help me in.

"I'm not getting in that."

"Can't you swim?"

"Yes."

"So what's the problem?"

"I left my sea legs in Boston."

He held out his hand again. "You'll be fine. We're only going to the other side. It'll be less than three minutes."

I glanced out towards the inlet. I let my hand drift toward his, all the while wondering what could go wrong. "I have my camera. It can't get wet."

His hand wrapped mine with a sure grip. "It won't." He pulled me toward him. I stepped down into the dinghy, but faltered when it shifted below my feet. I fell into Dusty's chest. I gripped his arms.

"Hey, watch the fingernails."

He laughed, but not in an amused way, more in an uncomfortable way. As he pried me loose, our gazes met…and held. I know my expression was one of pure fear, but I can't tell what I saw in Dusty's. Maybe it was fear, too.

I released my grip and sat down fast, hitting my butt on the rounded edge of the dinghy. "Can I stay here?"

"You can, but we'll be better balanced if you scoot a little to your left."

I inched over, stopped when the dinghy bounced, and then scooted a bit more. "This okay?" The prickly little millipedes were climbing up my neck.

He hadn't moved. But then he did, lowering himself down next to the motor. "Hold your camera bag in your lap. I'll go slowly so I don't splash you."

Splash?

Every muscle in my body seized as the motor roared to life. We quickly moved away from the boats and out into the bay. I held my breath, but eventually had to inhale. I guess I wanted to be ready when we capsized. I took another breath.

Three minutes was an exaggeration, ten minutes worth. When we tied up at the foot of the restaurant, I allowed Dusty to pull me up on dock. He slipped his hand under my elbow and guided me up the stairs to the outdoor patio. When he'd done that a few days ago up on the Bolinas ridge, I'd found it invasive, but this time the security was comforting. He dropped his hand when the hostess approached us. "Arkansas," he said.

The hostess checked her clipboard and led us to a table at the water's edge.

When had he made the reservation? Before I'd agreed or after?

I glanced once through the menu and put it down. Eggs Benedict was my brunch staple. I wondered how long it would take before we'd speak about the case. I'd put money on eight minutes tops. Our limited stash of small talk should run its course by then.

Dusty put down his menu. He interlaced his fingers and propped his elbows on the table as if he were leaning in to say something. Then he stopped. He dropped his hands and picked up the menu again.

A black bird dive-bombed the side of the table, disappearing underneath. I peeked beneath the tablecloth, but the bird was gone. I leaned back into my chair, closing my eyes and letting the sunshine warm my face. A few tables away, a child with a high-pitched voice argued with her parents. She ordered something and then refused to eat it because she said it wasn't what she'd ordered.

Ah, summer. Eating outside. Sun-soaked skin. Iced tea.

Dusty dropped the menu again. I opened my eyes. He ran his hand over his head as if he were smoothing out his hair, if he had hair instead of the stubbly growth of a shaved scalp. He fingered the menu with one hand and started tugging on his ear with the other.

What was his problem?

When the waitress came, he stopped wiggling around. He ordered French toast with hash browns and an iced tea.

"You can have a real brunch drink, it won't bother me," I said.

Lots of people don't like to drink around me because of my past, but I hoped, by now, Dusty knew he didn't have to be polite.

"Like what? A mimosa?" He twirled his index finger.

"For example."

"No thanks."

"Have a manly whiskey. I'm sure they serve it."

"At eleven in the morning? I'm not much of a drinker. A beer with friends. That's about it."

Yet another window into Dusty Arkansas. His hand flew back over his head again.

"Okay, say it," I said. "You're fidgeting. I know you want to say something."

He looked over his shoulder as if I were speaking to someone else. "Nope. Nothing." He tugged at his ear.

A server brought us our tea and some bread and butter.

"Fine. Tell me what you have on the case so far," I said. "I'm not working it, but I can help you brainstorm. You know I'm good at that. Have you found a link between cases?"

"Briana."

"Any forensics on the weapon used?"

He glanced down at his hands. "What's the deal with you and the surfer?" His voice rose. "Are you seeing him?"

Where did that come from? He'd just blurted it out. And loudly. The couple at the next table turned to look at us.

I reached for my glass and drained it. "I need more iced tea."

"You're right. None of my business." His hand shot into the air. "We need more iced tea over here," he said loud enough to shake the foundations.

Now everyone was looking at us. I wished I could turn to butter and slide under the table.

An uncomfortable-looking server delivered our food while I sat very still.

"More iced tea," Dusty said, pointing to my glass.

"Right," the server said and took off.

Dusty reached for the ketchup. With his gaze locked on his hash browns, he pounded the bottom of the ketchup bottle "I took his statement, remember? He said you two were in the sand, getting into 'it.' His words."

That TJ had a big mouth. I shifted in my seat. "A surfer. A kiss. It was a mistake. Haven't you ever made a mistake?"

Lord knows, I'd made tons of them in my short lifetime, many having to do with the male of the species.

Still not looking at me, Dusty appeared to have pulled into himself. Something in my chest felt sharp as if I'd been pinched. I rubbed the area and exhaled.

A few minutes later Dusty softly said, "The Dalai Lama says that we have relative truth and absolute truth."

Huh? Maybe now was the moment to tell him about Mrs. Grimes walking to the mailbox in the middle of the night. Or I could slather egg yolk all over my muffin and keep quiet.

The yolk tasted salty.

"More tea?" asked a different server holding a silver pitcher.

I nodded.

"Has it ever occurred to anyone working the case to check out the wives?"

Dusty put his fork down and sighed. "Of course. The spouse is always the first suspect, but with the evidence we have, it's clear all three murders were executed by the same perp."

"What evidence?"

"Not sharing."

"Besides being filthy rich, what do all three men have in common?"

Dusty reared back, puffing his shoulders out. "How do you know they were all rich?"

I grinned. "You just told me." I lifted my tea. "Thanks. I looked up Dr. Grimes. I have a full profile on him. The rest was a guess."

The air wheezed out of him and he picked up his fork. He was about to crack. Resolve oozed off him.

"We can't find a thing," he said. "Not a conference, not a vacation, nothing where the three might have come in contact. Three different walks of life. No lovers. Nothing." He took a bite.

"No lovers. Statistically one of them should have been stepping out."

"You'd think. But if so, he was very good at it. I think it was three men with happy marriages."

Not so happy according to victim one's wife. But I couldn't share that phone call either. "What about the wives? Could they have met somewhere?"

"None of the wives worked. One volunteered three times a week. Didn't look like they ever traveled without their husbands, either. Hmm, I guess that's another thing in common. So do you have a theory, Sherlock?" He popped a cherry tomato in his mouth.

"Where was Mrs. Grimes while her husband was being murdered?"

Dusty tilted his head. He paused. "Waiting for him to arrive at a charity event. Lots of people saw her."

"Well, if you're sure it's one perp, I don't have a clue. I was thinking the three wives offed each other's husbands."

Dusty chuckled and reached for his glass. "Oh. You're serious?"

The Connection

Monday morning I did the dishes piling up in the sink. I washed out the ashtray and opened the window. Then I started cold-calling. I needed work, not only for income, but to keep busy. Idleness breeds thoughts and thoughts give birth to memories and memories whisk me off to a painful place where I start looking for an escape. A mind and body-numbing escape.

Easier to stay busy.

First, I phoned a friend who'd used me as a stringer on a couple of stories. He was a story broker. Great ideas, but unable to run them all down. I pitched the shark attack as a human interest story, but he shot it down before it was out of my mouth. Second, I called the *Chronicle* editor who'd bought my article about Haylee's murder. She'd liked my work and said to let her know when I was back in town.

"The only human interest pieces we run contain either an amazing person who's dying or a celebrity," she said. "If it's a celebrity dying, even better. What else do you have?"

"A short piece on gang violence in San Rafael."

"Too common."

A sad state of affairs. "How about a serial killer?" Oh, great, Miss Big Mouth. Here I had nothing to sell, but I'd let the proverbial cat out. Now, she'd sic her reporters on the story and I'd have competition being the first to press.

"A serial? You have my attention."

"Something I was working on back East."

"We're not keen on stories outside of California, but if it's intriguing enough, I'll listen."

Next, I called the *Marin Independent Journal*. Mentioning Dr. Grimes's murder got attention. The editor offered me a dollar amount for every angle I wrote from. I told him I'd be in touch. I could write about the link to the two other murders. That was something no other reporter currently knew. I had names and addresses, but if I released them, Dusty would know I'd snatched them from under his nose. I'd never, ever, never get another piece of information. At this rate I was going to have to write for the tabloids. *Man found with no penis. Alien spotted with love stick necklace.*

I drove out to Ross. The only story moving was the death of Dr. Grimes and since Dusty had decided to play by the rules, one way to find information was to jump into the investigation myself. Despite my quick save, the *Chronicle* editor had surely called her contact in the FBI and either got confirmation or was lied to. I prayed to the patron saint of journalists, Saint Francis de Sales, for the latter.

I parked across from the Grimes' house to start my canvassing. Many of the homes sat behind gated fences. This required buzzing a lot of intercoms, where I was ignored or told they didn't know Dr. Grimes. A few homes had open access that allowed me to use my earnest smile and my Puss-in-Boots' eyes, but to little avail.

The last house I tried was the size of a French castle. I knocked on the very solid walnut door.

The woman who answered looked to be in her late forties. She wore her bleached blond hair straight and to her shoulders and she was dressed in a designer skirt suit cut slim to show off her figure.

"Hello, I'm working with the Sheriff's Department, collecting information on your neighbors, Dr. and Mrs. Grimes."

"Which house is theirs?" she asked, peering over my shoulder.

I turned and pointed. "Across the street. Third down?"

"Drives a silver Lexus?"

Ah, there was something. Where was Dr. Grimes's car found? "I believe so," I lied. I wrote my first question on my notepad.

"That's it. That's all I know. He drives a silver Lexus."

I shuffled back to my car. Of the other six neighbors I'd spoken with, only one knew who the Grimeses were and he knew Dr. Grimes because of a medical procedure. Did these people have gates to keep people out or to keep the world on the other side?

Only one question to follow up on—where was Dr. Grimes's car?

I shoved the key into the ignition of my rent-a-wreck. At the same moment a water delivery truck turned onto the street. I pulled the key back out and waited. Delivery people saw things that others never noticed.

The truck pulled into the driveway of the second house on the street. A snowcapped mountain was painted on the side and large water droplets were painted to appear as if they were falling from the snow. A guy with long blond hair, wearing a light blue shirt and dark blue shorts came around the truck with a five-gallon water bottle held on his shoulder. He walked to the door and was quickly let inside. No one had answered that door when I'd rung that bell.

I wondered if Mrs. Grimes was on his delivery route. The driver came out swinging an empty water bottle. He drove to each of the next three homes, all of which were behind gates.

He parked at the curb and was immediately let through the gates. Only one of those homes had answered my ring.

I waited. Two more houses and he'd be near my car. He drove passed the next two houses and parked behind my car. I hopped out.

I waved. "Hi."

Surprised, he stopped, but said nothing.

Up close I saw he was too old to wear long hair, but he still had the muscles to lift that water. Probably an old surfer.

"I'm here asking about the Grimeses." I pointed across the street. "Anything you can tell me about the occupants of the house?"

He frowned, then rang the bell on the gate in front of us. A buzz and a click and the gate popped open. "No," he said and stepped inside, snapping the gate closed behind him.

Cheerful guy. I waited.

He returned with two empty bottles. "I don't talk about my clients," he said and shoved the empty bottles into a compartment. He climbed into the cab and took off down the street. He skipped the next two houses.

Clients. I went back to my car and waited until he'd reached the end of the road and circled back. He glanced my way before turning into the Grimes' drive. Because I was behind the truck I couldn't see him deliver the water, but suddenly he and Mrs. Grimes were at the back of the truck, looking down the drive at my car.

Tattletale.

I drove off.

* * *

I stopped in the town center of Ross. A cute block with storefronts and stylish restaurants on each side. I parked. With Mrs. Grimes already knowing of my presence, maybe it was time for me to talk to her. She might slam the door in my face or she might be willing to talk and let slip something of value. Anger was part of the grieving process and angry people had a tendency to say more than they meant to.

My stomach growled. I walked to a café with outdoor seating and sat at an empty table. My cell rang with the familiar tune that signaled Mrs. Macklin.

"Fifi still isn't eatin'. I've booked 'er a flight tomorrow mornin'. Can yer pick 'er up at de airport?"

Could my day get any worse? "San Francisco?"

"Oakland wus cheaper. She gets in 'round noon."

"And what if she won't eat once she's out here?"

"That's not going to be a problem. Call me, darlin', when she arrives."

I put the cell back in my bag. A silver Lexus passed and darn if it didn't look like Mrs. Grimes driving. I leaned around a post to watch the car parallel park farther down the road. Mrs. Grimes got out and ducked into one of the shops.

"Do you know what you want?" a waitress asked, stopping beside me.

"I've no leads and a high-strung poodle coming to live with me. What do you suggest?"

"The Caesar's good. Only seven dollars."

"Add an iced tea." I glanced back down the sidewalk. Mrs. Grimes hadn't come out.

Dusty took the apartment for me because the landlord allowed pets, but when I'd decided to leave Fifi behind I hadn't put down the five-hundred-dollar pet deposit. I didn't want to put it down now. What would happen to Fifi if I accidentally on purpose forgot to pick her up?

Haylee would probably haunt me from the great beyond.

Mrs. Grimes stepped out on the sidewalk. She put something in her handbag. Before I was out of my seat, she was in her car and driving off.

The waitress brought my salad. "Are you leaving?"

"Do you happen to know what that store is with the red siding?" I asked.

She stepped around the post and looked down the sidewalk. "I think that's the salon."

"Hair salon?"

"Think so."

* * *

When I finished lunch, I walked down to the hair salon. It was a cozy place with only four stations, three of which were in use.

"Excuse me," I said, addressing the woman behind the reception desk. "I just saw Mrs. Grimes. I love her highlights and was wondering who did them."

"That'd be Bev."

I assumed Bev was the one who turned to look at me like I was Chewbacca.

"Hi," I said, wondering if I was really going to spring for highlights just to have a chance to talk about Mrs. Grimes. "Do you have any openings?"

Bev was about a foot shorter than me and close to three-hundred pounds. Her bare ankle was bigger than my neck. She strutted over to the desk. Holding her comb like a lethal weapon, she grabbed a patch of my hair and lifted it at the roots. "This is gorgeous color, when did you last have it done?"

"It's natural."

She dropped the hair and looked at me as if she didn't believe me. "Then why mess with it?"

Cornered.

"I really like Mrs. Grimes's...uh, highlights."

She waved the comb in front of my face. "She's blond. You don't want to go blond, do you?"

Did I? "No," I squeaked.

"You don't have the same color. You don't have the same texture." Her free hand flew to her hip. She angled her head and pursed her lips. "Anything else we can help you with?"

The other hairdressers and their clients had gone silent. The only person not watching me was a lone woman under a hairdryer. She was flipping through a magazine. I glanced at a shelf lined with products. A bottle of shampoo had a price tag marked twenty-seven dollars. "Ah, not today."

Bev stayed by the desk, hand on hip. "Okay then."

A bell clanged over the door as I left. I turned to see Bev drop the comb and grab the telephone from the receptionist. Guess Mrs. Grimes was about to receive a call.

The Voice

Dusty hadn't returned by dinnertime. The smell of roasting fish carried through my open windows from the barbeques down by the dock. My stomach howled.

I opened the refrigerator. A bag of carrots was all that was left after the stir-fry I'd made Dusty and Bob. The thought of climbing back in that loud car made me cringe. My ears were still ringing from my drive home.

I grabbed the carrots and left the apartment. Maybe someone would offer to trade a piece of fish for carrots. Everyone needed their veggies.

Downstairs, I followed a foot-worn path around the building out to the patch of green that stretched along the pier. Holding my carrots in full view, I greeted several men roasting their dinners on small grills. No offers yet. I probably didn't look pitiful enough.

I ruffled my hair and sat on the foot-high concrete wall that separated the green space from the upper parking lot. The parking lot served several buildings of low-income housing apartments. A Spanish melody wafted down the hill.

Later, this area would fill with the homeless who begged food from the barbequers. Oh, wait, wasn't that what I was doing? I chomped off the end of a carrot. I was pathetic.

"Yes," came a voice to my right.

I turned to find a woman lowering herself next to me, long white hair draped over her shoulders. Her eyes an opalescent white. She wore a red sequined cardigan and green knit gloves with the fingertips cut off. A pale peach scarf, spotted

with gray grime, wound her neck several times, the ends
falling over her chest.

"Star! You surprised me."

This was Dusty's "psychic" friend. Homeless and
completely blind. It was a little early for her to be wandering
around out here and I was surprised that I hadn't smelt her
before she sat. We'd met once while Dusty and I were
working Haylee's murder. Psychic was beyond my pay-
grade, but Dusty had an unwavering belief in her ability.

"Would you like a carrot?" I held the bag next to her hand
so she'd feel it.

She snatched the bag from me and clawed out a carrot.
"He who laughs last, laughs best," she said.

"Do you ever speak in anything but clichés?"

Without another word, she lifted herself off the concrete
like a queen rising to knight a warrior. I watched her walk
away and realized she'd taken my dinner with her.

He who laughs last, laughs best.

She was probably chuckling her heart out. She'd pinched
my carrots. Now I had nothing to trade. I was reduced to
begging. I hated begging, although I was somewhat
proficient in the art. The grocery store was still open. Oh hell,
I had to buy dog food anyway.

* * *

Dusty still wasn't home by the time I went to bed, so
when my cell rang at midnight I was expecting to hear his
gruff voice. Instead, the voice was mechanical and deep.

"You're asking too many questions. Stop now."

"Why?" I asked, confused by sleep

"The doctor died. Some men deserve to die. Leave it alone
or you'll join him."

The line went dead before I could point out that I didn't have testicles or a penis, so technically I couldn't join Grimes, but maybe I was over thinking the message.

I switched on the light and leaned against the wall. I needed to buy a mattress. This sleeping on the floor was getting old, fast. I thought about the phone message. Grimes deserved to die. What did that mean?

I punched in Dusty's number. A groggy growl greeted me.

"You sleeping?" I asked, realizing I couldn't tell Dusty about the call without letting him know why I'd gotten the call. That would lead to an argument and neither of us wanted that.

"What do you think?"

"Yeah, me too. I just wanted to let you know that Fifi misses me. She's flying in tomorrow for a short visit that…well…might be permanent. I don't have the cash to put down the pet deposit, so if we could keep this our little secret until next month that would be…swell."

"No problem. I saw a case on the desk today that might need some local coverage. I'll look into it and let you know."

"Super. I do need work."

"What about working as a photographer until things pick up?"

A serial killer threatening me and he thought things would pick up! "Good idea. I'll check it out. Night."

"Night."

As soon as I clicked off the oddest thing happened. Star's cliché popped into my mind. *He who laughs last, laughs best.*

If Grimes's murder wasn't random, the cliché might fit. Oh, hell. This was why Dusty thought she was a psychic. She'd say something weird and he'd make it fit into the case he was working. Now, I was doing the same stupid thing.

Probably because I didn't want to face what was really frightening me: How did the caller get my cell number? And if he knew my number, did he know my address? I'd go with a big fat "yes."

I shuffled to the kitchen and made a pot of coffee. I looked down at Dusty's boat. All the lights were out and two lower portholes were open. I carried my mug to the living room and looked down into the parking lot. Nothing moved.

Why did Grimes deserve to die? I switched on the laptop. The Internet. Our greatest weapon against the right to privacy. For a little more than a buck anyone could do a phone search. I'd once found a service for Haylee that did reverse name/address searches. She used it on every article she wrote. Said it saved her hours of legwork.

Question: Did he have my name first or my address? Answer: It didn't matter because he had both now. I sat and searched Dr. Grimes's name again. I'd read a few things, but now I was looking for reviews, specifically someone who was unhappy with his surgery. I was sure the FBI had read all the reviews. Even I'd thought of them before, but had dismissed reading them because they didn't explain the deaths of the other two men. What did a trucking company executive have in common with a corporate lawyer and a heart surgeon?

If Grimes deserved to die, did that mean that the other two deserved to also? Maybe the lawyer was handling the trucking company's business and Dr. Grimes operated on one of its executives. Stupid supposition. If this was the case, there would be a connection between the three and Dusty said there wasn't. Surely the FBI had gone through all the phone records and finance records with a fine-tooth comb.

By two a.m. the words were swimming before my eyes. I hadn't found anything of interest and didn't think I would. I only hoped that the killer wasn't scanning my laptop and knew I was continuing my exploration.

I crawled into the cold sleeping bag. I didn't want to die in my sleep, but I was too tired to care.

Soon Fifi would be here. She had a bad habit of barking when someone came to the door. She'd saved my life like that once in the past. Having the loudmouth around was looking better.

I closed my eyes.

He who laughs last, laughs best.

Oh, shit.

The Dog

I pulled into the Oakland Airport parking lot about the time Fifi's plane was scheduled to land. A Delta employee directed me to Cargo, which involved a long trek across a hot tarmac to a building that looked like a revamped airplane hangar.

Inside, two female cargo handlers in navy blue coveralls were playing with my new companion. Fifi was a white miniature poodle about as big as a Boston sewer rat. She stopped playing when she spotted me, stood stiff as a drill sergeant. She gave a loud bark.

I crossed my arms. "Really?"

She'd been trimmed the way Haylee had liked it, pom-poms on all four legs and one at the end of her tail. Her nails were painted bright fuchsia. She barked again, then ran to me and tried to jump up my leg.

"If you want," I said to the two handlers. "I can leave her here to be your mascot."

The women laughed as if I were joking. I wasn't.

"You need to sign here," said one of the women, shoving a clipboard at me.

I signed, while the other woman put Fifi back in her pink plastic travel cage. I picked up the cage and headed out the door.

"Wait!" called the handler with the clipboard. "You forgot her stuff."

Her stuff was in a brown box bigger than her travel cage. I stacked it on the cage. How to carry both back to the car? I might have to leave the travel cage or the box behind.

Decisions, decisions.

"Would you like a caddy?" the handler asked.

The other woman rolled an empty luggage cart over and put the box on and then Fifi's travel cage on top.

Fifi stuck her nose in the air as if to tell me she was ready to go.

* * *

Back at the apartment, I unloaded the box and travel cage and let Fifi tour the parking lot before taking her upstairs. When we reached the cast-iron staircase, she pulled up short and wouldn't budge.

"I live upstairs." Despite what Haylee believed, I didn't think Fifi understood English so I pointed up with the hope that she knew sign language.

She tensed.

"I can't carry you and the box and the cage. What's it going to be?"

She didn't move despite my yanking the leash.

"Great." I put down my load and tied her leash around the rail. I lugged the box and cage to the top of the stairs and came back for Fifi. When I lifted her in my arms, she licked my chin. *Yuck.*

Inside the apartment, she skulked around, sniffing every corner and piece of furniture while I unpacked her box. I thought about Dr. Grimes as I carried Fifi's water bowl and food bowl to the kitchen. What made him a man who deserved to die? The obvious was that he'd killed someone on the operating table, but my Internet search hadn't found any such report. Not even a complaint.

I carried Fifi's furry bed and squeaky toys to the guestroom. After all, she was the guest. Hopefully, temporary.

Dr. Grimes's practice was in Marin. He also operated at Marin General so there was one other place to look.

I picked up Fifi. She did feel slimmer. I carried her to her room and put her down in her bed, a dark blue round cushion with four-inch high cushioned walls. "I have to go out and you can't go."

She barked.

I ignored her and went to the kitchen to fill her water bowl. I sprinkled a few dry nuggets in her food bowl. She was set.

Fifi was waiting for me at the front door. "You can't go. Dogs aren't allowed and it's too hot to leave you in the car."

She made a strange sort of whining noise. I squeezed by and out the door.

She started barking. And barking. I locked the door and headed down the staircase. Her barking followed me down into the parking lot. No one would know there was a dog in there, right?

I stomped up the iron stairs. As I approached the door the barking stopped.

I tiptoed back to the stairs. The barking began again.

I stood there, fists clenched around an imaginary neck, waiting for her to stop. Surely she couldn't go on forever. One minute, two. Murderous thoughts spun in my head. I rushed to the door and threw it open. "I can't stay. You're annoying. Shut up!"

She silently sat back on her haunches and looked up at me with her big brown eyes.

"I know that trick. I perfected that trick. You're here to eat. Now, go eat!" I closed the door. No sooner had the lock clicked than the barking began.

I threw open the door. "You're going to roast in the car." I grabbed her leash and picked her up. She licked my cheek.

* * *

There wasn't an ounce of shade available in the courthouse parking lot. I cracked all four windows open and told Fifi I'd be back. Clouds were moving in from the west and I wondered if a summer rain was on its way.

The car's ugly paint job stood out like a boil on the tip of a nose. No matter where you looked your eyes always found it. Since the Sheriff's Office was housed in the courthouse, Dusty would surely see the car if he happened into the lot. I'd have to come up with another lie as to why I was here.

The Records Management Office was on the second floor. The man behind the window looked tired. He slumped forward but didn't look up to hear my request.

"I'd like to do a criminal search."

"Fifteen dollars for each case number," he said as if he'd been saying the same phrase all day.

"I don't have a case number, only a name."

He shoved two forms through the window. "Fill this out. We don't take checks. There's an ATM down the hall." He rolled his chair away.

All I had was the good doctor's name so the first form was quickly done. The second page was the Freedom of Information Act request. This one was a little trickier since I may not be entitled to this information. I filled it out with my name and my ex-position at the *District Dispatch*. Who would check? I returned to the window with my cash. The clerk was busy working on a computer at the rear of the office. He looked up once, and then went back to what he was working on.

I waited.

After another few minutes, he headed over to the window and held out his hand. I held out the forms and the fifteen dollars. "How long will it be?"

He looked at the first form. "Just the name? I'll have it for you by three."

Two and a half hours was too long to hang out and wait. I was about to leave when I remembered something. The clerk was already strolling back to his computer so I had to lean into the window for him to hear me. "What about incident reports?"

"If they weren't filed, they aren't here."

I was afraid of that.

When police responded to a call, but no arrest was made, an incident report would be written up. These reports normally ended up in the local police department. Dr. Grimes operated out of Marin General Hospital, which was in Greenbrae. From last night's Internet search I knew that Greenbrae didn't have its own police department. That meant the Sheriff's Office had jurisdiction.

I strolled down the hall toward the Sheriff's Office. I scanned the administration section for Dusty, but luck was with me. He wasn't around. At the desk, I waited for the female officer who was explaining to a harried-looking woman where she had to go to post bail.

The woman kept insisting she had the money and the officer kept insisting she had to go to another office.

As I waited for the officer to give up and come help me, Special Agent Clark burst through the front doors, rushed past the desk, and pressed the buzzer to the offices. I watched until the heavy door that cut off the public and private offices closed behind her. She hadn't seen me.

"May I help you?" the female officer asked.

I'd been so keenly aware of Agent Clark that I missed the end of her other conversation. The bail-seeking woman was gone. "I need to do an incident search."

The officer reached under the desk and pulled out a form. "It's ten dollars. We don't take checks. There's an—"

"—ATM down the hall. I know. I just have a name so where do I put it?"

She pointed to an empty space a third of the way down the form. I filled in the name and handed her ten dollars. The last of my cash. "How long?"

"About an hour."

I turned to leave and the heavy door off to the side opened. I looked up expecting to see Agent Clark, but spotted Dusty coming through. He was looking straight at me as if he was expecting to see me.

"Looking for me?" he said as he came around the desk to join me.

I had the quick sense to nod.

"What's up?"

"Ah…oh, I picked up Fifi and she was restless so I brought her to visit you. She always liked you."

"She snarls any time I get near her."

"Come say hello. She's in the parking lot."

"I'm busy. Killer on the loose and all that. I'll stop in when I get off tonight."

"She'll be disappointed."

"Okay. I'll walk you out." He pushed open the door for me. "I read about that robbery case I was telling you about," he said, falling in beside me. "In Novato. A jewelry store, but what makes it interesting is that the store hadn't opened yet.

It had to be one of the contractors or someone else connected with the store. Maybe a scam for the insurance."

"Worth looking into," I said, thinking over the different angles I could write from. My mind drifted back to my original question. "Hey, how did you know I was in the office? I hadn't had time to ask for you."

"Agent Clark said she saw you in the waiting area."

She hadn't once looked in my direction. "Impressive."

"She can be. She's not actually as dull as she comes off." His expression took on a dreamy quality that felt like a punch in the nose.

I stopped. Dusty took a few more steps before realizing that he was walking alone.

My hands flew to my hips as I reared back. "How impressive is she? Does she have a line on the killer? Are you about to make an arrest?"

Does she have the killer calling her in the middle of the night?

"Whoa, chill," he said.

I dropped my hands and started for the car. "Well..." On some level, I knew how ridiculous my outburst sounded. I turned down the aisle where I'd parked. "If the case is coming to an end, I'd like to hear about it *before* it makes the five o'clock news!"

We reached my car and I opened the door. Fifi took one look at Dusty and started growling. When he reached to pet her, she snapped at his fingers.

Good dog.

The Reports

There were no criminal warrants filed against Dr. Marshall Grimes. No incident reports filed with the Sheriff's Department either. There was one last place to check and I had an hour and a half before the Ross Police Station closed to the public.

I drove to Ross, but had to pull over on Sir Francis Drake Boulevard. The GPS image on my phone showed the police station was right here. I looked up. Near the corner was the Fire Department, an adobe-looking structure with two over-sized garage doors for the fire engines. So where was the police station? Around back?

I glanced over the building again. At the far left, a handicap ramp led up to a glass door. On the door, Town of Ross Police and Fire was stenciled in black. I made a U-turn and pulled into the front lot, parking in one of the two parking spaces. The other one was designated for handicapped drivers. I put Fifi on her leash and we walked up the ramp. The door was locked. An intercom with a buzzer and a sign that said "Press for service" was mounted by the door handle. I pressed. After a long silence and then a clicking sound, the door popped open enough to release the latch.

Fifi and I stepped into a four-by-six waiting area. A wooden counter divided the waiting area from the administrative office. Two chairs were squeezed into the corner; one held a red donation bucket big enough to put Fifi in.

The counter was cut low enough in the center for wheelchair visitors, but was higher on the left and right side. The only way into the admin office from here was over the counter.

An officer in a blue uniform was standing over a copy machine by the back wall. The machine was spooling off copy after copy. He occasionally tapped the pages to keep them from overflowing the tray. When the machine went silent, he walked over to the counter. "What can I help you with?"

He was a good-looking man, tanned and fit and close to my age. I wondered if he surfed.

"I'd like to file a request for an incident report."

The officer disappeared into a part of the office cut off from view. A metal file cabinet rattled open and then closed. He walked back with a sheet of paper in his hand.

"That'll be ten dollars," he said, sliding the form across the high part of the counter. "Make your check out to the Town of Ross."

I thanked my lucky shamrocks because I'd forgotten to take out more cash. "Glad someone takes checks around here."

"Excuse me?"

I waved him off and pulled out my checkbook. I wrote out the check and filled in the form with Dr. Marshall Grimes's name. "Can I get this today?"

The officer looked at the form. He turned and looked at the empty office behind him. He faced me. "I'll see what I can do. Come back at 4:30."

I strolled outside with Fifi by my side. I started to walk toward the business center of the town, and then stopped, remembering my threatening phone call of the previous night. No need to announce that I was in town. Although I might just be here for a cup of coffee or to buy a bottle of that twenty-seven-dollar shampoo, but why tempt fate? There's an Irish saying that goes something like: Don't break your shin on a stool that's not in your way.

I loaded Fifi into the car and drove a mile north to San Anselmo. It should be safe to have a cup of coffee there. I found a café with outdoor seating and ordered a latte.

* * *

To my surprise, a domestic disturbance had been written up against Dr. Grimes back in 2003. Obviously, no charges were filed or they'd be found at the Records Office. So maybe Dr. Grimes wasn't a nice guy. Maybe the Mrs. took care of him herself, except Dusty had said Mrs. Grimes had been at a charity event with lots of witnesses.

My three-wives theory was looking more convincing. If only there was evidence linking the widows. Details. Always the details that ruin a good theory.

Well, now I had another question that needed answering. I drove back to the apartment, but Fifi had some exploring to do before she would even look at the stairs. We walked down to the dock and across the wide expanse of green.

She stopped and sniffed every rock, pine cone, and blade of grass as if one of them might contain a sweet treat.

Last night's caller had said, "Some men deserve to die."

Dr. Grimes knocked his wife around. Did victims one and two knock their wives around? There was a good chance victim one did. That could have explained his wife's remark about him being a sicko. Sacramento, where victim one had lived, was less than a three-hour drive northeast. I could drive up and request criminal reports and incident reports. Bel Air, where victim two had lived, was down in L.A. and that was a much longer drive. I didn't think my rent-a-wreck would make it there and back.

"We're done here," I said to the dog and started up the path to the apartment. Fifi took a stand, and the leash became taut.

"Do you want to eat today?"

That was all it took for her to trot on past me and up the path, stopping only when she reached the iron stairs.

"I'm going to have to take you to doggie cross-fit because I'm not picking you up every time we go up or down." I picked her up. She licked my chin.

I snapped my teeth at her.

Once inside, Fifi jumped onto the psychedelic sofa and struck a pose. I went straight to the laptop and found the website of the Sacramento Criminal Court Records office. But to request a Criminal Background Research I had to supply a couple of things I didn't have, such as Victor Schuss's date of birth and social security number. I was able to do a general index search for free and came up with a reference number for a white male named Victor Schuss.

How many Victor Schusses could there be in a county of…oh, let's see, one-point-four million people? I started to fill out the online form for the request when I realized I was going to have to shell out another twenty-five dollars and I had no idea how long I'd have to wait to get the information.

Phooey on that. I strolled to the kitchen and pulled my hidden copy of Dusty's file from under one of the cabinets. I found where I'd written the ex-Mrs. Schuss's phone number. I punched it into my cell phone.

"This is Special Agent Clark again," I said. "I spoke with you Saturday about your deceased husband, Victor."

"I have nothing else to tell you that I didn't tell you years ago."

"You never told us about the warrant you swore out against him," I lied, hoping I was right.

She was silent on the other end and I was starting to fear that she'd hang up.

"It was a long time ago. I don't remember the particulars," she said more softly.

"Tell me what happened. It probably means nothing now, but we have to research every detail."

"We'd been married a few years. Two, I think. We had a blowup and Victor hauled off and hit me, knocked me against the kitchen counter and broke a couple of my ribs. He was arrested, given probation, and it never happened again."

Her voice hoarsened when she said "it never happened again." She was probably lying, but I'd only found one reference number in the records search, which probably meant there was never another warrant served, so there hadn't been a second arrest. I thanked her and wished her well.

Unlike criminal reports, incident reports still had to be requested in person. I could drive up and check out how many incident reports were filed in the seven years between Victor's arrest and the date of his death, but I had my confirmation. On to victim two, Stan Henry.

I sat back down at the laptop. As I did, a strange whine filled my ears. I turned to the sofa, but Fifi was gone. I looked down at my feet; she wasn't there either.

"Fifi?"

Nothing. I started to think she'd passed into another dimension, perhaps sucked down into the psychedelic sofa print, when the whine came again. I walked to the kitchen and there she stood beside her empty food bowl, head up, muzzle forward.

"Oh, you thought I'd come in here to feed you." I checked my watch: 6:30. I was about to tell her it was time, when I realized it was a dog. She didn't actually understand me.

I picked up the bowl and carried it to the counter. I had no clue what was the right amount of food to put in, but I was sure that no matter how much I put in, she'd eat it all. If the human stomach was the size of my fist, her stomach must be the size of a knuckle.

I spooned in one tablespoon. Much larger than a knuckle, but it looked meager in the big metal bowl. Mrs. Macklin had said she wasn't eating. I didn't want to overwhelm her shrunken stomach.

I placed the bowl on the floor next to her water bowl. She looked at the food and back at me.

"You're on the anorexic plan."

She barked and I heard a slurping sound. I looked at the empty bowl. She barked again.

"Faster than the speed of light." I snatched up the bowl and added another tablespoon. This time Fifi didn't hesitate. She nose-dived the bowl as soon as it hit the floor.

Back at the laptop, I searched Bel Air in L.A. County. The county covered eighty-eight cities and numerous communities. I kept clicking sites and following the trail, but ended up on the page where I started. I tried again and within minutes was back on the homepage.

This web designer mistook me for a patient person. I picked up my cell phone and called Paulie, the private investigator who was looking for my no-good husband.

He started in with excuses. "I haven't got an eye on him yet, but I have a guy going by his last known address. I'll be on him tomorrow."

I'd heard that one before. "You let him get away. I'm not paying you any more money until I have that signature."

"You'll have it soon. Don't worry. I'll find him."

"Yeah, yeah. Listen, do you ever deal with anyone in L.A.?"

"Like California?"

"Is there another L.A.? I'm looking for someone who specializes in records. It's for the Marin County Sheriff's Department," I added. Paulie wasn't licensed and didn't particularly like doing things legally. The mention of the Sheriff's Office would keep him from suggesting he do the search I needed.

"You have a pen?"

Paulie gave me two names and numbers and his opinion of each of the contacts. He said he'd email me tomorrow if Conor turned up. I'd heard that before, too.

I punched in the first contact's number. It went to voicemail. I punched in the second. A woman answered. Mavis. She had a gravely voice.

"I need to track down some criminal warrants or incident reports in L.A. County," I said after telling her how I got her number.

"L.A. County's a big place. Can you be more specific?"

"Bel Air."

"Six courts service Bel Air and several police stations. You have an address?"

"I do." I read over Stan Henry's information and noticed he'd been married to wife number two for five years at the time of his death. If he beat wife number two, he probably beat wife number one. Something to think about. "The address I have is five years old. Would you be able to search by name?"

"How many searches you want? Twenty-five dollars a search."

"Twenty-five!"

"Fifteen for the county, ten for me."

From what I'd found on the Internet I was looking at five or six searches, maybe more if I added incident reports. "I can't afford that. I have to find out if this guy beat his wife. Can we trade something?"

"Like what?"

My legwork could save them travel fees. "I have contacts with the press and I'm a pretty good researcher. Need any research done in San Francisco?"

I heard her draw in on what I assumed was a cigarette and exhale heavily. "Hold on."

The line filled with the voice of Tom Jones singing *Delilah*. I brought up my bank account on the laptop. Less than two hundred to last me until the end of the month. Next month I'd have one last paycheck from the *District Dispatch* before I'd have to crack open my meager savings. I really didn't want to dip into the savings.

Mavis came back on the line. "You near a place called Petaluma?"

"Pretty close."

"I can get the price down to fifty dollars total if you can do a title search for me on a Petaluma property."

Since Paulie gave me her name, she was assuming I was another P.I. "Works for me. You have an email address?"

We exchanged email addresses and disconnected. As soon as I put the phone down it rang. Hopefully, Mavis hadn't changed her mind so soon.

"I'll be heading out in about an hour," Dusty said without a greeting. "Planning on picking up some Chinese. Want me to get you some?"

This was the fourth meal Dusty had offered to buy me since I arrived. He must be feeling mighty guilty for limiting my income.

"Sure."

We disconnected and I looked around to see what I'd need to hide before he got here.

The Rose

It was almost dark when Dusty knocked at the door. I'd been reading the only book I'd brought with me, a seven-hundred-page tome on Albert Einstein, but my stomach was growling so loudly it was hard to concentrate on the words.

I threw open the door and found Dusty bent over.

"You said an hour," I snapped.

With his free hand, he lifted a black rose off my welcome mat. "Looks like you've already pissed off a neighbor." He handed me the rose. "What did you do?" He stepped in and closed the door behind him.

Fifi came running in from her room. As soon as she saw Dusty, the barking started. "I tell you, the thing hates me." He flicked his fingers at her. "Shoo. Shoo."

I stared at the black velvety petals. They looked so natural, but black roses weren't natural. They were created through a dying process. I knew this because I'd wanted them for my daughter's funeral. They represented death.

Was this another threat from last night's caller?

I was pretty good at spotting a tail so I was sure no one had followed me to the courthouse. Even if someone had, he couldn't have known why I was there unless he was in the office when I made my request, and no one had been there, but the clerk. "I didn't do anything." My voice cracked.

"Then why do you look like you're going to faint?" He set the bag of food on the carpet and looked as if he was ready to catch me if I fell. Fifi approached the food. "You!" he said and pointed at her.

I ignored both of them and thought back to my short trip to Ross. I'd been careful. No one else had been in the station when I asked for the incident reports. Afterwards, I'd come straight home. I'd used the Internet. Was the killer tracing my Internet searches? Possible, but that was a pretty complex operation. Then the light bulb came on. "Oh shit!"

"What? You remember now?"

I sure did. The phone call to the ex-Mrs. Schuss. Had she told someone about the call? I'd used a fake name, one of a very real agent working on the case. Had the real Agent Clark telephoned the ex-Mrs. Schuss? Was that how she knew I wasn't Clark?

"Put the food on the table before Fifi snatches it," I said. "I'll grab some plates."

I dropped the rose in the trash and took out two plates and two glasses. How stupid could I have been?

Dusty had placed three boxes on the table when I came in with the plates.

"Why are you so late?" I asked, trying not to worry about the rose, but failing miserably.

"I spoke with the sergeant working the Novato robbery. Haven't you seen? I emailed the case info to you. You okay? You're pale."

"Stood up too fast. Don't worry about me, but it is odd that someone put that rose outside my door without Fifi getting curious. She's usually very annoyed with strange noises."

Dusty looked down at Fifi. She growled at his attention. "I reserve comment."

I offered Dusty my only chair and I sat on my stacked suitcases. Fifi disappeared under the table.

"How's it going, working side-by-side with the Feds?"

"We've divided the work up. They're concentrating on the past victims and we're concentrating on the last one."

So Clark might have spoken with the ex-Mrs. Schuss—I had to find out her new name. But I wasn't going to call back. Not now. If Mrs. Schuss told Agent Clark that someone else had called using her name, could Clark be the one threatening me, for the fun of it or maybe to warn me away from the case? If Mrs. Schuss told Clark, could the killer have access to Clark's investigation? Not likely, that stuff only happened on television. What if Mrs. Schuss didn't tell Agent Clark, but told someone else that two different people were calling using Agent Clark's name?

That sounded plausible.

As Dusty opened a box of steamed rice, I fretted over whether to come clean with him or not. In the morning, I might be too dead to tell him my suspicions. But if I told him that I'd learned enough to make someone very nervous, my article and the paycheck I'd been fantasizing about would be history. I needed that money. I had another mouth to feed.

He spooned some rice on his plate and exchanged boxes with me. "Well, it can't be noise," he said, "because all the noise from these places carries out over the harbor. I would have heard if you were blaring your stereo." He raked some chow mein onto his rice.

"What are you talking about?"

"Your gift, the rose."

"Oh. You haven't been around a lot lately. Too busy trying to find a serial killer in a haystack. I had a wild party just last night. My last night of freedom."

"Freedom from what?" He handed me several small packets "Here, try some of this sauce."

"The you-know-what." I glanced down at Fifi. She batted her lashes at the rice box passing from my hand to Dusty's, and then licked her lips or nose. It's was hard to tell which.

I tore off the edge of the sauce packet with my teeth. "I have another job."

Dusty stopped eating. "I'm afraid to ask."

"Freelance work. I have to do a land search for a Petaluma property. Since you used to live there, I thought you could tell me if I do it at the courthouse or elsewhere."

"Naw, Petaluma's in Sonoma County. You'll have to drive up to Santa Rosa, the county seat, to do a land search."

I stood and walked to the front window. "Did you see anyone when you arrived?" Nothing moved down in the parking lot.

"Hey, you haven't finished your pot stickers. I saw the guy downstairs. Pretty sure he's a stoner. Let me know if the smoke comes in and I'll do something about it."

I walked back to the table. "Maybe it's medical marijuana. You can't bust him for that."

Dusty swallowed then said, "I'm not going to bust him, but I can block your air vents."

"Thanks." I picked up the box of pot stickers, but put it down next to Dusty's plate.

"What? You don't want any?"

I trailed my fork through the chow mein. "Not so hungry any more."

He dumped the last two pot stickers on his plate and stacked the empty box inside another empty box. "You snapped my head off for being late and now you aren't hungry?"

I glanced back to the front window. The vertical blinds were wide open and anyone hiding in the darkness had a clear view inside.

"It's that damn rose, isn't it?" Dusty asked. "You have done something." He pushed his plate away and leaned back in the chair.

I got up again and closed the blinds. When I sat back down Dusty was watching me.

I knew I should tell him. But if I told him about the threat, I'd have to tell him how far I'd gotten in the investigation. If I told him that, he'd figure out where I got the information on the first two victims. I'd be banned from the courthouse for the rest of my life. "I've only been here a few days. I don't have a television or stereo. What could I have done?"

What I was warned not to do.

Dusty rubbed the blond stubble covering his head. "You want me to stay?"

"Right. And where exactly are you going to sleep?" I started stuffing the empty containers into the paper bag.

He picked up my plate and stacked it under his. "Same as you. The floor."

"Fifi will protect me."

Dusty snickered.

"Besides," I added, "the rest of my stuff should arrive tomorrow."

Dusty carried the dishes to the kitchen. He saw the rose in the trash. "I think it's a prank, or one of the weird neighbors' way of welcoming you to the building," he said. "Looks like something Mr. Stoner downstairs might do."

"Yeah, probably."

I walked to the window and peeked out through the closed blinds.

"You sure you don't want me to stay?" he asked, picking up his laptop bag.

I shook my head, but a cloud of fear, just left of my shoulders, was waiting patiently to envelop me.

"What about the dog?"

"What about her?" I asked.

"Doesn't it need to go out again?"

Fifi tilted her head sideways.

"No."

"When was the last time it went out?"

"After eating about 6:30."

He huffed. "Come on, I'll walk her with you. There's no way she can hold it until tomorrow, and I don't want you tripping around out there in the middle of the night."

Fat chance.

"Grab the leash," he said when I didn't budge.

"I think it's too late. It's like ten p.m. Who walks a dog that late?"

"You're really scared." He clamped his forehead with his hand and looked down. "What have you done?"

"Nothing. I swea— Okay, I'll get her leash. Come here Fifi."

I snapped the leash on her collar and picked her up. She leaned in like she was going to lick me. "Don't even think about it," I said, then whispered. "I'm probably going to die because of your bladder, then who's going to feed your scrawny self?"

I passed Dusty in the doorway.

"You might want to lock up," he said, holding the door handle. "You have your keys?"

I tapped my jeans pocket, and he pulled the door closed and tested the handle. "What about the deadbolt?" he asked.

"We're just going down to the parking lot." Plus, I wanted to be able to get inside as fast as possible.

We clomped down the stairs and I put Fifi down next to an oleander bush. She ignored the bush and trotted over to a red Camaro. I glanced up to make sure no one was hanging around my door.

"He who laughs last, laughs best," I said. "Does that mean anything to you?"

"Should it?" Dusty asked while watching Fifi sniff the Camaro.

Fifi squirted the tire and Dusty laughed.

"It's something your friend Star said to me last night."

Dusty started walking toward the corner of the building as if he was walking up to the harbor parking lot. "Star. I haven't seen her in a long time. If she said it, then it must be important."

"I figure it lightly translates to having the last laugh, right?"

He looked up and around the building before turning back to me. "What was it in reference to?"

"How would I know? I don't speak bag lady psychic. She sat beside me and said, 'He who laughs last, laughs best.'"

He shrugged. "Want me to walk you up?"

"No." *Yes.*

I picked up Fifi and started for the stairs. "Thanks for dinner," I said as I pulled out my keys.

With his laptop case tucked under his arm, Dusty stood watching me unlock my door. I took one more look around before closing it and locking both the handle and deadbolt.

The deadbolt on the door was a good one, but I knew people like me who could get in with a pick gun. I'd lost confidence in Fifi, so I stacked clean plates behind the door. On the plates I stacked glasses. If someone came in I'd hear them. Not that I planned to sleep.

Fifi was already curled in her bed when I dragged my sleeping bag from the bedroom to the living room. She lifted her head as if to ask what I was doing, but quickly dropped it to let me know she didn't care.

I switched off all the lights and sat on the sleeping bag with my back propped against the seat of the sofa. I faced the door. After about ten minutes I grew restless and knew there was no way I could spend the next eight hours like this.

I stood, stretched, and then ambled to the front window. A new arrival down in the parking lot. The car was backed into a parking space. The driver was in the car, a pale light lit his face. He had a full view of my apartment door. Tears swelled in my eyes. I sniffed and swallowed hard. Then I walked back to the sleeping bag and smoothed it out across the rug. I crawled inside and closed my eyes.

With Dusty standing watch, I should sleep.

The Watchman

A strange breathing sound woke me. I opened my eyes to a cotton ball of fur waving like a metronome in front of my nose. I stretched my head around to find Fifi panting and watching the door.

The black rose.

I shot up to a sitting position, startling Fifi. She barked and dropped a squeaky rabbit in my lap. I threw the toy across the room and she galloped after it as if this were a game. I shoved off the sleeping bag and staggered to the window. Blinding sunlight caused me to jerk away as I opened the vertical blinds.

Squinting, I looked down. Dusty's black Sentra was where it had been last night.

I dragged my feet to the kitchen, switching on the coffeemaker as I passed. From the back window, I saw the shiny lock on the outside of Dusty's boat, which meant he was still in the car. He didn't drink coffee, had a prejudice against caffeine.

Silly man.

All I had in the fridge was a Diet Coke and an apple juice bottle. I poured the rest of the juice into a glass and grabbed Fifi's leash. She dropped the squeaky rabbit and ran to the door.

Dusty's car was parked underneath a carport structure that ran the length of the rear lot. Because the car was now shaded from the sun, I half-expected to find Dusty asleep. I carried the glass to the car, but when I got there, the front seat was empty. I peered in the back. No Dusty. Maybe I'd just missed him. I led Fifi down the grass path toward the harbor. Dusty's boat was still locked from the outside.

I drank the apple juice while Fifi examined the eight-inch concrete wall that ran along the back of the sidewalk. The water in the harbor was low and smelled like rotten eggs. If Dusty had walked off without his car, then someone had picked him up. Maybe he'd driven home last night in a sheriff's mobile because he had official business this morning. I finished the juice and returned to the apartment.

I checked the doorframe before going inside. My lint ball was still wedged between the door and the frame so no one had snuck in. For a brief moment I wondered if the killer could have nabbed Dusty, but he'd had his laptop with him and it wasn't in the car. Also, Dusty was a pretty big guy, quite a bit taller and more muscular than the other victims. And he carried a gun. Someone would have a death wish to mess with him.

I locked the deadbolt and tapped Dusty's number into the phone. It went to voicemail.

"Hey, I read the case info on the jewelry heist. Looks squirrelly. I think I can sell an article on it. Can you set me up with the detective on the case? Call me back."

Fifi stood in the kitchen doorway and barked.

"You have to stop with the barking. I have neighbors and you're not supposed to be here."

She barked again.

"My boxes are arriving today. The rest of my earthly belongings."

She cocked her head to the side.

* * *

The drive to Santa Rosa took over an hour because of road work on 101. The Recorder's office was across the street from the District Attorney's office and parking was plentiful. Mavis's title search was actually a mining claim that I had to verify. I thought all the mines these days were owned by corporations. If the personal claim was genuine, I then had to check the land deed and notices of default. Checking the land deed turned out to be the pricey item. Two hundred dollars. Luckily, my temporary employer was footing the bill.

Waiting for each document and setting up the wire transfer for payment took more than half the day. Fifi and I stopped for lunch at a strip mall near the highway. We ate outside in the great concrete wasteland. The roar of traffic and the smell of gas fumes reminded me of D.C. and I felt a twinge for the life I'd left behind.

In the past, I'd had offers to hire me away from the *District Dispatch*; one of which I almost took when my idiot editor kicked me off the crime desk and demoted me to photographer. In the end, I'd stayed for Haylee. We'd made a good team and she was sure we'd earn a Pulitzer one day.

God, I missed her. I kept waiting for the day I'd wake up and she wouldn't be the first thought in my head. I barely remember losing my mother, but I've lost enough loved ones to know that time was the great healer—if one could ever be considered healed. Each loss was like losing a chunk of yourself. Some days I felt as if I were walking around with buckshot holes right through my body.

I dropped the rest of my fries on the ground. A snort and they were gone before they hit. I looked at the half-eaten sandwich and wondered if Fifi wanted that, too. Of course she did, but I wrapped it in my napkin and carried it with me to the car.

Dusty's car was still in the apartment parking lot when I drove in. No sign of Dusty. This late in the afternoon I assumed he'd spent the day in the city with the FBI. With Agent Clark.

The iron stairs rumbled as I stomped up. I hated being out of the loop.

It was time to clue Dusty in on what I'd found. He was my partner, after all, not Clark's. Actually, he wasn't. I wasn't a detective and I had no right to work this case.

Details.

Upstairs my doormat was clean. No black roses, but no boxes either. They were already a day late. I unleashed Fifi and locked the deadbolt behind us. The apartment was stuffy and I opened the windows to get some air moving through.

At the laptop, I pulled up the tracking number on my boxes that were supposed to have been delivered yesterday. The new tracking information said they'd be delivered tomorrow. "Shit!"

I felt like punching something.

"Fifi. Here, Fifi."

Curled up on the sofa, Fifi lifted her head as if to say, "Quiet, I'm sleeping," before dropping her head back down on her outstretched paws.

Great. I really needed those boxes before I continued with my investigation. I clicked open my email to send Mavis the document numbers she needed for her client and to ask for an L.A. address where I should send the documents that I'd collected in Santa Rosa.

She'd already emailed me the reports on Stan Henry. Victim number two. No criminal reports were ever filed and no incident reports mentioning his current wife. But three incident reports had been filed involving his previous wife, Ina, one of which had been written up at Sherman Oaks Hospital after Ina Henry had been treated for an exposed fracture of her left arm. The report said that Mrs. Henry promised to file a criminal report. Clearly, she didn't. The report was dated fourteen years ago.

Interesting.

Now that I had a name, I went to work researching anything and everything on the first Mrs. Henry. Ex-wives could be a great source.

Twenty minutes passed and I hadn't found anything. I had to assume Ina Henry was remarried and living under her current married name. I was about to throw in the towel when I remembered an older news source I sometimes used. It was an archive of newspapers from across the country. The group that had originally started it back in the late eighties had gone out of business some years ago, so the records hadn't been updated in years. Maybe I could find the wedding announcement and thus Ina Henry's current name.

The search found Ina Henry's name right away. She hadn't remarried. She'd disappeared. Twelve years ago. I read article after article. The official search lasted almost a month. If these stories were any indication, Ina Henry had never resurfaced. Either she'd been whisked away by one of those organizations that help women escape abusive relationships or she was dead.

Stan Henry and the new Mrs. Henry had been married five years. Seven years to declare a missing person officially dead. Twelve years. He must have remarried the day after the declaration on his first wife. Seven years to find a new partner. Nothing odd about that.

Was he reformed? Right. The lack of records would say he was. No incident reports for turning wife two into a punching bag.

Some men deserve to die.

Now, I had proof all three victims physically abused their wives at some point. Was that the link the FBI was looking for?

Time to tell Dusty. I punched in his number, but the call went to voicemail. I disconnected without leaving a message.

I never quite understood the abused wife syndrome. Maybe because I was raised with six brothers and I learned early on to fight back. If a man ever lifted a hand to me, he'd find himself in a world of hurt. Even if I was knocked out cold, when I came to he was going to be sorry. Luckily, I'd never had to test this theory. Right around the time I turned sixteen, my father wouldn't let my brothers fight with me anymore. He'd knock them around for "hitting a girl." If I tried to hit one of them just to prove I wasn't "a girl" they wouldn't hit back. My brothers feared my father more than my little whacks.

That was then. In college I'd taken four self-defense classes and learned a few tricks. And after that, working so many cases with police officers, I'd learned to shoot. Fight fire with a bigger fire was my motto.

I opened a new document on the laptop and started typing out a new article for the *Marin Independent Journal*. I added a few juicy adjectives since the editor said that he would pay me by the word. Dr. Grimes was a local and this was a local story for all the editor knew. Hopefully, there'd be more articles down the road.

On the sofa, Fifi leaped to her feet and started barking, her little body shaking. She jumped off and ran to the door, howling as if someone had stolen her Alpo.

Dusty?

I gathered my notes together and shoved them into the file folder. I saved the document and out of habit, emptied out the archive list of my Internet search. While waiting for his knock, I closed the laptop and shoved the folder under the sofa.

I'd have to leak the information to him slowly, let it excite him so maybe he'd forget about being mad at me.

One last glance around. Fifi was still at the door barking. I started to unlock the deadbolt and froze. What if it wasn't Dusty?

I rushed to the front window. The parking lot was full of cars. Two nondescript sedans, a San Rafael Police car, and one Marin County Sheriff's car. A group of people huddled around Dusty's car. I spotted Agent Clark and Agent Wagner right off, but didn't see Dusty among the others.

I scooped up Fifi, grabbed her leash, and ran down the stairs.

The Car

"Where's Dusty?" I asked a female deputy. Her sheriff's uniform was the color of grass stains.

She looked at me, then down at Fifi before turning back toward the group of officers. No answer. The Sentra's driver's door was open and stubby Agent Wagner was leaning inside the car. I hadn't checked this morning to see if the car door was locked.

The Marin County Sheriff's SIS van pulled into the parking lot, stopping next to the San Rafael Police car. Two men got out and joined the group by Dusty's car. Agent Clark was wearing a skirt. She almost looked like a woman. I wondered if that little bit of femininity was for Dusty's benefit. I started to turn away, but as I did, Agent Clark pointed to the privet bushes behind the car, and the two SIS men went over and deposited an orange marker. Both men put on gloves.

I ran to the nearest San Rafael police officer, a clean-cut guy of about thirty.

"What's going on?" I asked. For some unknown reason, Fifi chose that moment to squeeze through my ankles, causing me to lose my balance and fall into the officer.

The officer snatched me by both shoulders, steadied me, and gave me a warning look.

"I'm sorry," I said, unwrapping the leash from around my leg. "I'm not good with dogs. I'm more of a pet turtle kind of person. You know, those little green ones." I was obsessing, something I tended to do when I was worried. I pinched my lips closed and glanced back over to Dusty's car.

One of the Scientific Investigation guys pulled something rectangular out of the bushes. The carrying case for Dusty's laptop. I recognized the Buddhist bumper sticker stuck to the front. I'd read it a million times and it hadn't changed my life.

Be vigilant; guard your mind against negative thoughts. - Buddha

The SIS guy dropped it into a plastic bag and sealed it shut. He returned to the bush and lifted another object out. Dusty's open laptop.

"Shit!" I rushed forward, but the San Rafael officer's hand shot out, his arm catching me across the stomach.

"Ma'am, you have to stay back."

"I know the owner of the car. Has something happened?"

The young officer left his arm blocking me. With his free hand, he motioned to Agent Wagner, who rushed over.

"This woman says she knows the Sentra's owner."

Wagner looked at me and squinted as if he realized he'd seen me before, but couldn't remember when. He made a smacking sound with his lips. "The journalist, right?"

"Where's Dusty?"

"That's the big question. When did you last see him?"

"Last night, after he got off work. We had Chinese."

"Do you live on one of the boats?"

I pointed to the upstairs apartment.

That seemed to make more sense to Wagner. He nodded. "Does he always park his car here?"

"Where's Dusty?"

"We don't know," Wagner said. "Does he park here?"

Red and white signs were posted every two car lengths declaring that parking was for residents only. Maybe the agent figured because I lived here I allowed Dusty to have my space.

I backed away and shook out my hands. I needed air. I had to think. Last night. I'd seen the flash of the laptop's screen. Dusty had been working on it after he parked. Agent Wagner was speaking to me, but his words didn't break through the multitude of images rippling across my memory. The rose. The dog. The hesitant expression. The laptop.

Finally, he grabbed me and shook my shoulders. Fifi tried to bite his leg and he jumped back, letting me go. "Hey!" he yelled.

"What!"

"Parking."

"No. He parks in the harbor lot out front." I pointed past my apartment building.

"Did someone pick him up this morning?" Wagner asked.

A Sheriff's Department SUV pulled into the lot. The officers milling around went silent. The Marin County Sheriff got out of the passenger's side. He was a tall, wiry guy and although he had a reputation for being laid back, he didn't look as if he'd take any sass.

Wagner tensed. "All right," he said to me. "I need to speak with you some more, but I have another matter to take care of first." He addressed the San Rafael officer. "Can you put her in the rear of your cruiser until I'm ready to finish this conversation?"

The young officer slipped his arm in mine. Wagner took off across the lot toward the Sheriff.

"Let's go," the officer said, tugging me forward.

"You don't have to put me in the car. I'm not going anywhere."

"I have to do what the man says. Come on."

I let the officer lead me to the black and white. He opened the rear door and I bent to pick up Fifi.

"The dog stays outside."

"She'll run off."

He took the leash from my hand. "I'll tie her up over there," he said, nodding to the staircase rail.

Because his car was parked next to the SIS van and I'd have a birds-eye view of whatever they brought back, I didn't fight him. He shut the door and I turned to face the action, which was mostly a bunch of law enforcement personnel standing around a car.

Dusty had disappeared while protecting me. That wasn't okay. No. Not okay. I started to rock, bounce actually, off the rear seat. I had to find him.

He who laughs last, laughs best.

Star's stupid cliché popped into my head. Was this what she'd meant? Was the killer laughing best because he'd nabbed a person I cared about? I shook my head as if to empty the crazy thoughts. Star was a bag lady with no magical predictions. There was absolutely no way the killer could know what I thought about Dusty. He was taken because he was a man and this killer kills men.

The sound of a heavy engine behind me pulled me out of my contemplation. I turned to see a delivery truck jammed half in and half out of the lot. The police vehicles had choked off the entrance. I reached for the door handle, but there wasn't one. I banged on the window and screamed at the top of my lungs. "Hey! Over here!"

The San Rafael officer was only a few feet away. He must have heard my cries because he turned. I slapped at the window again and pointed to the delivery truck. He probably thought my franticness had something to do with Dusty's disappearance because he ran to the car and threw open the door.

I hopped out.

He shoved me back in. "What?"

"That guy," I pointed to the delivery driver. "Grab him."

Agent Wagner drew up behind the officer.

I pointed again. The delivery driver was clearly looking to back out and forget my delivery for today. "Grab him! Now!"

Agent Wagner didn't hesitate. He ran to the truck and drew his weapon. The driver killed the engine and threw up his hands.

"Step out," Wagner said, motioning the driver out of the truck. "Slowly."

The driver stepped down from the truck. He was skinny with pasty skin and hunched shoulders, his brown uniform looking two sizes too big.

"May I go?" I asked the officer. He released me and I ran to Wagner. "Put the gun away."

Wagner looked at me. Doubt washed over his features, but he didn't lower the gun. "Why did you tell me to stop him?"

"He has my boxes." I glared at the driver, his hands still in the air. "You were going to leave without delivering my boxes."

The driver pinched his mouth and shook his head ever so slightly.

Liar.

Agent Wagner holstered his gun. "You don't appear to be aware of the seriousness of what's going on here."

"I'm more aware than you think, agent. That's why I need my boxes." I turned back to the driver. "You can put your hands down and deliver my boxes to that apartment up there," I said, pointing.

To Wagner I said, "Get on with your questions so I can start looking for Detective Arkansas."

Wagner waved away the driver, who ran to the rear of his truck. Once the driver was out of hearing, Wagner leaned into me. "This is a police matter."

"And I'm a civilian. I can do whatever I like as long as I don't get in your way."

"You need to tell us everything you know."

"I don't know anything."

"Why did Detective Arkansas park in this particular lot last night?"

I pictured the black rose by my door, but I'd already decided not to tell him about it. Should I tell him that Dusty had parked there to guard me? Not yet. I needed time to think.

The driver passed me with my four boxes stacked on a dolly.

"It's the one upstairs," I called after him.

"You're evading me," Wagner said. "Are you and Detective Arkansas lovers?"

"What? Pssss. No!"

My skin grew cold despite the heat. I rubbed my arms and walked back to the police car. Wagner followed. The night that Haylee's death finally sank into my soul, Dusty had sat with me until dawn, making sure I didn't drink, but also soothing the crazies that sometimes roamed my brain. He was a friend, the dearest friend I had.

The autopsy photos of the first two victims popped into my mind. Oh, god. I had to find him.

"You two seem to know a lot about each other," Wagner said. "So what aren't you telling me?"

I remembered how Dusty had tried to shield me from Haylee's crime scene photos and how he'd let me smoke in the non-smoking building despite a sergeant's complaining. That had been the first day I'd met him and I'd learned a lot about him just by those simple gestures.

"I don't know what to tell you. He brought Chinese. We ate and then he left. Maybe he was tired and decided to leave the car there."

"So, he might have disappeared while returning to his boat in the dark? Do we need to dredge the harbor?"

Oh, great. Wasted time and taxpayers' money. I shook my head. "No. He helped me walk the dog and afterward, I saw him from my window. He was in his car working on his laptop. He wouldn't have left it in the car."

Agent Wagner stared at me for a long time. I tried not to think about where Dusty could be or with whom. I tried not to think about anything because even though everything I'd said was true, I knew that Wagner knew I was lying.

The Box

I shoved the four boxes across the carpet and bolted the door. With a parking lot full of officers, I was probably safe, but I'd thought Dusty was safe last night, too. I turned around and kicked the bottom box. I punched the top box and when it didn't hurt enough I punched it again. The second time broke the skin across my knuckles.

I leaped over Fifi and ran to the kitchen. I ran the water and when it was icy cold I put my busted hand under it. I used a leftover napkin from last night's Chinese to dry my cheeks. I turned off the water and used the same napkin to dry my hand. The pot of coffee I'd made before the police arrived smelled burnt. I switched it off and poured a mug.

Yuck.

I grabbed a cutting knife and carried the mug and the knife back to the living room. If I'd been smart, I'd have thought to mark the boxes, but as it was, I had to cut into each one and dump the contents on the floor.

True to form, the metal case I wanted was in the last box I sawed into, the one busted by my boot. I picked the case up and tore off the electrical tape that Haylee had used to seal it a year ago when she'd taken it away from my drunken self. Inside, on a piece of red velvet cloth, was my Smith & Wesson revolver. I lifted it and felt its weight in my palm. It was a small weapon; a point-and-shoot gun for self-defense. It probably needed cleaning, but Smith & Wessons were forgiving. That was why I'd chosen it.

I finished the burnt coffee and kicked through the junk at my feet, looking for the box of bullets I remembered packing. When I found it, I put down the mug and loaded all the chambers. I didn't know who had Dusty, but I had a good idea that the same person had left the black rose and I knew of only one way to contact him quickly.

I shoved the gun in my camera bag along with a few extra bullets, not that I was planning a shoot-out, and headed for the door.

Fifi blocked my way.

"You can't go this time," I said as if she understood. "One of us might die."

As soon as I locked the door the barking started, but with a parking lot full of police, I figured my stoner neighbors might have something other than a loud dog to worry about.

My car was blocked by the San Rafael Police car. I walked around it, trying to see if I could squeeze out. Wagner saw me and jogged over.

"I have a few more questions for you," he said.

"Now?"

He looked over his shoulder. "In about ten minutes. I have something to finish up first."

"Ten minutes is good," I said, burnt coffee firing all cylinders. "I have to buy some dog food and I thought I'd grab a cup of coffee. Want one?"

He pulled out his wallet. "Sure. I take it black." He handed me a ten-dollar bill. "Grab one for Clark, too."

And fill it with Windex. I pocketed the money. "Will do. But the thing is, my car's blocked in. I think if this San Rafael guy rolled forward I could inch by the SIS van and get out."

Wagner waved over the young San Rafael officer. "I'll handle it."

"Great. Thanks." I ran to my car.

* * *

Rush hour traffic had the Miracle Mile jammed bumper to bumper. Once I reached San Anselmo and turned left toward Ross, I was going against traffic. I pulled into the drive of Mrs. Grimes's house, and drove right up to the side door. I banged on the door until Mrs. Grimes answered.

"You!" she said.

I was surprised she recognized me, but she probably recognized the ugly car.

"We need to talk," I said.

She tried to close the door, but I rammed my foot in, blocking her. "I'm calling the police if you don't leave," she said.

I shoved open the door and stepped inside. "Please, call the police." I closed the door. "We can tell them how you hired someone to kill your son-of-a-bitch husband."

She froze, standing in the middle of a laundry room. The color had faded from her skin and I didn't think it was because I'd pulled the gun, but I realized I had it aimed at her chest. The doorway behind her led to what looked like a massive kitchen.

I motioned with the gun. "Let's go."

She backed up and turned to walk through the doorway into the kitchen.

Off to the right was a dining room with a table big enough to seat twelve. I motioned for her to go that way.

"Sit," I said.

She pulled out a polished cherry wood chair and sat.

Still holding on to the grip, I shoved the gun back in my camera case to keep it covered, but ready to draw at a moment's notice. "Listen, I don't care about who or why you hired someone to kill your husband. The guy knocked you around, he probably deserved what he got. My problem is, whoever you hired has kidnapped a good friend of mine. A good guy. Not someone who beats his wife. Not someone who deserves to die."

Across the table, I pulled out a chair, but was too restless to sit.

Mrs. Grimes licked her bottom lip, and bit it. "I don't know what you're talking about," she said, her voice pleading.

"Put your hands on the table. Flat."

Her hands went straight to the tabletop. Abused women were good at taking orders. "How do you know Mrs. Schuss?" I was sure the wife of victim number one had been the person who'd led the killer to me.

Mrs. Grimes licked her lips again, then shook her head. "I swear, I don't know any Mrs. Schuss."

"She goes by another name." I really needed to find out what name she was living under. "She lives in Sacramento."

"I swear."

"What about Mrs. Henry of Bel Air?"

There it was. A flinch. A tightness in the throat. Mrs. Grimes was connected to the wife of victim two. I pulled the gun back out and pointed it at her again. "I'm in a bit of a hurry." I wanted to shoot, not her exactly, but someone. My mind was racing. I was having difficulty putting my thoughts together into sentences. Dusty was in danger, serious danger. If I was too late, if he'd already lost his junk, I'd …well…I couldn't think like that. I had to get him back.

Mrs. Grimes's hands flew in the air as if that would keep me from shooting her. "There's a website! I met her there."

I formed my words slowly. "A website for abused women?"

She nodded and lowered her hands back to the table. "She suspected her husband had killed his first wife, but she couldn't prove it. You can't know what it's like for women like us."

"You can always pack up and leave."

"It's not that easy. I tried once. Went to a shelter in San Rafael. They said they would protect me, take me out of the state if I wanted. But Marshall found me. He nabbed me on the way back from the drugstore." She huffed, a laugh cut short. "I'd gone to buy something to reduce the scarring on my breasts. He dragged me back here. Tied me to a chair for over a week. No bathroom or tampon breaks. Pure humiliation. Afterwards, it took three days before I was able to walk normally."

As she spoke, her face was ridged with anger and fat tears spilled down her cheeks. "I knew Marshall would never kill me. He enjoyed inflicting pain way too much. What fun would he have if I was dead? I thought about killing myself. Lots of times."

She wiped her cheek with two fingers and bit her lower lip. "It was the only escape I could think of until…"

She looked longingly at the gun as if she wanted me to do what she'd been unable to do. I put it back in the camera case. "Look, I admit that I don't understand this whole abused wife thing. It seems to me there's always a way to get away—"

"—you really—"

"Let me finish." I paused. "That said, I once fell into a bottle and couldn't find my way out."

"You could have stopped drinking," she said, not bothering to hide her sarcasm.

"My point exactly. We can't ever truly understand another person's plight. I'm not here to judge you. You did what you felt you had to do."

Mrs. Grimes looked down.

"Now, *I* have to do what *I* have to do."

Her head jerked up. "But you said—"

"I said your hired killer has taken someone that means a lot to me and I have to get him back. Now. Before that killer hurts him." I took out my cell phone and slid it across the table. "You need to contact that person and make him understand that he can't hurt Dusty."

She didn't reach for the phone, only stared at it. "I don't have a number for him."

"How do you reach him?"

"It's complicated."

I reached across the table and snatched back the phone. "I'm going to make it real simple for you." I shoved the phone in the camera case. Despite my boldness, there was a vice grip squeezing the center of my chest. It felt as if each breath would be my last, but I would fight to the very end.

"I'm leaving now," I said. "But you should know that I've written an article and emailed it to a friend of mine," I lied. This was a trick Haylee had perfected. I hoped to pull it off half as well as she used to do. "It's a story about a group of women, a Mrs. Schuss, a Mrs. Henry, and a Mrs. Grimes, who hired a killer to murder their abusive husbands. If this killer hasn't returned Dusty, safe and sound, by eight a.m. tomorrow morning, my friend will run this article in a nationwide newspaper."

Mrs. Grimes dropped her head into her hands. "You can't do that," she said, peeking through her fingers. "Do you have any idea how many people you'll hurt by running a story like that?"

"I figure your killer will start killing the wives. First, you, Mrs. Schuss, Mrs. Henry, and who knows how many others. He'll want to get rid of the evidence. And yes, there may be collateral damage—innocent people, family members, et cetera, but I'm confident that the FBI will nab him while he's hunting down his witnesses. Also, I'll be sharing everything I know with Agent Clark of the FBI."

I stood and pulled the camera case strap over my shoulder. "If you don't save Dusty, all those other deaths will be on your head. Here's your chance to clean up this mess and keep your illegal activity a secret. Once I have Dusty back, tell your hired killer that no one needs to know what I know. Fair enough? That's my trade. Dusty for my silence."

I started for the rear door. "Oh, your killer has already threatened me. I'm not an idiot. If anything happens to me, my friend has instructions to run the article."

The Bluff

My shaking grip rattled the steering wheel as I backed out of the driveway. I managed to coast to the corner before I had to pull over and park because my knees bounced so hard I couldn't keep pressure on the gas pedal. I stepped out and walked around to the front of the car. I leaned against the dull black hood.

What had I done?

I replayed our conversation in my head. Had I said anything that might cause Dusty more harm? Nothing came to mind. I only hoped he was still alive and …intact. I squeezed my temples as his mutilated image pushed its way into my brain.

"Journalism is about truth," Haylee had said many times. "But sometimes we have to lie to get to the truth."

Okay, think! What else had I said?

I actually had a friend from college who'd been hounding me for the last year to write for the slag rag he ran. It was a nationwide piece of garbage journalism that earned him the big bucks. I didn't, however, trust him to hold onto an article until I wanted it released. Ethics weren't his strong suit.

All in all, it wasn't a bad plan. Completely fabricated, but not insane. First thing I needed to do was write the damn story. If it ever went to press, Agents Wagner and Clark would know without a doubt that I'd gotten Dusty's information, and they'd probably wrongly assume he gave it to me. But if the story went to press, that piece of knowledge would be the least of my problems.

* * *

Back in San Rafael, the only official vehicle left in my parking lot was a Sheriff's Department cruiser. The female deputy who'd refused to answer my earlier questions was standing beside it.

I walked up to her and didn't say a word.

She looked me up and down then stared into my eyes. I stared back. Silently.

"Can I help you?" she asked, raising one hand to the hip where her gun was holstered.

"Yes, you can. Have Agents Wagner and Clark left?"

"Do you see them?"

"Not an answer, but I'll take that as affirmative."

"Are you the coffee girl?"

"Coffee? Oh, guess I am."

"Wagner says you owe him."

"I owe him a cup of coffee, that's about it."

"He wants you to stop by the Sheriff's Office, says he has more questions."

"Will do." *When leprechauns fly.*

I walked over to Dusty's Sentra.

"Not past the tape," the deputy called, referring to the yellow crime scene tape wrapped around two poles and a pair of traffic cones, boxing in Dusty's car.

Standing by the tape, I peered into the driver's window. Why hadn't I checked to see if the door was locked? Dusty never left his car unlocked. Why hadn't I looked around more? I would have spotted the laptop case if I'd only walked behind the car. If I'd been more curious, the investigation into his disappearance would have begun six hours sooner. Six whole hours. An eternity to someone who liked to cut off weenies.

I walked to the passenger's side. The door handle had been dusted for prints. Mine would be among the ones they found. Why hadn't I heard a commotion? Surely, Dusty put up a fight.

Why hadn't Fifi heard something? Maybe she had; she never liked Dusty.

The seat backs were clean. No blood spatter. He hadn't been hit over the head like victims two and three. So how did the killer get close enough to nab him?

I glanced up at my apartment. If he'd seen something strange, maybe someone lurking near my door, he would have put down—maybe even turned off—his laptop and gotten out to investigate. If the killer then surprised him, would the killer have wasted time coming back to Dusty's car and tossing the laptop into the bushes? I didn't think so.

The killer must have come up to the car. Dusty would have been on his guard. How did the killer get the jump on him? Was it someone he knew? No way. Dusty wasn't friendly with that many people. Maybe a cop. Maybe someone from his Thursday night club. Perhaps there was a reformed wife beater in the group and to make up for his sins, he hired himself out to kill other wife beaters.

That sounded just crazy enough to be plausible.

A tow truck pulled into the lot. The deputy directed the driver to Dusty's car. That was why she was still here. She was staying until they towed Dusty's car to wherever they would finish the forensics. I'd sort of hoped she was left behind to protect me, but no one knew I needed protecting.

I rushed for the stairs. I had to walk Fifi before the deputy left.

After that, I wasn't leaving my apartment until my fake article was in someone's mailbox.

* * *

"Oi don't understand," Mrs. Macklin said, her County Cork accent sounding thicker than usual. A sign she was upset.

"I've emailed you an article. I don't want you to do anything with it."

"Nathin'?"

"Not unless something happens to me. I've listed you as my next of kin—"

"Waaat ye saying, child? Yer in trouble?"

"No. It's insurance."

"Doesn't soun' like insurance, does it? Waaat ye be scared of?"

"Nothing. Nothing at all. Detective Arkansas has gone missing. You remember him, he worked Haylee's case."

"De idol worshipper. Has de man gotten yer into trouble?"

I could almost hear her crossing herself every time she mentioned Dusty. "He's been kidnapped and I'm using this story as a way to get him back."

"Oi don't like it."

"You'll be keeping me safe," I said, knowing that would appeal to her. She hadn't been able to save her daughter and that pain still lived inside her. It lived inside me, too. "There are three email addresses at the bottom of the article. If anything unforeseen happens—"

"Don't be throwin' words raun tryin' ter confuse me. 'ow dangerous is dis, child?"

"It's very dangerous for Detective Arkansas. No one will want to hurt me as long as they know I have this article."

"But ye don't 'ave it, oi do."

"Same thing. That's why it's insurance." I paused. How could I make her understand how important this was without worrying her too much? "You shouldn't need to use the three email addresses, but if you do, one is to a magazine editor who will print the article, another is to the Marin County Sheriff's Department, and the last is to an agent at the FBI. The article will give everyone the information they need to find me."

A little white lie. If I disappeared, I'd be knocking on the Pearly Gates long before my email merged onto the information highway and I'd be hauling Dusty along with me. Or did Buddhists go to a different gate?

Mrs. Macklin was talking and I'd missed most of what she'd said. As I tuned in, I realized she was repeating my instructions. "That's right," I said when she was finished.

"On a scale of wan ter foive, 'ow worried shud oi be?"

"One."

"Don't ye fib ter me."

"Okay, two. No, one. There are a lot of people who don't want this story to go public. I really think I'm safe."

"Can oi read it?"

"I'd rather you wait until you hear from me."

She huffed. "Briana…"

"Fifi's perked up. She's eating again. Do you want me to send her home?"

"Oi told ye, she misses yer. You're 'er home now so take sum responsibility. Waaat will 'appen ter 'er if somethin' 'appens ter yer? She'll starve and it will be your fault. Poor darlin'."

She was acting like I was already dead.

"Nothing is going to happen to me."

"Den why ye send me dis article?"

Oh Lord. We danced through the same conversation two more times before she let me off the phone with a promise to call her every morning and evening.

The Confusion

I looked out my kitchen window as rays of reddish gold light shot across Dusty's closed-up boat. The last rays of the day.

The police had cut the lock on his boat, probably to go through it, and then relocked it with a big gaudy brass lock.

What if Dusty came home and couldn't get on his boat? I thought, but at the same time realized that wasn't going to happen. He might never see his boat again. He'd spent his last night on earth watching over me.

My eyes filled with water, blurring the image of his boat into a swirls of blue and white.

Behind me, Fifi whined.

"Give-me-a-minute." I snatched Fifi's bowl from the floor and scooped in half a can of dog food. I set the bowl down and watched her scarf up the chow. Suddenly her head came up and her little body froze.

"What do you hear?"

I wasn't stupid enough to wait for an answer, but rushed into the main room. I'd closed the blinds after the sheriff's deputy had left. I was tempted to peek through, but I didn't think it was a good idea. I was hiding out. Just as I started to argue with myself, there was a loud bang on the front door.

Barking, Fifi skidded across the kitchen linoleum and made a bee line for the door. The second knock was harder and longer, mirroring the pounding of my heart. Four, five, six raps.

"Briana. You home?"

I inched forward.

"Briana!"

"Who's there?" So much for hiding out.

"Bob. Let me in."

I unbolted the door. Bob stood there, his gut hanging low over his belt, his brown waves looking like he combed them with a hand mixer.

"You okay?" he asked. "I just heard about Dusty." Stains marked the front of his shirt.

I grabbed his arm and pulled him inside, bolting the door behind him.

"This is serious shit, ain't it?"

"You might say that. Fifi, shut up!"

Fifi clamped her jaws and looked up at me as if she might pee on my leg. I glared back until she turned and trotted off to the kitchen.

"When did you get a dog?"

"Oh, that old thing. Take a seat. Can I fix you anything to drink?"

"Don't guess you have a beer?"

"Negative. Coffee and water are about all I can offer, and I don't recommend the coffee." I'd made two fresh pots since the burnt one, but a bitter taste and smoky smell still lingered.

Bob dropped down on the sofa and dust particles flew up around him. Another thing I needed to take care of. I should make a list: find Dusty, buy mattresses, clean sofa.

"Have the police interviewed you?" I asked, dragging the chair over from the table.

"Naw." Bob made a face. "Why would they interview me?"

"You're his friend."

"Oh. Yeah. Guess so. I saw it on TV. They showed his picture and asked for news. That kind of stuff."

"Do you know where he'd go if he just took off?"

"He wouldn't just take off."

"That's what I thought, too. Let me ask you something. In your Thursday's club—"

"We call it Thursday Nights."

"Right. In your Thursday Nights…group, are there any men who have been convicted or charged with spousal abuse?"

"I can't talk about the others. It's one of the rules. I can only speak for myself."

"Even if Dusty's life is in danger?"

He stood, ran his hand through his curls, and paced before the sofa, small steps. "Dusty's life is in danger?"

"Ah, he's a sheriff's detective and he's…missing. My theory is that it was someone he knew that approached him."

"He's not tight with a lot of people."

"Exactly! So, knowing that this Thursday Nights is all about anger management—"

"But it's not. I don't have anger problems. I'm what Dr. Ford calls passive aggressive. I can't let my anger out until I don't know I'm doing it."

"Yes, but it's still anger whether you know it or not."

He sat back down, placing his elbows on his knees and clasping his hands together. "Reckon that's true."

Looking at him straight on, I suddenly wondered if I was looking at the killer. He'd managed to get me to open my door. He certainly could approach Dusty without alerting him. I slid out of the chair and walked toward the hallway. My gun was in the bedroom. "Bob, what's your story. Why are you in the group?"

He looked upward, as if waiting for the angels to give him a clue.

On the Einstein scale, he was probably a two, but who said a psychopath had to be bright?

"My mu-th-er," he said in a low, exaggerated voice.

The blame game. "What did your mother do?" Dare I mention that she wasn't the one in therapy?

"She's a planner. Every year she plans a big birthday bash for my birthday. This year she planned four days in Vegas. She bought us tickets to Cirque de Soleil, to see Celine Dion, and one for a cool magic show. A rip-roaring time right?"

I leaned against the wall by the hallway. From here, my gun was closer to me than I was to Bob. "Sounds like fun."

"Yeah, well, of all the birthdays she's planned, maybe three have worked out. This year, though, she convinced me. She said nothing would tear her away because she felt so bad about having to cancel last year. She bought new dresses for the shows, bought me a new suit. Then two days before we were to fly out, she dropped the bomb. Some unexpected meeting had come up and she couldn't possibly leave on Thursday. She would be able to leave by Saturday though. That meant no Cirque de Soleil, no dinner at Nobu, no Celine Dion and only one full day in Vegas."

"So what did you do?"

His smile spread so far across his face, I knew he wasn't sorry for whatever it was he'd done.

"My mother's assistant kept my mother's calendar online. I knew the password. I went in early and called everyone on her calendar for Thursday and Friday and told them she had to cancel those meetings due to an emergency appendectomy. We canceled the trip and my mother sat alone in her office for two days. No one showed up. Turned out one of the appointments I canceled was for her accountant and an IRS representative. When she couldn't prove that she'd had an appendectomy, the IRS fined her for canceling the appointment."

"That doesn't sound too bad. How did you end up in the group?"

"My mom said she'd disinherit me if I didn't get help."

"So you took action. You got help. Good for you."

"Sort of. First, I crashed her Mercedes into a lamppost."

I clamped my lips to cut short my smile. Instead of taking out his anger on the person who deserved it, he took it out on her car. Not the type to kill wife beaters.

I walked back to the chair and sat. "Listen, I don't need you to tell me the specifics, just tell me if any of the men in the group have abusive issues toward their wives or women in general."

Bob appeared to be thinking. He lifted his index finger, then his second finger and his third as if he were counting off. I waited, realizing I'd tensed up.

I stretched out my neck and shoulders. I lifted my feet and flexed them, nicking Fifi's bottom. She growled.

"Sorry. I didn't see you. Geez."

She stretched up and strutted to the door, then stopped. That was a bad sign. She was hoping to go back out once more. I went to the kitchen and looked out the back window at Dusty's boat. Still locked up tight.

When I sat back down, Bob had seven fingers held high. His face was scrunched into an expression of total concentration. "Only one I can think of is Dusty."

I lurched forward. "Dusty abused his wife?"

"Naw. Not that way. It was the divorce. At first he was okay with it, but then something snapped. He thinks it was because of all the teasing he got at work, but I think his anger was boiling below the surface. You know what I mean? Anyway, California is an equal...something state."

"Community property state?"

"That's it. So Dusty's lawyer told him to go home and divide up the belongings on a sheet of paper. Cars, dishes, TVs. Stuff like that, then bring him the list. Dusty started writing, but the more he went through the house, the madder he got."

"Do I want to hear the rest of this?"

"Oh, this is the good part. He went out and rented a chainsaw, actually two because he needed a special one to cut through the bathtub."

"He cut the house in half?"

Delight poured from Bob's face as he shook it up and down. "Isn't that cool? But that's not the best. He rented a mini-backhoe and dug a pit in his half of the yard and then he tore down his half of the house and buried it in the pit."

"You're kidding." I was calculating the property damage in my head, although I didn't know the value of his house. Since arriving in Marin, I hadn't seen anything for sale less than $600,000.

"He built this wooden tombstone and placed it on top of the mound. It said, 'Do what you must'...no wait that's not it." He pulled out his phone. "I have a picture of the quote. I've been trying to memorize it."

He flitted through his phone log. "Here it is." He turned the phone, showing me the photo. The words read:

> *Do what you have to do*
> *Resolutely, with all your heart*
> *The traveler who hesitates*
> *Only raises dust on the road.*
> —Buddha

"Cool, huh?"

I read the quote again. "So he was doing what he had to even if it was illegal?"

"Actually, it wasn't illegal because no papers had been filed. Dusty gave a list of everything he buried to his lawyer and his wife agreed with all but two objects. He had to pay for the loss on the house. He's still paying for that, I think. But he got off easy because the house was devalued with the housing crisis. If a separation had been filed, he would have faced charges."

"Sounds like his wife cut him a break. She could have kept him in court for years with that stunt of his."

"All's well that ends well."

"Except that Dusty is missing." I couldn't tell Bob that Dusty'd been nabbed by someone who held a grudge against spousal abusers.

He looked thoughtful. "Yeah, 'cept that."

Would the killer know Dusty's history? Since no charges were filed, I doubted it. I was back to suspecting this Thursday Night group. "Are you sure there's no one in the group that has an issue with spousal abuse?"

He shook his head and the index finger flew up. "There's me, Dusty, Randy, who can't keep a job because of his…anger. There's another guy with sex issues."

A light bulb went on. "What kind of sex issues?"

"They don't involve abuse."

"How can you be sure?"

"It's…well, it's kinda…it's a guy thing and I don't want to talk about it. So then, there's Yann. Guy has an accent. I can't figure out what he's saying half the time."

"What's his problem?"

"Politics. Goes off on these tirades, gets everyone yelling."

He had five fingers up. I remembered seven the last time he'd gone through the group.

"Who are the last two?"

"Dr. Ford, of course. And…oh, James."

I waited for him to tell me James's issue.

"James didn't take Dusty," he said. "He couldn't have done it. He just couldn't."

"How can you be so sure?"

"They don't get along. They're not friends like me and Dusty."

"What's James's story?"

"Ex-crackhead. Kind of a real hothead."

Fifi stood up and barked at the door. We both turned to look. "She wants to go out. Why don't you think this James couldn't take Dusty?"

"Dusty would be on guard if James approached him. They really don't like each other. An ex-druggie and a cop."

"Will you go with me to walk the dog? I'm kind of spooked since Dusty disappeared."

"No problem. I'll protect you."

I shook my head as I walked to the bedroom for my jean jacket. Fifi could pin Bob in less than sixty seconds. Bob was not an aggressive man, more likely the type to run away, but a second person with me would hopefully deter any would-be attacker.

"This will keep us safe," I said, showing Bob my revolver before shoving it into the jacket pocket. The pocket covered most of the weapon while my hand on the grip covered the rest. The good thing about a jacket was that I could fire through the material with a minimum loss of power.

* * *

The smell of roasting sausages floated down from the hill. I'd been too worried to eat dinner and I wasn't hungry now, but I followed the smell like a hungry dog. Actually, Fifi followed the smell and I followed her.

Only two barbeques burned near the boats. The earlier police presence had scared off most of the locals. Plenty of homeless roamed the hill. They usually showed up later in the evening, so they'd missed the police cars.

Fifi visited both barbeques, but came away empty. It wasn't a social evening. People were keeping their food and their remarks to themselves. I glanced across the wandering homeless, looking for Dusty's friend, Star. If ever I needed a psychic it was now, not that I believed in psychics. I didn't believe in her crazy clichés either, but I was desperate for any connection to Dusty, even a blind bag lady.

A woman pushed by, her grocery cart stuffed high with newspapers and filled brown paper bags.

"Have you seen Star this evening?" I asked her.

"Who?"

"Star. Blind lady with long white hair."

"Don't know her," she said and shoved her cart away.

"Who are you looking for?" Bob asked.

"Dusty's psychic friend, Star. Do you know her?"

He shrugged his shoulders.

"She has long white hair. Look up the hill and let me know if you see her."

While Bob cut across the sidewalk and headed up the slope, I stopped another one of the regulars that I recognized and asked if he'd seen Star.

"You need to lay off the weed," he said and kept walking.

Look who's talking, I wanted to call after him, but I figured his response was standard for whatever I might have asked. Did you pay your electric bill? *You need to lay off the*

weed. Did you call your mom? *You need to lay off the weed.*
Do you know who kidnapped Dusty? *You need to lay off the
weed.*

Another homeless man wearing a knit cap was curled up
against the concrete wall. His head drooped over his left
shoulder and his mouth hung open. His right hand clamped a
whiskey bottle with brown liquid still left in the bottom. I
walked toward him. He didn't stir. A sip of whiskey might
cool the fire that had been burning my stomach all afternoon.
Two sips might extinguish it for good.

I bent before the man. He was breathing heavily. I inched
the bottle out of his hand and stood, backing a few feet away.
He never moved. I unscrewed the top and took a whiff. The
hairs on my arms rose. Saliva filled my mouth.

Just one sip, I told myself. With the cuff of my jacket, I
wiped the bottle rim clean. I licked my lips and took another
whiff. It was like greeting an old friend. But something was
nagging at the back of my brain. I knew what it was and I
tried to ignore it. *Not all friends are good friends.*

One sip. One, to calm me down, to turn off the thoughts
that had been bombarding me since I found out about Dusty.
One bloody sip!

But after one, I'd want another one and another until I
couldn't think at all. I'd lose my edge. If I did, Dusty would
lose his life. No, I had to stay in the game. I had to buy Dusty
time. The top screwed on as easily as it had come off. I
squatted and slipped the bottle back into the man's hand. He
slept on.

I climbed the hill and took a last look around. As I
glanced from the homeless to the boaters, from the wanderers
to the grillers, glances greeted mine. What better place to
blend in. Was the killer out here? Was he moving
camouflaged among these people?

Was everyone watching me or was I paranoid? Wherever I looked, someone looked back.

One hand tightened on the gun grip, my other tightened on the leash. "Let's go."

The Lie

When the call came I was so deeply asleep that I don't remember answering it, but as soon as I heard the synthesized voice, I shot up.

"I want to speak to Dusty," I demanded, kicking my way out of the sleeping bag.

"Have you published the story?"

My tears had dried and left my eyes swollen and crusty. In the darkness, I rolled to my knees, the rug hard beneath me. "I promised I wouldn't as long as Detective Arkansas is safe."

"He's safe. For now."

Was that really true? "I want to speak with him."

"That's not possible. He's in a safe location as long as the story isn't published."

"Nothing will be published as long as he and I are both alive. But I need proof you aren't lying."

"You'll get your proof, but I want something in exchange."

"You're getting something in exchange. My silence. I'm not publicizing what I know about you and your clients."

Static burst through the line and I jerked the phone from my ear. I brought it back, but couldn't hear his voice. "Are you there? I can't hear you. Are you there?"

The static died away.

"I've left something in your mailbox."

"You mean my email…" And all I heard was a dial tone. I switched off the phone and went to my laptop. The time on the monitor was 3:43 a.m. I checked both of my email accounts. The only new arrival was a penis enhancement ad called "Willy Wanker."

"Cute," I said to no one. I slid it to the junk folder and slid around on the chair.

My mailbox.

Downstairs was a row of mailboxes for the apartments, but I'd yet to open mine because I hadn't given anyone this address and because all of my correspondence went through email.

My keychain lay on the table. The two larger keys went to the front door—the handle and the deadbolt. A blue aluminum key went to a narrow storage closet downstairs that Dusty had said was for my bike or surfboard. Funny guy. The last key was half the size of the others. I reached for it and walked to the front door.

I was about to open the door when my intelligence switched on. Did the caller want me to open the door? Was he waiting on the other side with a switchblade to cut my throat? I backed up until my calves hit the sofa and I dropped down, staring at the door. Was there something in my mailbox or not?

I could grab the gun, but going out there in the dark with no one around was just stupid. If this guy could haul a big guy like Dusty away, I figured that I'd be light housekeeping. I could call Bob and give him the key, but there was no guarantee he'd be safe. If the killer was waiting for me, he might kill Bob for the fun of it.

I walked to the kitchen and looked out over Dusty's dark boat. I'd balked about him living so close, but now, keeping watch was the one thing that helped soothe me. Oh, what had I done? If I'd told him about the caller in the first place, would he have been more prepared?

I'd once told him that I was cursed. He'd said bad things happen and that I wasn't the source, but I was having a hard time believing him right now. My mother, my daughter, my best friend, and now my new friend, all lined up like rifle targets at the fair. As soon as one falls the next one goes down.

I went back to the sofa and picked at the crust on my eyelashes. My muscles were vibrating beneath my skin. I'd never been wired this tight. No amount of caffeine could do this.

I-can-not-fail.

Those words ran through my head over and over. As did the image of Dusty's enthusiastic tour of the apartment on the day I arrived, looping like a broken video. His boyish smile. Hands flying as he pointed to the picture window. The way he rushed from room to room. His mischievous smirk at unsaid innuendos.

I-can-not-fail.

* * *

At seven fifteen, Fifi trotted through the room toward the kitchen with the remains of what had once been a squeaky giraffe toy in her mouth. When she spotted me on the sofa, she dropped the headless giraffe. She cocked her snout to the side and sniffed the air as if trying to figure out if my presence meant something important. Like breakfast.

Satisfied that my smell hadn't changed, she snatched up the giraffe and continued her trek to the kitchen.

Through the apartment's thin walls, I heard my neighbors beginning to stir. Even the stoner downstairs was up, because I heard him fall over and then curse loudly. Maybe all this noise was what woke Fifi so early every morning.

I went to my room and pulled on a pair of jeans. Earlier, I'd thrown a sweatshirt on over my tee shirt. I came back to the sofa to wait for my neighbors to get up and out. I wasn't going down to the mailboxes without someone else around. Fifi walked to the door and barked as if she wanted to go out. I shook my head and she came and joined me on the sofa, curling into a ball against my thigh.

The first apartment door opened at eight fifteen and the first car engine came to life soon afterwards. Then a second door opened and voices carried up between the buildings. It was now or never. I hooked Fifi's leash on her collar and picked up the gun. I unlocked my door, and in case the killer was waiting, I raised the gun. I counted to three and swung open the door.

"Holy shit!" Agent Wagner yelled, reaching for his weapon.

Fifi started barking.

I quickly lowered the Smith & Wesson to my side. "What are you doing here?"

Agent Wagner raised both his hands and pushed them at me as if to shove me out of the way. I held my ground. Fifi kept barking.

"Do you have a license for that?" he asked, pointing.

"Of course."

I had a license for the state of Massachusetts, even one to carry it concealed. Luckily, I hadn't tried to conceal it today because a California license—if I had one—didn't allow for concealment. "I'll ask again, what are you doing here?"

"Shut the dog up!" he said and we both looked down.

"Fifi!"

Fifi sat back on her hind legs and closed her jaws. She puffed out a single growl.

"Who are you expecting?" Wagner asked.

"Not you." I moved out of the doorway and he rushed past me. "I'll be right back," I said, and made a beeline for the kitchen, pulling Fifi by her leash. I shoved the revolver in the drawer with the forks and knives.

When I came back into the main room, Wagner had closed the door and was standing at the picture window with the blinds pulled wide open. "Nice view of the parking lot," he said. "Deputy Lee said that she relayed my message."

I unhooked Fifi's leash. "Right, I owe you some money."

"Don't mess with me. Why didn't you come by the Sheriff's Office?"

"A friend of Dusty's came by and then it was dark. Maybe you noticed, I'm a little jumpy since Dusty disappeared."

"Where's the weapon?"

"In the kitchen. I put it away."

Wagner turned away from the window and walked over to me. "When were you planning on coming in to answer my questions?"

"After I walked the dog. Now, you've saved me a trip. Would you like to sit down?" I walked over to the sofa and plopped down. Fifi walked back to the door and stared at it. Wagner stood.

The sofa was so low, my eye level was at his crotch. I figured it wouldn't take him long to get nervous and sit. He had a choice of sitting beside me on the sofa, which I hoped he wouldn't do, or sitting in the only chair at the table. I really needed to get a second chair for when Dusty came back.

Wagner shifted to one foot and looked around the room. He strutted to the chair, carried it across the carpet, and sat facing me. The chair height allowed him to tower over me by a foot. He probably felt like the "big man" because at five-seven he didn't have the opportunity to tower over many people.

"Now, why don't you tell me what is going on with you and Detective Arkansas?" he said.

Fifi lifted her head and burped out a bark.

"She's right," I said, nodding to Fifi, who had gone back to resting on the carpet. "There's nothing going on. A few months back, we worked a case together. We're friends, that's it."

"Agent Clark will be happy to hear that. I think she's sweet on Arkansas. Can't see it myself, but there's no accounting for taste, is there?"

His words rippled through me like an electrical shock, maybe because I didn't particularly like Clark or maybe because I wasn't ready to lose my new friend to a romance just yet. I tried to picture the two of them together, laughing, flirting, but a foul taste rose up in my throat and I shook off the image. I'd worry about Clark later. Now, I had to stay focused on getting Dusty back.

"It's always bothered me that you were in that original case meeting. Why would Detective Arkansas allow you in the meeting, when you were a witness? It didn't make sense."

"You've already asked Dusty and he told you."

"Ah, so you know about that conversation also. How much do you know about the killer we're looking for? Do you know he has a penchant for dismemberment?" His grin was more of a smirk. "Very specific dismemberment," he said, slowly.

"I found the last body, remember?"

Agent Wagner scooted forward, perching on the chair as if he were a viper about to strike. "We don't have much time if we want to find Detective Arkansas alive. Tell me the truth."

I thought about what might be downstairs in my mailbox. Was it something that could help Agent Wagner find Dusty? I'd have to see it first. I wasn't going to risk Wagner screwing up my agreement with the killer. Wagner, the alpha dog, would never play by my rules, even if they were better than his.

"I've told you the truth. He brought dinner over, we talked, we walked the dog, and I saw him sitting in his car working on the laptop. I don't know what else to tell you."

"I think you do."

I closed my eyes and exhaled. I was growing tense again. "And why's that?"

"Because every time I mention Arkansas and Clark in the same sentence your eyebrows pinch together."

"They do not."

"And each time I mention dismemberment, your eyes go all wiggly. It's personal to you, isn't it?"

He was leaning in so close I had no room to stand, but I couldn't sit still any longer. I slid my legs to the side and pushed up with my arms, sideswiping his knees as I stood.

Fifi stood too.

"Look, I have to walk the dog. If we're going to go around in circles, I'd rather be in my car looking for Dusty. Have you spoken to any of the men in his men's group?"

"What men's group?"

I hooked the leash onto Fifi's collar. "They call it Thursday Nights. They should be meeting tonight. Oh, and there's a guy with sexual issues. You might want to interview him first."

I didn't like the idea of going out of the apartment without my gun, but I didn't want Wagner to see it again. He might ask to see the license.

"Let's walk the dog," I said.

I stood behind the door as I opened it. That way if the killer was waiting for me, he'd kill Wagner first.

The Story

An early morning fog curtained the parking lot and apartment building. My muscles tensed as I turned toward the harbor and realized I couldn't see Dusty's boat anchored out there in the mist.

Agent Wagner asked me about the members in Dusty's men's group as Fifi sniffed the grass, the wall, the sidewalk, the bushes.

"Talk to the Sheriff," I said over my shoulder. "He may know more than I do." I'd rather have the Sheriff tell Wagner that Dusty was ordered into the group because of anger issues. I didn't want Wagner thinking I was closer to Dusty than anyone else because it just wasn't true. The men in that group probably knew more about him than I ever would.

Wagner strutted to his car while I walked back to the narrow row of mailboxes. I pulled out the key and stuck it into the miniature lock and turned until it clicked. What if the killer had left me an ugly surprise? What if I was about to pull out a bloody stump?

"Wagner," I called.

He stopped and turned, aggression held in his shoulders.

My brain spun into overdrive. Anything I said would have consequences.

Wagner took a step toward me.

"Let me know if you learn something," I said.

He snickered. "You'll be the first."

I took a deep breath and opened the mailbox. If I was going to scream, I'd better do it while Wagner was close.

But I didn't scream. There was no blood. No mysterious envelope or box. Only a green and white USB flash drive.

I snatched it up and shoved it into my pocket. Wagner didn't bother to look my way as he drove past and out of the lot. Fifi growled.

"I don't like him either." I picked her up and climbed the steps to my apartment.

* * *

After feeding Fifi and brewing a pot of coffee, I lit a cigarette and turned the flash drive over and over in my hand. There was a risk something on this would crash my laptop. Maybe the killer thought that would be enough to destroy my article, but I didn't think I was dealing with someone that simple-minded.

I went to the bedroom. Under a stack of folded pants, I found my backup drive. I plugged it into my USB port and started a complete backup. As my laptop and backup alternately hummed, I lit a second cigarette and poured a second mug of coffee. Dusty had been gone for more than twenty-four hours.

My stomach growled. I should eat, but the thought of food made me nauseated. The thought of Dusty locked away somewhere hurt or half-alive made me nauseated, too. The thought of his johnson… Okay…enough.

When the drive stopped humming, I checked the laptop. The process was complete. I unplugged everything and shoved my backup between the pants in my closet. At the laptop, I plugged in the flash drive and waited. A window prompted me to open the contents. I did.

Nothing exploded.

I exhaled. Two files popped up. One was a picture file, the other an audio. I clicked the picture open first.

I jumped up so quickly I knocked over the chair. When it thumped down on the carpet, Fifi came running from the other room. "Not good. Not good," I repeated, clutching my stomach and staggering away from the table.

From across the room, I looked back at the laptop. I had to go back.

In the photo filling my screen, Dusty was propped up in a corner, his chin tilted downward, his eyes closed. A thick brown rope attached his hands to a steel ring mounted on one wall. A piece of cloth was tied over his mouth. By his feet was yesterday's *San Francisco Examiner*, the date circled in red.

I walked across the room again, the image burned into my brain. Nothing about it said Dusty was still alive. Okay, there was no blood and he looked to have all his parts, but his eyes were closed and there was no hint of life.

Fresh tears spilled over my lashes. After last night, I was surprised that I had any tears left. I walked to the window and looked out over the parking lot. I remembered an Irish saying my father used to tell one of my brothers: You'll never plough a field by turning it over in your mind.

I touched the dimple in the middle of my chin. *A dimple in the chin, a devil within*. His saying for me. And this devil was going to kill a killer.

I righted the chair and sat. I clicked open the audio file and listened.

The voice was the same mechanical voice of the two phone calls. The killer wanted me to write an article and publish it. He said if it wasn't published in the *Examiner* by Saturday, I would start receiving small parts of Dusty in my mailbox. I'm pretty sure the "small" attached to "parts" was a joke. Maybe not.

"You are to tell the story of Jean Newman," the voice said. *"Jean married one of her classmates from the police academy. Her husband, Tommy, found work first and they moved to Boone, Oregon. The Boone Police Department didn't have any other officer openings, so Jean went to work as a civilian in the department. After a year, she was hired by the department as a traffic officer. That's when the arguing started.*

"Although Jean was little more than a meter maid and Tommy was a deputy, Tommy wasn't about to compete with his wife for promotions. His arguments quickly escalated into violence. By their third year of marriage, Jean was sleeping with a gun under her pillow, afraid to fall asleep before her husband arrived and she knew what mood he was in.

"The police chief went to Tommy when another officer position opened up. He told Tommy he was thinking of Jean for the spot. He was getting heat to hire a woman for the position. He asked Tommy if he'd have a problem working with his wife. He assured Tommy that the department was big enough that only in a large-scale operation would that happen and the last time Boone saw a large-scale operation was in 1982.

"Tommy raved about Jean, how well she'd done in the academy, how she loved working for the department. That night he beat Jean to within an inch of her life. She called in sick the rest of the week and the chief hired someone else.

"When Jean recovered, she tried to find an ally in the department. She told the new female officer

how Tommy was treating her. Whether it was because the officer was new and didn't want to ruffle feathers or because she wasn't sure Jean was telling the truth, the woman kept the confession to herself.

"The next time Tommy beat Jean, he broke her leg. Because it took two days before Tommy allowed her to have it looked at, the doctors told her she might never walk normally again. Her lifelong dream to become a police officer was gone. That night Jean asked her husband, a man twice her size, for a divorce. When he came at her, fist clenched and ready to strike, she fired three rounds into his chest at point-blank range. Tommy would never hit anyone again.

"Everyone in Boone stood behind Tommy, the nicest guy on the force. No one believed Jean's story of abuse and she wasn't allowed to present evidence of her abuse at trial.

"Jean went to prison for seventeen years to life. She died in a prison fire five years into her sentence."

I listened as he repeated his instructions, but my mind raced ahead. Was the story true? I tended to think it was, because why give it to me otherwise? Internet snooping would answer that question. How did the story relate to Dusty? Maybe it didn't. Why was this story important to the killer? Did he know Jean? Love Jean? Relate to Jean in some way?

I had no way of knowing Dusty would survive even if I got this story into print, but I had to try. The problem was it was an old story and who would be interested? How could I pitch it in a way that would make an editor want to print it?

Fifi barked once. I slid around on the chair and found her standing by the door. "You went out an hour ago. I know your bladder is bigger than that."

She sat on her hind legs, nose pointed.

"There's someone out there who wants to kill me. Who's going to carry your butt up and down the stairs then? Think about it."

Had I just told a dog to think? I had to get out of the apartment. I couldn't spend one more night locked away like a prisoner.

I unplugged my laptop and pocketed the flash drive. I grabbed one of the packing boxes from Fifi's room and carried it to the bedroom. The laptop went in first. On top I added a nice pair of pants and a clean pair of jeans. Lots of undies—who knew how long I'd be gone—and a few sweaters. The box was half full.

I pulled on my jean jacket and shoved my Smith and Wesson in the pocket. Hopefully, I wouldn't run into Agent Wagner this time.

I topped the box off with two packs of cigarettes. Then, for good measure, I threw in the rest of the carton. I seemed to be going through them faster than normal. I added two cans of Fifi's dog food and closed the box. I'd need wi-fi, but Dusty had said most of the libraries had that for free.

"You ready for a new home?" I asked Fifi. I'd say *with or without me,* but I didn't want to upset her.

The Escape

"I need something more... monochromatic," I said to the car rental agent. It was the same somber guy who'd stuck me with the multicolored Ford.

"But those bright colors suit your personality," he said.

In my pocket, I tightened my fingers around the gun's grip and wondered what he'd look like with a hole in the middle of his forehead. "What else do you have in the same price range?"

He moaned and pushed himself out of the comfy leather executive chair as if the effort took every ounce of his strength. He moaned again as he straightened up and his hand gripped the center of his back. He stretched his shoulders up. He was taller than Dusty and heavier and he walked with a slight limp to the right. I followed him into the narrow parking lot of used and abused cars.

He pointed to an orange 1998 VW bug. Cloth window trim, tasseled with little red balls on the end, ran along the inside top. A wobbly hula dancer was mounted on the dashboard.

"A classic," he said.

"Does it run?"

"Like a charm." He gave me a disapproving glance. "You don't need fast, do you?"

Fast enough to outrun a killer. "How fast?"

"Forty, maybe forty-five if you top off the oil."

"What else?"

He hobbled past the VW, his head turning side to side. "Oh, the G5." He sauntered over to a silver Pontiac and ran his plump hand over the pristine finish. "2009."

A four-door sedan, all one color. I looked in the driver's side. "What's wrong with it?" The interior looked almost new. "Does it have an engine?"

The agent leaned against the rear door and crossed his beefy arms. "How could I rent a car without an engine?"

How indeed? This guy was slick enough to sell oil to the Saudis. I walked to the hood. The passenger side of the car was parked against a wall. I couldn't see that side. "Why is it so cheap?"

He nodded to the far side. "Has a tiny scrape on the passenger side. That's all I've got for the same price, you want it or not?"

I glanced back at the bright green-and-black Focus. Fifi was watching from the front seat, her paws poised on the dashboard. "I'll take it."

* * *

I drove west because I couldn't think of anywhere else to go. Traffic in both directions was fairly steady as I passed through the neighborhoods of Fairfax and into the flatlands of San Geronimo. I checked the rearview mirror often. When I reached the state park, the road narrowed and began to zigzag through the tall trees. I glanced at the rearview and waited until there were no cars visible behind me. Around the next bend, I pulled over onto a shoulder used to let faster traffic pass. If the killer was following me, he wouldn't have seen me pull off the road and he'd have to drive by before he saw me. I got out and walked to the back of the car and waited.

I patted the gun in my pocket.

No one went by for the longest time until a pickup sped past. The driver didn't turn my way.

As I started to relax, another car approached going slowly. It slowed even more when the driver saw me. At the last minute it pulled onto the shoulder. The driver, a man of maybe twenty-eight sporting a shaved head, opened the door and started to get out. I was already by his passenger's door.

"You need some help?" he asked over the roof of his car.

The FBI's profile: white male between the ages of 30 and 40. I pulled out the Smith and Wesson and pointed it at his head. "You need something?"

His eyes looked as if they might pop out of his head. His skin went from rosy to chalk in two seconds flat.

I pocketed the gun. "Sorry, I thought you were someone else."

He slid back behind the wheel and burned rubber getting back on the road. Bet that was the last time he'd try to help out a stranger.

When I reached the ocean road, I drove past the Bolinas cutoff. My GPS ordered me to turn around and try again. Heading back toward Bolinas, I recognized the road from when I'd driven from Stinson Beach with TJ. After two more wrong turns, I found the main street that led into the sleepy beach town. I parked in front of the café where TJ and I had had dinner.

I tied Fifi's leash to the car's bumper and dug my laptop out of the box. Too early for lunch, the café was empty. I took a seat by the window to keep an eye on Fifi, not that I thought anyone would steal her. No such luck.

"Are you alone?" a voice asked.

I looked across the empty tables. I slid my hand into my jacket pocket and gripped the gun. "Yes."

A head popped up from behind the bar. Long brown hair. TJ's sister, BJ. She held an empty plastic tray, like the ones used to stack dirty glasses for washing.

"What can I get you?"

I pulled my hand out of my pocket. "Do you serve lattes?" It was a mom-and-pop kind of place. I expected to be laughed at.

"One?"

"One for now, then keep them coming. You wouldn't happen to have wi-fi?"

"You think you're on Mars? I'll bring you the code with the latte."

Better and better. "Could I also get some toast?"

"Just toast?"

"My stomach's upset."

"Okay, butter on the side."

I cranked up the laptop and opened my word processor. I didn't think I needed to replay the audio file to remember the story. It was a classic tale of Battered Women's Syndrome, sometimes associated with Post-traumatic Stress Disorder.

When I'd worked as a journalist for the *Dispatch*, I'd written an article titled *Women Who Kill*. The article had been based on the very public murder of a minister by his God-fearing wife. The polarity of the case generated lots of interest. So-called experts argued the case for both sides. Had it been cold, calculated murder, or self-defense?

As I'd told Mrs. Grimes, I had a hard time grasping the reasons why these women stayed in their violent relationships. The one reason I'd heard most often was that the women thought it would stop. The husband always profusely apologized, cried, and even begged for forgiveness. By the time the woman realized it wouldn't stop, her self-esteem had plummeted so much that she didn't have the emotional energy to walk out.

In some cases, the abused was so financially dependent on the abuser that she couldn't see a way out. Others, like Mrs. Grimes, feared the danger would follow them wherever they went. The abusers would find them, or their children, or their relatives, and the violence would be worse.

BJ slid a glass mug across the wooden surface and set a plate with two toasts and a cup of butter in front of me. "That your dog?"

I glanced out the window. "It's complicated."

"You can bring her inside if you want. It's okay with the owners."

"Really?"

"Everyone does."

I went outside and untied Fifi. When I brought her in, BJ had left a bowl of water on the floor beside my chair.

I picked up the toast and took a bite. I could barely swallow it. I put it down and pushed the plate away.

I wiped my hand on the napkin and turned back to the laptop to finish putting Jean's story into my own words. Trying to hype up the article, I threw in a few facts from my previous piece. Once spousal abuse was brought out into the light of public debate in the 1970s, reported abuse against wives dropped 27 percent over the next ten years. That still left 1.6 million abused wives, which I hoped might raise an editor's eyebrow.

I added that a woman was abused every nine seconds in this country. A much bigger problem than gun violence. Spousal abuse and gun violence added together were evidence of the violence we were passing down to our children.

I removed the part about gun violence. The article needed to focus on Jean's story of spousal abuse. Her loss of self, career, and ultimately, loss of her life.

I'd have to come up with a timely pitch and I had to do it quickly. Staring at the completed article, I figured I should first verify that Jean's story was true.

A quick Internet search brought up a list of titles that told me Jean Newman had been arrested for killing her husband. I clicked open one of the later news articles, hoping to find a review of the case and the conclusion at the same time.

The café door closed. I looked up and there stood TJ. He smiled generously, but didn't seem at all surprised to see me.

"Hey," he said and squatted to pet Fifi. "This your dog?"

He was scratching behind her ears and her nose was stretched so far to heaven you'd think she was having an orgasm.

"It's good to see you," I said.

He stood and pulled out the chair across from me. "I'm glad you came back."

"You won't be when I tell you why."

"Why, you hiding out from the police or something?"

I held his gaze, letting it sink in slowly while judging his reaction.

His face lit up. "No way!"

"Technically, I'm not hiding from them yet, but I'm about to do something that will make me number one on their throw-her-in-jail-and-throw-away-the-key list."

"Cool. What are you going to do? Rob a bank?"

"Print an article."

His smile fell. "You're joking?"

I shook my head. "Journalism is a powerful thing. A friend taught me that." I reached for my latte. "I was about to ask your sister if she knew of any dirt-cheap B-and-Bs in the area. The man who killed that guy we found is staking out my apartment, and once this article goes public, the FBI and the Marin County Sheriff's Department will be on my trail."

"Cool."

"TJ, it's not cool. That nutcase who killed the guy we found has kidnapped a dear friend of mine. If I don't get this article published, my friend's going to die. Hell, he might be dead already."

TJ sat still for a minute, which was strange because he always seemed to be in motion.

"Come on," he said, standing. "I know the perfect place."

"Harboring a felon is against the law. I don't want to get anyone in trouble."

"Psss. This is Bolinas. No one cares. Sis," he called over his shoulder.

I closed down the laptop.

"You never saw us," he said to BJ.

She puckered her lips and shook her head as if she was used to his theatrics.

The Hideout

TJ navigated as I drove up a twisting mountain road. The fog had burned off, but was hanging out on the horizon. The air was warm and smelling of wildflowers. TJ had me turn into a one-lane road and we passed a shingled house and then a field of orange poppies and purple lupine.

"Where are we going?"

"You'll see," he said, stroking Fifi. "Keep straight."

The weeds at the side of the road were higher and starting to scratch the car. We passed another shingled house on the left, this one smaller with wind chimes hanging across the front porch.

"Okay. Turn in behind here."

About a quarter mile from the last house, I turned left into an even narrower road, deeply rutted and unpaved. I slowed to a crawl, squeezing the car between patches of evergreens. After a hundred yards, I pulled up in front of a wooden shack with an aluminum roof. Windsurfing boards and poles laid scattered around the ground.

"Park anywhere," TJ said.

I let Fifi hop out without her leash. The air was thick with the sound of buzzing, but I didn't see any bees.

"What happened here?" TJ asked, looking at the passenger side of the car.

I walked around. Running from the front tire to the rear was a red scrape, eight inches high. It looked as if someone had sideswiped a big rig. The scrape dented the car body so badly, I was amazed the interior wasn't messed up.

"I didn't do it," was all I could say. The car went from nondescript to being highly noticeable unless I kept the passenger's side hidden. "Where are we?"

TJ pointed toward the last house on the road, its roof barely visible through the trees. "Down there's my mom's place. This shack here is where I used to work on my boards. I lived in it, too, for a while back in my terrible teen years."

He was an old man of twenty-one.

"Come inside, let me show you around."

Fifi was already running down the road toward TJ's mother's house. "Here, Fifi," I called and clapped my hands.

"She probably smells our dogs. They're pretty big. She'll turn around when she sees them."

"Big enough to eat her?"

"Don't worry, they're gentle."

"Who's worried?"

The door creaked open and a cloud of dust flew up as we stepped inside. Tools, fast food wrappers, and plastic drink bottles were scattered across the floor. Against one wall was a cot with a slim mattress on it.

TJ bent and scooped up a handful of trash. "I'll grab you a sleeping bag from the house and a pillow. If you sit outside you can get the house's wi-fi. I've tried it, it works." He piled together more trash, then walked over and dropped down on the mattress. "There's a generator." He pointed. "You can charge your phone and computer on it. You can come to the house to use the toilet, or if you don't want to walk that far, you can just go in the woods behind here."

"Pee in the woods? Really?"

"Well, yeah. Like camping."

"I grew up in inner city Boston. My dad was a cop. No woods. No camping."

"No worries. Geez." He threw up his hands in surrender. "The back door is always open."

"Sorry." I sat beside him on the mattress. "I don't mean to be snippy. I'm worried about you getting into trouble. I don't know how safe this is. The killer has already taken one person who tried to help me. I don't want him to take you, too."

"How's he going to find us?"

"He knows Bolinas. He dropped a body here."

"Good enough reason not to come back."

"True." I thought about the other risk to TJ. Harboring a fugitive. My record of keeping my friends safe was hovering somewhere around zero percent. And here I was about to put someone else in danger.

Where else could I go? I hadn't much money for a hotel and I had to do what I could to free Dusty. Just a day or two. By then, either Dusty would be safe or I'd be in jail. "Whatever happens, I'll always deny that you knew I was in hiding. As far as you are concerned, I'm only here visiting."

TJ draped an arm across my shoulders. He smelled like the beach. "Want to fool around?"

I pulled away and shoved his arm off. "It's not going to happen." I turned to him and saw what Dusty had seen that night on the beach. He was a kid. A suntanned, sun-bleached surfer kid. What had I been thinking?

"Does that change things?"

"No sweat," he said, slumping into a crestfallen pose. "It's that cop, right? The one on the beach. You in love with him?"

"What? No? He's a detective. We're just friends." I was getting tired of everyone thinking there was more than friendship between us.

"Whatever. I saw the way…wait! Oh, man, is he the one missing? I saw his picture on TV."

"He's my friend and yes, he's missing. My friends tend to disappear, so you should think long and hard about my staying here." I took the gun out of my jean pocket and set it on the mattress.

"Whoa." TJ stood, took a step away, and slipped on an empty potato chip bag. "What's that?"

I glanced at the Smith and Wesson. "My gun. I did mention a killer was stalking me."

"You can stay, but the gun has to go."

"I need it for protection."

"When I was a kid my friend's dad had a gun for protection. One Saturday he was cleaning it and blew a hole in my friend's face."

I picked up the gun and put it back in my pocket.

"Don't do that," TJ yelled. "You'll shoot yourself." He was pulling on his hair and shifting from foot to foot. "My dad always says that the way to get killed with a gun is to have a gun."

"It has a safety. I've had this for several years and never shot anyone, not even myself." I didn't tell him that Haylee had believed the same thing as his dad and had taken it away from me a year ago. "Okay, I'll put it in the glove compartment. Will that be okay?"

Maybe he'd kick me out after all.

"Do it now."

I went out to the car and shoved the gun in the glove compartment. I had to mash the rental agreement folder to make it fit.

TJ was still standing when I came back in.

"Grab your laptop," he said. "Let's go up to the house."

* * *

As we hiked through the tall grasses toward the house, a breeze carried the scent of wild lavender. When we were about twenty feet away, two large dogs came out and stood at attention on the back porch of the house. One was black and gray and looked as if he could tear my head off without a second thought. The other, caramel brown, looked as if he wouldn't tear my head off unless the gray one did. Both were mixed breeds and neither from the same family.

When Fifi spotted them, she barked and took off running toward them. TJ's dogs split up, the gray one going right, the brown one going left. Fifi clamored up the steps to find herself alone at the top. She looked side-to-side, surprised. She lifted her muzzle to show her contentment. My fierce warrior.

"TJ, if anything happens to me, would you look out for Fifi?"

"No problemo."

Easy for you to say.

The inside of the house was eclectic with sculptures, ceramics, and other original pieces of art. Every surface had something interesting to look at. There was a painting of Uncle Sam baring his bottom. There was a set of ceramic goblets with sparkling rims. There were several mobiles made from driftwood and sandblasted glass. And the famous Bolinas-sign coffee table that TJ had told me about last week at dinner.

"Don't tell my mom about the gun. Wait here, I'll get her."

He was still worried about the gun. When people were irrational, it made me nervous and I had enough to worry about right now. I sank down on the plush, green velvet sofa. The two lattes I'd drunk were beginning to wear thin and I needed a cigarette in the worst way.

Glass pieces from one of the mobiles tinkled together.

Outside, Fifi was barking. I wondered if I should check on her, but heard TJ's footsteps coming down the hall.

TJ's mother was the same height as he was. Her hair was greasy, her face sunken-looking, and dark circles ringed her eyes. He'd said that she'd recently gone through chemo for breast cancer and was having a hard time regaining her strength. She walked slowly, leaning on TJ's arm. He helped lower her to the sofa beside me.

For a second time, I realized this arrangement wasn't going to work out. TJ's mother needed him here, not in jail. I couldn't take the risk of the FBI finding me here.

"Briana, mom's a lawyer. I told her everything."

My heart hit the floor. My back went rigid. He couldn't have told her everything because he didn't know everything. But as a lawyer, she'd taken certain oaths that could work against me now.

Mrs. Quentin smiled. Although her facial skin looked thin and fragile, I sensed that smile had once been warm and soothing. "I'm sure he hasn't told me everything, but it sounds like you're in some trouble."

"I'm not in trouble yet because I haven't done what the killer is demanding that I do, but—"

"Isn't withholding information during an investigation illegal?"

Her body might be slow, but her mind was clear enough.

"A friend of mine has been kidnapped by a serial killer—"

"Serial killer, whoa," TJ said.

I clasped my hands over my mouth. Suddenly, I was Miss Chatterbox. "You didn't hear that," I said through my fingers. I dropped my hands. "I'm not supposed to have that information, so you definitely shouldn't have it. Don't even say the words serial killer again."

"What's the big deal?" TJ asked.

I glanced at his mother. Her furrowed brow let me know that she got it.

"TJ, the police leave out information to try to make people slip up," I said. "You found the last body. People who find the bodies are always suspect."

"You were with me."

"But I alibi-ed out. I'd just arrived in town. You, on the other hand, led me to the spot under the tree. Get it? If you know something you're not supposed to know, they'll throw you in jail and ask questions later." I debated telling him that Dusty originally had suspected him.

"Whoa."

Mrs. Quentin brought her hands together in her lap. "Go on with what you were saying," she said.

I couldn't take my eyes off TJ. He was muscular enough to lift a body. But could he have approached Dusty without causing alarm? No. I didn't think so. Dusty had taken an instant dislike to the guy. He would have arrested TJ for being near my apartment.

"Briana?" his mother said.

I felt horrible for even wondering and hoped it didn't show on my face. "The killer is demanding that I release an article about an old case in order to save my friend's life. My friend is a detective in the Marin County Sheriff's Department, and I truly believe that the department would support me in doing whatever I must, to save Dusty."

"Ah, Lieutenant Arkansas."

"You know him?"

"Heard of him and I've seen the news. But that doesn't explain why you need a place to hide out."

"I don't mean to be rude, but I've already said too much. I don't want to say anything that may make you have to break a vow or would put your career at risk."

She reached out and took my hand in hers. Her skin was on fire. "I used to be a litigation lawyer. Now, I mostly work with immigrants trying to earn legal status. I understand better than most that the law doesn't serve everyone."

"Well, there's the withholding information thing, but the biggy is that I can't see a way to pitch this article to an editor without revealing its...importance."

She nodded and looked at her son. She had kind eyes. "I've been ill," she said, her voice soft. "I spend most of my day in my room. I think this is the last time we'll talk. I know you came out here to write an article and if asked, I'll say you wouldn't tell me about what."

"Thank you."

"One more thing. I don't want you involving TJ any more than you already have."

"I won't, I promise. I'll keep my mouth shut." With my free hand, I made a zipping motion across my lips.

She released her grip. "TJ, will you help me up?"

TJ rushed to her side. I slid my arm under hers and helped TJ lift her. "I'll go, if you think it's best."

"Don't be silly. Nothing illegal about writing an article. Not in this country."

TJ led her out of the room, and a sadness washed over me.

The Editor

I went back to the shack and straightened it up enough to move around without stepping on anything. Outside, I tied Fifi's leash to a pine tree and she lay down under its shade and went to sleep. I turned over one of the windsurf boards, brushed it clean, and set up my laptop. As TJ had said, I connected with the wi-fi from the house, but the signal was weak.

I read down the list of the *San Francisco Examiner's* editors. I didn't see a metro desk and figured one of the managing editors handled it. There was a tip line, but even though I considered this story a tip, I doubted anyone else would. I called my connection on the *San Francisco Chronicle*, but she wasn't in.

Enough procrastinating. I would have to be checked out and the story would have to be fact checked before it went into the cue for Saturday morning. The editor-in-chief. I punched in the number and he answered himself. More evidence of a dying medium.

"Briana Kaleigh. Up until April I worked for a daily out of D.C., The *District Dispatch*."

"We're not hiring," he said and the line went dead.

I was speechless. I hit redial.

"I have an article for you," I said before he could open his mouth.

"What kind of article?"

"The murder kind." I told him the gist of Jean Newman's story. As I did, I realized that I hadn't finished verifying her story myself. I'd been so anxious about Dusty that I let the first rule of journalism slide—accuracy.

"It doesn't sound like anything we'd want to print. Have you tried the *Chronicle*?"

"It needs to be printed in Saturday morning's *Examiner*."

"You have a problem then because we only publish Sunday through Friday."

Had the killer thought of that? Was I guaranteed to fail? "Then you have to publish it tomorrow morning."

He cleared his throat. "And why is that?"

This was what I'd been dreading. To say anything more I was compromising an open investigation. But what choice did I have? There was no interest in an old story like this unless it was linked to current events.

"Could you take my word for it if I gave you references that checked out?"

"I'm a busy man and I don't like my time wasted."

"I know I sound like a quack, but I'm not. In April, Debra Kirkland over at the *Chronicle* bought an article from me, a murder that I helped crack. I worked the metro desk and the crime desk at the *District Dispatch*." I gave him my name again and told him to look me up.

"Let's say all this checks out. We're a free paper. We mostly print local news. This story's out of Oregon *and* it's not current. I can't print it unless you give me a reason that stirs my soul."

Down at the house, I saw TJ step out on the front porch. I wanted to end this call before he came this way. Time to break the law. "Last week there was a murder in Bolinas of a Dr. Grimes."

"We ran something on it."

"The killer of Dr. Grimes has demanded that this story be printed in the *Examiner* by Saturday morning. If not, he will kill another man."

"Does this have anything to do with the missing detective? Wasn't he working on a murder case?"

I stood and circled the windsurf board. "The killer has kidnapped Detective Arkansas."

"Kidnapped? I heard he was missing, but I didn't hear anything about a kidnapping. I'll need to verify this with my FBI source."

"If you do that, the article will be dead and so will Detective Arkansas. If you have a FBI source, you know how they work. The killer called me directly."

"Like the Zodiac?"

"What?"

"An old case, you're probably too young. How do you know it was the killer and not some crazy? I can't print an unverified article."

"If I can verify that Jean Newman worked for the Boone Police Department and that she died in jail after being convicted of killing her husband, will you print it?"

"You haven't done that yet?"

"Partly, I admit I've been lax." The words stuck to my tongue like cotton because I knew I was better than that. "This whole thing has shaken me up."

He didn't say anything for the longest time.

"I still can't see why you think this old story has anything to do with Dr. Grimes's murder," he finally said.

"The next thing I tell you is off the record and you have to keep it to yourself."

"Thrill me."

"Dr. Grimes was a wife beater, and so were two other California men that this killer has murdered and mutilated."

"A serial? Just like the Zodiac."

I vaguely remembered the Zodiac case. It was journalism school legend. But I didn't remember the particulars, only that a journalist was involved. "Will you help me?"

He was silent, but I heard the sound of a pencil moving across paper. "Email me what you've got and call back in an hour. I need to check you out and see what we have here."

"Don't talk to the FBI or you'll be signing Detective Arkansas's death warrant. I'm serious."

I walked over to where TJ was petting Fifi. She really liked him. She'd probably be happy with him when I went to prison.

"I've done it. I've compromised the investigation. This editor will either let the FBI know what I know and they will be after me, or he'll print the article and the FBI will be after me. Either way, I'm officially on the run from the Feds."

"Cool."

"Yeah, cool." I imagined Wagner's tight little face when he learned of my involvement. "How's your mother?"

"She's sleeping. Want to go down to the beach? Thought I'd try to catch some waves."

Off to the west, the fog bank was rolling in. The wind had picked up and the air had a chill to it.

"You go on. I have to make some calls and verify this story in case the *Examiner* is actually going to print my article."

* * *

I read through several newspaper articles on Jean Newman's arrest. She'd been a fairly attractive woman with big blue eyes and blond shoulder-length hair. Her story made quite a stir in the feminist population. The evidence against her was overwhelming because she'd confessed. In 2002, she was confined to Oregon's only women's prison, which caught fire in 2005. Two cells burned, one was Newman's. Three bodies were recovered, Jean and two other prisoners. It was thought to have been set by one of the female guards, who disappeared afterwards.

Another article said the guard had been Newman's lover. I looked at the prison photo. Jean's transformation after three years in jail was amazing. She'd been working out. Her hair was cut short and her neck was as thick as a linebacker's. Maybe she was working out to protect herself from the guard's advances. Unfortunately, abused women tended to repeat their history.

I mapped directions to the prison. It was an eleven-hour trip from San Rafael. Why was Jean's story so interesting to this killer? It wasn't the first time I'd wondered, but now I had time to think about it. Maybe he was related to her. He must have known her somehow. This was where the FBI might come in handy. With any luck, they'd have this info by morning.

I called back the editor-in-chief. "Did you get my email?" I'd sent him everything I'd found as well as my article of Jean's story.

"Got it. You checked out…sort of. The editor at the *Dispatch* said you were just a photographer."

"Before that I worked the crime desk for two years, but I didn't leave on friendly terms. Long story."

"I don't want to hear it."

"I sent you links to a few of my old stories. Check the byline."

"Jean Newman's old information checks out," he said. "What doesn't check out is the link to the Grimes's murder."

"I told you—"

"You didn't let me finish. I have verified Grimes was mutilated, which wasn't previously known to the press, so

I'm going to take a chance on you. Front page of tomorrow's edition. Now, what about a byline?"

"Can you use Anonymous?"

"Don't usually. I'll see what I can do, but if this is legit, the Feds are going to be beating my door down and anonymous won't be anonymous. You get me?"

"I do, but I don't want my name on it."

"You're coming to me, right, with any further communication?"

"You're my guy, but my first priority is to protect Detective Arkansas, not get you a news story." I gave him my phone number and he said he'd call after the article went public.

190

The Toilet

Around seven a.m., engulfed by a thick and chilly fog, I
hiked the trail down the hill and into town. TJ had shown me
the trail the night before when he told me he usually slept
until ten. I couldn't wait for him to wake up. I had to see if
the article had been printed. Only then would I have my
bargaining power back.

As I approached the ATM sign hanging on the corner of
the town market, sirens roared toward me. I ran under the
awning and turned to find a row of Marin County Sherriff's
Department vehicles bursting through the feathery clouds. I
ducked into the market as the sales clerk rushed to the door to
see what the commotion was.

"Lots of police," I said and pushed past him.

While he stood in the doorway watching, I shot through
the market and out the rear. I ran for the café, three buildings
down. I half-climbed, half-fell over the little white picket
fence that went around the back of the outdoor dining area.

The café's back door stuck, but I could tell by the
movement that it wasn't bolted. I shoved my shoulder into it
with all my might. It gave and I tumbled into the café. BJ,
who'd been at the window, came running. "What's going
on?"

"Hide me."

She helped me to my feet. "This is about you?"

I brushed off my jeans. "Your brother didn't tell you?"

"How would they know you're here?"

"Good question. I have no idea."

Outside, a car skidded to a stop.

BJ grabbed my arm. "Come on."

She led me out the rear and down a concrete path to what looked like a garden shed. A sign with the outline of a woman was stuck to the door. She pushed me into the restroom and pulled a set of keys from her apron pocket. She unlocked a storage closet and shoved me inside.

"Keep quiet until I come back."

"They could be here all day."

"Then you better get comfortable."

She closed the closet door and the lock clicked.

A few minutes later my eyes adjusted to the darkness. A strip of light filtered in at the bottom of the door. I'd briefly seen shelves lined with bottles and paper products as I came in and I didn't want to knock anything over. I bent my knees and tried to drop straight down into a sitting position. Since I'm only graceful in a skewed world, I fell to the side, but caught myself without making too much racket.

The floor beneath me was cold and smelled like a used toilet. I hoped I wouldn't be here long, but if the deputies were looking for me, they'd certainly do a thorough search of the city. How had they tracked me? Traffic cameras? Through a state park? I didn't think so.

We'd hidden my car in the woods behind the shed. TJ had given me an old vinyl tarp to throw over it. Everything else I'd brought was at TJ's: my clothes, my laptop, my phone. If the deputies found those, TJ might have to tell them where I was. I'd told him not to risk jail time; his mother needed him.

I heard voices and tried to get a direction. Although the toilet was behind the café, it was also to the right side of the building. Were the voices coming from the street? As hard as I tried, I couldn't make out any words. I leaned forward and pressed my temple against the door. I had to relax. Anxiety wouldn't do me any good.

A little later the restroom door whooshed opened and I held myself still. Someone stepped over to the toilet and relieved herself. A faucet came on. Ah, a hand-washer. After the door bumped closed, a throbbing silence again surrounded me. I was stiffening in my cross-legged position. Just as I was about to wiggle my legs to the side, the restroom door opened again and the aroma of coffee filled the tiny closet. My mouth watered. The smell was strong; she must be carrying a large cupful. I took a deep breath. Oh, what I wouldn't give for a latte.

A loud fart echoed across the room. I clamped my mouth. Then a grunt. Another grunt. The next smell to fill the closet was of something dead and rotting. I pinched my nostrils closed. How to ruin a pleasant coffee buzz. I'd never drink coffee again.

Yeah, right.

The stink lingered long after the woman had gone. My knees ached so I used the door handle to pull myself up. The restroom door swung open again.

"Oh geez," someone said. It sort of sounded like BJ.

I heard the window hinges creak. A fresh breeze blew in under the door and freed my nostrils from assault. The person walked over to the closet door. Her shadow blocked the crack of light at the bottom. I froze.

"The breakfast rush is over," BJ said in low tones. "But the town is still full of cop cars. I'll come back when it's safe."

The restroom door closed.

I figured it was somewhere between nine-thirty and ten. I was possibly looking at another couple of hours in here. If they'd found TJ, or any of my stuff, surely BJ would have said.

Pressing my back against the door, I slid down and closed my eyes. By now, the killer should have seen the article. Dusty should have been released. Unless the editor went to the FBI and the article hadn't been printed. In that event, I had one more day to get the article published. I should plead my case before Agent Clark. Maybe she cared enough about Dusty to do the right thing.

I must have drifted off to sleep because the flush of the toilet startled me. Brighter light filtered in from under the door and shapes formed in the closet. A bucket. A mop. A plunger.

I had more room than I'd thought. When the restroom door closed, I scooted around to face the closet door again. Sleeping wasn't a great idea; it might give me away.

For the next few minutes the toilet stayed busy. I must have slept a good bit if it was already lunchtime. I stood and pulled off my sweatshirt. The closet was growing warmer.

Two girls or women—I couldn't tell by their voices— came in together.

"You go, I can wait," one said. She had a high shrill voice.

"You sure?" the other asked.

"Go. So what's with all the cop cars?"

"Haven't you seen the picture? They're passing around a picture of some chick."

"Think she's the one who murdered that guy out on the beach last week?" Shrill Voice asked.

They thought I was a killer?

"Must be. Why else would the cops be looking for her? The guy I talked to was FBI."

"Was he cute?"

"Kinda. I'm done. I didn't flush to save water. You flush when you're done."

Their soles shuffled across the concrete.

"Maybe it was her husband," Shrill Voice said. "Sometimes I think I could kill mine."

They both laughed. The toilet flushed.

I rocked back and forth on the balls of my feet. I stretched my arms up over my head and clasped my hands. Me, a killer. If the article wasn't published, I might just be one. If only I'd seen the *Examiner* before the militia arrived. I wiggled my fingers and stretched my face by making a huge smile. I really wanted to move, not a little but a lot. Not knowing what was happening was making my skin crawl. I rubbed my arms and thighs.

I spread out my sweatshirt and sat on top. I leaned forward and pressed my temple into the cold, smooth wood. I wished BJ would come back, but she must be in the middle of the lunch crowd. The restroom door didn't open for the longest time.

He who laughs last, laughs best. I wished that stupid cliché would stop popping into my head. Ah, Dusty, please forgive me. I should have told you about the caller. I should have told you about the link I'd found.

The door swooshed open and thudded on the stop.

"Shhhh," said a man.

A female giggled. "Lock the door."

Are you kidding me?

The sound of a heavy belt buckle hitting the concrete. "Remove this," the man said.

Another giggle. A snap of elastic.

Someone slammed against the closet door, causing my temple to bounce against it. I sat up and massaged my forehead.

"Mmmmm. Mmmm. Be careful," the female said.

"Put your leg here," the man said.

The closet door thumped again.

And again.

Whoa. They were going to burst through the wood. This wasn't the way I wanted to be found. I stood. I shook out my hands. I needed a cigarette.

"Ah, yeah, baby, like that. Ah, baby."

Bump, bam, bam.

I wasn't the one having sex and I needed a cigarette. Badly. Dusty hadn't been released. If he had, the police, the FBI, they would be with him and not so interested in me. The editor had lied or the killer had lied. Either way, Dusty was still in danger.

Bump. Bump.

"Faster."

Bump, bump, bump.

Oh, Lord. I crossed myself and said a prayer to one of my favorite saints, Saint Rita, patron saint of desperate causes. As soon as I realized the irony of my prayer, someone knocked on the restroom door.

"Anyone in there?" a voice called.

"Shit," the female said, and then in a hushed voice told her companion to stop whatever he was doing. "Just a minute," she called to the person at the door. "Put your pants on," she said softly.

"But…"

"Now."

I heard the rustling of clothing and couldn't imagine what they were going to say to the person at the door. The restroom door opened and nothing was said. The door closed and I didn't hear any new footsteps come in. I was alone again. My thoughts drifted back to Saint Rita.

Because my life was an open invitation to desperate causes, I'd grown up praying to Saint Rita, who'd been introduced to me when I was fourteen. I'd been expelled from school for fighting and my father had been livid. He sent me to Vermont to stay with my Aunt Eileen. She taught me about my Irish heritage, the mythology of the Druids, Finn MacCool, and the Earth Goddess. But being a pious woman she also taught me about Jesus, the Bible, and the saints.

"A girl growing up without a mother needs to know about Saint Rita," she'd said. "Saint Rita of Cascia was born in Italy and despite wanting to become a nun, she was married off at a young age to an abusive man. For eighteen years, she remained devoted to this cruel man until he was murdered by an enemy. When she was unable to stop her sons from seeking revenge on their father's killer, she prayed for their deaths rather than have them continue the cycle of violence. Her prayer was granted and afterwards she joined a convent where she lived until dying of tuberculosis."

After all these years, I'd completely forgotten about the abusive husband. Aunt Eileen had also said that after joining the convent, Rita prayed so fervently that a small gash opened on her forehead and remained open for the last fifteen years of her life. That was the first time I'd heard about the stigmata.

For the few months I'd lived with Aunt Eileen, I went to bed and prayed so hard to be good, so I could go back home to my father and brothers, that I gave myself a headache. Every morning, I ran to the mirror to see if I had an open wound in my forehead.

Every morning, I was disappointed.

The Getaway

Now, my head was pounding from a serious lack of caffeine, and if I didn't have a cigarette soon I was going to kill someone. Yes, really.

Either the fog was rolling in or the sun was setting because the air had grown cooler. I put on my sweatshirt. No one had come to the toilet in a long time, more than an hour. I was jumping up and down and shaking out my hands to try and keep sane. It wasn't working.

The restroom door opened.

"Briana?"

BJ. I was saved. *Thank you, Saint Rita.* I clasped my hands. *May God bless you.*

"I'm still here." She'd locked me in; where did she think I was going to go?

"Most of the cops are gone. TJ's going to take a drive around town. If it's safe, he'll come to the back with Mom's car. The trunk is big enough that we can put you inside and he'll take you to the house."

"Have you heard anything about Dusty?"

But she was gone. The restroom door bumped shut.

I closed my eyes and pictured the cigarette pack on the floor beside the cot. My mouth watered. I licked my lips, and imagined lighting one up and inhaling. The crazy thing was, I felt calmer. My muscles relaxed with the imagery.

The restroom door opened again. The lock on the closet door clicked open. TJ stood before me, his sun-bleached curls backlit and making him look like a breathing statute of Saint Michael.

"So this is what the ladies' room looks like," he said, glancing around.

"Get me out of here." I rushed to the restroom door, but stopped short of opening it. "Is it safe?"

"There are two police cars left and they're stationed at the only exit from town. We'll get you to the house and decide what to do."

I didn't say anything. There was no deciding.

I had to move on. I wouldn't risk getting him or his family in any more trouble than I already had. I stepped away from the door. "I'll follow you."

His mother's sedan was parked by the white picket fence. The trunk was open.

"Do you think that's necessary?" I asked. "I can lie in the back seat."

"And if we're stopped?"

I lifted a leg into the trunk. "Wait! Have you heard anything on the news about Dusty?"

"No. But I read your article in the paper."

I hoisted myself onto the spare tire, a fat screw cutting into my butt. As the hood dropped down and clicked shut, panic rolled through my chest. Total darkness. This time, there wasn't a crack of light. I said another prayer to Saint Rita.

The ride was smooth at first with only a slight amount of exhaust fumes leaking into the trunk. When we reached what I assumed was the hill towards TJ's house, I started getting tossed around and the fumes were causing me to cough. Then the car slowed. I rocked over the fat screw as the car pulled to a stop. The trunk popped open. I couldn't climb out of the warm fumes fast enough.

"Where are you going?" TJ called as I sprinted across the field to the shed.

Inside, the place was cleaned out. All my stuff gone. TJ ran in behind me.

"My stuff?" But for the instant my cigarettes were all I cared about. It was times like this that I knew I had to quit, but it was also times like this that I didn't think I'd ever be able to, and that was more frightening to me than dying of lung cancer. I hated knowing that something as meager as a roll of tobacco could hold me captive.

"It's all at the house. I took everything to my room so I could say it was mine."

"Did the police come by?"

"The FBI. A man and a woman.

"Did they find my things?"

He shook his head. "They looked through my room, but didn't take anything."

He removed something from his pocket. "Here's your phone. I removed the battery and the SIM card."

"Why?"

"I don't know. That's how the cops always trace people on TV."

I'd left my phone on. I was waiting for a call from the editor. "Good thinking," I said, feeling like an idiot. If that was how they'd traced me to Bolinas, I deserved to go to jail. What was wrong with me lately? I was usually more on the ball than this.

"I took it to Stinson and made a call before I removed the battery and SIM," TJ said, smiling. "The police moved on an hour ago."

"You're quite the super spy," I said.

"We should be partners."

No. I had a partner. And he was in trouble. "I know you're against the whole cigarette thing, but I need one, badly."

"Guess you do, you're sweating. Come on."

"About the phone, you only need to remove the battery. It's so the GPS chip won't get any juice," I said as we walked to the house.

When I stepped into the kitchen, Fifi leaped up my leg. I bent and picked her up. "Did the agents see Fifi?" Wagner should have recognized her.

TJ shook his head. "We had a story prepared, but we didn't have to use it."

"That's good. I don't want you lying."

"I put Fifi in mom's room and when the agents came I asked them not to disturb her."

"You're kidding? They didn't bother her?"

"They wanted to meet with her. She came out for a few minutes and answered their questions, and then she went back in her room."

A cold chill rolled down my spine. "What did they ask her?"

"If she'd seen you. They had a picture of you. It wasn't very good."

"Did your mother lie?"

"No. Here are your cancer sticks and your phone battery and SIM. Let's go outside so you don't stink up the house."

I put Fifi down and sniffed my sweatshirt. It smelled like burnt gasoline. I probably shouldn't light a cigarette around it, but the cig was lit before I was out the door. I inhaled twice as I paced before the house. "What did your mother say when they showed her my photo?"

"She said you'd come here yesterday to see me and then you'd left and she didn't know where you were, which was true. I knew where you were because BJ had called."

I inhaled two more times, my muscles softening with each lungful of poison.

"Years ago, Mom was working on this big litigation case against an oil company and we got raided by the Sheriff's Department. They waited until mom was at work, then they frightened BJ into opening the door and letting them in. My mom went ballistic. I've never seen her so mad."

I stubbed out the cigarette. "Do you have a copy of the *Examiner*?"

"Let me get it."

I lit a second cigarette, but only took a few puffs before TJ came back with the paper. The article was page one. *Marin Detective Kidnapped by Killer* was the headline.

"I need to get out of town tonight."

TJ rubbed his chin. "Guess you do."

"But you said the only exit was barricaded by two deputies."

He grinned. "No problemo. I'll drive your car out of town and park it farther up Route 1. Then we'll take my friend's dirt bike up the coast. You'll have to hike about half a mile. No sweat."

"Something tells me you're enjoying this."

"It's kind of fun trying to outwit the Feds. Can I listen to the recording the killer sent you?"

"TJ, you're already in enough trouble. I promised your mother."

* * *

We waited until dusk to leave. TJ had moved my car with little trouble. The police stopped him, checked his license, and made him pop the trunk, but let him through. His friend brought him back on the motorbike.

"They must not have a description of my new rental," I said, pulling on the backpack that TJ had lent me. "That's

good news. Hopefully, Wagner still thinks I'm driving the
ugly Ford, but it won't take him long to figure out it was
rented. Soon he'll find the clerk, who'd switched the rental
cars."

"By then you'll be long gone," TJ said. He patted the seat
behind him on the dirt bike. "Hop on."

The initial thrust of the bike made me swallow my heart,
but as we traveled north, the breathtaking view of the coast
squashed any fear I had about TJ's driving. When we cut east
into a national park, redwoods towered over us and pines
scented the air. Beneath the heavy branches, it quickly grew
dark. At one point, the bike was unable to make it up the
mountainous incline with both of us so I got off and walked.
When we reached the bottom at other side, TJ pulled over
and killed the engine.

He handed me my car keys. "This is the end of the trail.
You'll have to go the rest of the way on foot. Follow this
path to a footbridge across the creek. Keep going until you
hit the road, then go north. You should see your car in the
lookout parking lot."

We hugged. My last sniff of his ocean scent now so
familiar that I wished I could bottle it and carry it with me.
"There are no words for what you've done for me." I pulled
him close and kissed his cheek. "Thank your mother. Be nice
to Fifi."

"I'll see you when you come for the dog."

"Or you can bring her on jail visits."

"Where are you heading?" he asked.

"L.A.," I lied. I wished I could say I really, really trusted
him, but Dusty had shoved a grain of doubt in my brain and
that was all it took to sprout a field of paranoia. Then, there
was Wagner, who could probably break TJ if he figured out
I'd been to TJ's house. All it would take is one eyewitness.

I'd told TJ not to risk jail for me and I'd made him promise. What he didn't know, he couldn't share.

I turned away and started down the path. The dirt bike's motor revved when I reached the footbridge.

The Prison

I'd managed a few hours of sleep in a dark highway rest stop, and was buzzing with two lattes. A little after one p.m. when I pulled into the parking of the Oregon Women's Correctional Facility, I suddenly wished I'd eaten the other half of my breakfast burrito.

I'd called ahead for an appointment. The warden didn't work Saturdays, but I was assured someone would be available to help me.

From the lot, I watched prisoners playing soccer in the yard. Not a jumpsuit in sight. They were dressed in blue jeans and tee shirts of various colors. Half a dozen women sat on two concrete picnic tables cheering the players. A guard was cheering, too.

In another area of the yard, several women were on their knees working in the soil of a massive vegetable and flower garden. If not for the fence and barbed wire, I'd have thought I was at an unfunded private school.

Inside, I signed in with my old *District Dispatch* press badge and a female guard led me to a locker room and told me to remove any metal jewelry, belts, and an underwire bra, if I had one. I'd been told when I called not to wear jeans— didn't want to confuse the visitors with the inmates. At a rest stop, I'd changed into my black linen Eileen Fisher slacks. I don't know why I'd grabbed them when I was rushing to leave my apartment, but they were comfortable and I almost looked official.

After I stored my personal things in the locker, another female guard ran a wand across me and then patted me down. I'd been to prisons before, but this always felt invasive. She unlocked the first gate and passed me off to a third guard, a man, who opened the second gate.

"C-2," the female guard said to the male.

"You're here for Laetitia?" he asked me.

I nodded, although that wasn't the name I was given on the phone. "The person in charge," I said.

We walked down a corridor of raw concrete walls, fluorescent tube lighting the only light source. He led me to a windowless room with rows and rows of wooden desks. He switched on the lights and gestured me inside.

"Someone will be with you," he said and closed the door between us.

Muted sounds carried through the walls, but nothing I could make out. For all I knew I was hearing the cheers of the players in the yard.

Walking around the desks, I read the pencil-carved graffiti. *Riot! SWAG. Love rocks. Me & Eddie.*

I imagined the teacher counting the pencils as they were handed out and counting them again before anyone left the room. Pencils made good weapons. I'd learned that in grade school when I fell carrying one and it went into my palm. Hurt like crazy.

The door opened. A woman, dressed in black pants and a white blouse tied at the waist, came in. She led with her shoulders and moved with an air of authority. Her dark skin was flawless and her hair was a mass of dreads held together in a ponytail at the back. Draped around her neck, like a necklace, was her ID badge. "Hi, I'm Laetitia," she said.

I took her hand and introduced myself.

"I'm glad Jean's case is finally getting some attention," she said. "It'll help others like her."

"Would you mind if I made some notes?"

She smiled. "You'd need a pen for that."

I waited. She had to know I wasn't allowed to carry anything in with me.

She walked over to a metal cabinet and, using a key attached to her ID badge, she opened the doors and took out a ballpoint pen and a sheet of paper. "Will this do?"

"Thank you. I have a fairly good memory, but sometimes I write things that only make sense later. It'll keep me from having to bother you down the road."

I sat down at a desk and she turned around the desk in front so as to face me.

"I guess the first thing I'd like to hear about is the fire. I understand that a guard set it."

"That was never proven," Laetitia said. "Please don't make us look bad in your article. We really do a lot of good for these women."

"I can see that by looking around. Trust me, it's not my goal to make you look bad, I'm here looking into something that should have been looked into a long time ago."

Laetitia's features warmed; she almost smiled. "Arlette could be a handful. That was the guard. Because Jean had worked for the police department, part of Arlette's job was to keep her safe. Arlette was a bodybuilder and she got Jean into a training program. Jean knew it was in her best interest to get stronger and after a few months she started to have a passion for working out."

"Like a runner's high."

"I suppose you could call it that. It wasn't uncommon to find her doing pushups or sit-ups in her cell. She was always pulling a muscle or getting some type of sports-related injury."

"So what happened?"

"No one knows. Jean's roommate was released from our jurisdiction two weeks earlier and it was rumored that Arlette was spending more and more time with Jean. Touching and sex, consensual or not, is forbidden here, but let's face it, women need physical contact. They need to be held. It happens, that's all I'll say."

"They became lovers?"

"I was told that Arlette wanted to, but Jean wasn't sure. Jean wanted to take it slow, but Arlette could be a bird dog when she wanted something. I know that firsthand." She blew out a breath of air. "Now, all this is supposition. What our investigation turned up was black and white. Jean's cell caught fire, killing Jean and the two inmates in the adjoining cell. Cameras show Arlette leaving the prison right before lockdown and she never showed up at her apartment or at the prison. She just disappeared."

Laetitia pressed her hands flat on the desktop. Her nails were professionally done. "It's still an open investigation. A FBI guy called, wanted us to fax him the file. Maybe now someone will do something about finding Arlette. When women die, it's never taken as seriously as when a man is killed. If the woman's a prisoner, well, who cares?"

That sounded as if she'd lost someone close to her, but I had to stay on track. "When did the FBI guy call?"

"Yesterday. I copied everything and sent it to him. Isn't that why you called?"

She assumed that I knew about the case because the FBI had put me on to it. Too bad it didn't work that way. But I was glad to know the FBI was taking Jean's story seriously, and I was happier that they were ahead of me instead of trailing. It made it easier for me to stay invisible.

"How did the fire start?"

Laetitia didn't like the question. She squirmed sideways in the desk and crossed her long legs. "The investigation turned up accelerant."

"Where was it found?"

Her jaw tightened; she was grinding her teeth. "On Jean." She rubbed her hands together. "Someone would have had to bring it into the prison. The thought was Arlette brought it. She torched Jean, for whatever reason, and by the time the alarm rang, the fire had broken into the next cell and killed the other two sleeping inmates."

"What type of accelerant?"

She pressed her fingers back down on the desktop as if stretching them. "I'd have to read the report again, but it was some type of fuel."

"Fuels burn pretty hot. How was Jean identified?"

Laetitia glanced down. Was she remembering or wondering whether or not to answer?

"In the worst way," she said in a soft voice. "Dental records."

What would cause Arlette to do that to a woman she'd known for years? Could it all come down to a lover's quarrel? It wasn't as if Jean was going anywhere. Couldn't she try another way to resolve the problem? She had all the time in the world.

"What if it wasn't Arlette? What about Jean's roommate?" I asked. "Could she have taken revenge for some earlier vendetta?"

"Not likely. On the day Peppi was released in Oregon, California deputies came to take her to California where she served two more years. She was a petty thief and a con artist with no violent tendencies and she was behind bars at the time."

I wrote Arlette and Peppi's names. Both had a reason to avenge Jean, but I couldn't see a woman hauling off Dusty, not even with a wheelbarrow. "What about Jean's lawyer? Do you have a name?"

"I have it in the file."

"Do you remember if he was a public defender?"

"Oh no, he was top of the line. I met him several times when he was appealing Jean's case. Working in the police department, Jean knew the best lawyer to hire and she hired him. He fought for her like a cat in heat. He would have kept on fighting if she hadn't given up."

"What do you mean?"

"After the first appeal, she told him she was done."

"When was that?"

"About a year before she died. It was as if she knew she didn't have much time left."

* * *

I drove south to Eugene where Jean's lawyer lived. I had no idea if Mr. Robert Underwood Esquire would see me, especially on a weekend, but I wasn't going to call ahead. I couldn't give him time to verify my name with the FBI.

Eugene was a charming city. Bright, clean, and well laid out. I got turned around once because of a large farmer's market, but using the map I'd picked up in a service station, I quickly found a side road that led me to the university suburb where Mr. Underwood owned a brownstone.

I parked in front and waited for signs of life.

After ten minutes my patience wore out. I climbed the steep steps to the door and knocked. A tall thin woman with wild gray curls answered the door.

"I'm looking for Mr. Underwood," I said.

"Are you selling something?" she asked with a broad smile.

"No, ma'am. I need to speak with him about one of his old cases."

She stepped out on the porch with me and pulled the door closed behind her. "Are you a lawyer?"

"A journalist."

She raised a finger. "Ah, is this about the case that was in the paper?"

"It is," I said, surprised. The *Examiner* was a Bay Area paper. "Did you read it?"

"No, but my brother told me about it. It pleased him very much. He's in the back, tending to his orchids. Go on around, the gate is unlocked."

I found the latched gate and the narrow alley between the two brownstones. The back garden was a ten-by-ten square of grass, neatly trimmed. A white round, plastic table and set of chairs, grayed from the elements, were the only lawn furniture. On the far side was a single-car garage. A row of levered windows had been added to the garden side. Many were open and moist. That must be the greenhouse. A green garden hose snaked its way from the main house, across the garden, and into the door of the garage. I walked over and knocked on the doorframe before entering.

The inside smelled of wet dirt and moss, like the smell of the woods behind TJ's shed. A hot, humid mist fixed to my skin as I walked over to the lawyer. Mr. Underwood was six-four or five, at least. His dirty tee shirt revealed thick, muscled biceps. If he didn't want to speak with me, he could squash me like a gnat.

I introduced myself, and he removed a soiled garden glove and shook my hand with a firm grip. The thick white hair looked as if it belonged on an older man.

"I should have assumed Jean's tale would have brought out the reporters," he said, shoving a thin stake down into the dirt next to the orchid's stem.

The trays holding the orchids were higher than usual, almost three-quarters of my height. I assumed this was to adjust to Underwood's height so that he wouldn't have to constantly bend over, although he was bent over a fuchsia-colored orchid.

"Why do you think the story was only published now?" he asked.

"The article said why."

He reached into a bag of soil on a rolling cart beside him. "The missing detective? Do you believe it?" He made a disparaging sound.

"You don't believe it?" I asked, trying not to let my voice give away my surprise.

"Reporters aren't the most honest people in the world. They'll write anything for a byline."

This coming from a lawyer.

His bulk was more terrifying bent over the delicate orchid blossom. I felt as though I'd climbed up the beanstalk. "Do you believe Jean was innocent?"

"As her lawyer it was my job to prove she was."

You didn't do a very good job, did you?

Hard to believe I kept that thought silent. Sometimes, I amazed myself. "She confessed."

"Listen, I fought in Vietnam. I know firsthand what PTSD is and how it skews your thinking. It was a case of self-defense in every sense of the word."

He had a strong belief in Jean's innocence. He was big enough to haul off Dusty. He fought in Vietnam so he probably had killed people. And his tenor voice was distinctive enough that he might use an electronic device to hide it. He sounded like a TV announcer: *That number again is 1-800-445-6161. Call within the next hour and receive not just one, but two boxes at no extra charge. That number again is...*

Despite the mist soaking my skin, the hairs on the back of my neck prickled. What had I walked into?

I stepped back. "When was the last time you saw Jean?"

"About four months before the fire."

"Why did she give up on the appeals?"

"Don't know the real reason, but what she said was that life inside was safer for her than life on the outside."

"Did you agree?"

He looked at me as if I were an idiot, then returned to clipping his orchid with a miniature pair of clippers.

"I couldn't help but notice the radical change in her looks in the article," I said. "Have you seen the pictures?"

He straightened up. "Seeing her so often, I hadn't noticed. It really hit me when I read the article yesterday. I was always telling her she had to get stronger. I meant it mentally, but she took it differently. She started lifting weights in prison."

"Did you go to her funeral?"

Another bored look. "Me and the undertaker."

Besides his strong belief in her innocence, plus his size, and his distinctive voice, he was the only one who cared enough about Jean to go to her funeral. I swallowed hard and took another step back. A perpendicular aisle opened to my left. If he pulled a gun or rushed me, I could dart down the aisle, turn left at the wall and make it out the door before he could. Of course, he might be a good shot.

"If I wanted to talk with someone who knew Jean well, who would you suggest?"

He bent back over his orchids and didn't say anything while he pruned.

I watched him closely as I waited, my feet poised to run. Sweat popped up in the hollow of my back.

"Other than myself, I'd have to say that would be Peppi, Jean's last cellmate."

"Bob, dear," his sister called from the doorway. "Phone call for you. Says he's FBI."

Time to run.

I stuttered out a thank you and rushed to the door. I was in my car with the engine running, hopefully before Mr. Underwood had cleaned himself up enough to enter the house.

The Hotel

According to Mr. Underwood, Peppi Rodriguez, Jean's old cellmate, was the only one around who knew Jean well. The more I thought about the audio file the more I was willing to bet money that the killer personally knew Jean. That put Mr. Underwood and Peppi on the short list. I pulled into a service station, gassed up, and bought a pack of neon orange crackers that looked as appetizing as toxic waste. With my ten dollars change, I bought a roll of quarters. There was a pay phone at the far side of the lot, next to the air hose and vacuum. I used it to call the California Institution for Women.

The prison's message gave me very little information other than its address and hours of operation. If I wanted to speak with someone, I had to call back during business hours. The message said Sunday was a visiting day.

On the hood of the car, I spread out my Oregon map. Below it, I laid the California map that TJ had left in the backpack. The good news was that the California Institute for Women was a straight shot south on Interstate 5. The bad news was that it was a fourteen-or fifteen-hour drive. Even worse, the prison wasn't far from Los Angeles, the fake destination I had given TJ in case he had to give the Feds something on me. It wouldn't do me any good to turn up there if they were looking for me in the area or along the road heading that way.

I reread the notes I'd made at the prison. Peppi's sentence had been for two more years. She'd be out by now.

I went back to the pay phone and called the Marin County Sheriff's Department. "I'm calling to ask if you've found that missing detective," I said in a voice so low it pained my throat.

"Detective Arkansas is still missing. Do you have any information?"

I hung up.

I checked in with Mrs. Macklin, cutting the call short when the mechanical pay phone's voice asked me to deposit another quarter.

I was out of ideas so I got in the car and headed south toward California. The murders were in California and Dusty had disappeared from California. Unless I seriously thought the lawyer did this, it made sense to head back.

Almost four hours later, I crept across the line back into the Golden State, where I half-expected to find a police barricade, but apparently no one was looking for me. That meant Wagner had yet to realize that the black and green Ford had been a rental.

Or maybe the Feds had forced TJ to tell them where I was headed and he'd sent them south to L.A.

Or better yet, maybe they'd found Dusty. But I knew they hadn't. The tightness that had clamped my gut when I learned of his disappearance was still there. My muscles and nerve endings were still vibrating, although I sensed a change was coming. And not a good one. My search for Dusty was taking too long. The odds that he was still alive were getting smaller. I'd done what the killer asked; I could only hope he was good to his word.

Powerless wasn't a good state for me. It made me jumpy and reckless, but worst of all, it left the door open to a paralyzing depression that was already trailing me. I had to find Dusty before it caught up to me. He mattered too much.

I pulled to the shoulder to wipe my eyes. I was falling apart too often and I didn't have time for such weakness. Dusty needed me to find him. What would he do?

I veered back onto the interstate. I was starving and I could barely keep my swollen eyelids open. I'd never make it back to Marin without falling asleep at the wheel. But without access to Mrs. Grimes, I had no way to contact the killer and find out what was going on. I could print the article I'd threatened Mrs. Grimes with, but that might guarantee Dusty's death.

I took the next exit and continued south along the local roads while looking for a cheap motel with wi-fi. Now wasn't the time to sleep, but I needed to do more research and I had to find out if there was any news on Dusty. I might have to risk a call to Wagner.

Luckily, the area around Mt. Shasta was full of motels, all with availability and many with wi-fi. I chose one that was way back from the main road, buried in a copse of pine trees. I parked so that my dented passenger side was beside a large triangular pine that looked like a Christmas tree.

I had my choice of rooms, so I picked one closest to where I'd parked. I asked the desk clerk a second time about the wi-fi service and he assured me, over a blaring TV, that it worked.

The room smelled like a wood fire and had only one window. The ragged bedspread was worn around the edges. I closed the single curtain and plugged in the laptop. The time had come to send everything I had to Agent Wagner. It was Saturday night and the *Examiner's* website didn't have any further info on Dusty Arkansas.

I was pretty sure the Feds were verifying everything in the original article, but they didn't know I'd put together the fact that the victims were all abusers. Once Wagner and Clark had that information they might also leap to the possibility that the wives hired someone for the hits, but why wait for their collective brain to crank up. I'd give them everything.

It would mean cutting off my contact with Mrs. Grimes and therefore, the killer, but I had to do something and fast.

The trick was to send the information to Wagner without giving away my location. For that I needed a fifteen-year-old kid who sometimes helped out the Boston P.D. I knew that because he was my nephew and his father, my brother Garrett, worked for the Boston P.D.

But in Boston, it was already nine p.m. on a Saturday night. I'd be lucky to catch my nephew at home. I used the hotel phone to make the call.

"Aiden, I'm glad I caught you. I need your help with something."

"I'm on my way to the movies, can you call back later?"

"It's urgent. Life or death. Police business."

He made some huffing sounds then spoke to someone in the background. "Okay, what is it? Like fast."

"I need to send you an email and have you reroute it before sending it to the receiver. The same thing that you did for me last year."

"Figures," he said sullenly. "Just a minute."

He spoke with someone near him because I heard both voices. He asked the person if he had his phone with him. The friend said he had it.

"All right, Auntie, I'll use my friend's phone and do it on the way to the movie. What's the destination email?"

I read off Wagner's email address and Aiden read off his friend's email address. I had no clue how all this worked. He'd done it for me once before when I wanted to send an anonymous letter to the White House.

218

"Aiden, I'm not kidding about this saving someone's life.
It's very, very important."

"I know. The Feds are looking for you. Dad's fit to be
tied."

"Then we should keep this between us."

Aiden laughed, a haughty teenager laugh that sounded like
something between a guffaw and a snort. I had nothing to
worry about; he wouldn't tell his dad if the house was
burning down.

I sent the email and lay back on the edge of the bed.
Several hours later, a chill woke me. I scooted up the
mattress and crawled under the covers.

* * *

A dog barked.

"Shut up, Fifi," I said and rose to unfamiliar surroundings.
The flood gates opened and a barrage of anguish rushed in. I
leaped from the bed, my shirt and pants more wrinkled than a
shar pei. I yanked back the curtain. Clouds huddled over Mt.
Shasta.

My stomach growled, then cramped. The only
nourishment I found was a slim bag of nuts in the mini bar. I
poured the contents into my mouth and chewed as I stripped
down for a quick shower.

It was Sunday. The *Examiner* went out today. I needed a
copy, but a free paper such as that probably wasn't delivered
this far from San Francisco. But it might be updated online. I
switched on the laptop and showered while it booted.

My sour mug spanned the *Examiner's* webpage. Where
had they gotten that photo? I looked as if someone had farted
and I was trying to get away from the smell. Were those lines
on my forehead? I didn't have lines on my forehead. I
glanced up but couldn't find a reflective surface nearby. I
went back to the article and read the text attached. Still no

sign of Dusty. I read all the other articles related to the search for Detective Arkansas.

By now, Wagner had all my research, but nothing was mentioned about the other two dead abusers or their wives. I wasn't surprised Wagner hadn't shared the new information with the press, but I was starting to worry. If Wagner had already sent someone to talk to my brother, Garrett, he might learn about his talented son. I needed to get back on the road. Fast.

But first, I had to find an address for Peppi Rodriguez. I logged onto the same search service I'd used to find Mrs. Schuss's phone number. Nothing came up. Was Peppi a nickname? I tried again but Rodriguez was too common a name for a general search.

Sweat broke out on my upper lip. A flush scorched my skin. I could almost hear Wagner's guys pulling into the drive, but I had to finish this.

There was another service. A pricier one. It accessed driver license numbers. If Peppi had been out of jail for a few years, maybe she'd filed for a license.

I'd start with California, then Oregon. Each state was another hundred dollars. I hit gold with California. Peppi Rodriguez. Valley Road, Sonoma, California. I did a map search and scribbled out the directions.

The Ranch

Peppi Rodriguez had hit it big after leaving prison. She lived on a sprawling piece of land, the nearest neighbor two miles back up the road. At the door, I ignored the bell and knocked. She was an ex-con. On the off chance this was actually a meth lab, I didn't want to blow anything up. I knocked again, harder.

When no one answered, I stepped off the porch and walked around to the side garage. The garage doors were locked. Standing on my tippy toes, I could see in the window. Two cars were inside and there was room for a third. I walked around to the back.

Behind the house was an open, circular field. The house and the garage formed the six o'clock position and directly across the field in the twelve o'clock position were two large buildings that looked like stables. Another large building was in the three o'clock position and a barn was in the nine o'clock position. The clocklike layout created a certain amount of privacy and the woods that stretched beyond the circle of buildings created even more.

Laetitia had said Peppi was a petty thief and a con artist. Had she conned someone out of this beautiful piece of property? Identity theft maybe.

The afternoon sun beat down on my shoulders. I smelled horses although I didn't see any. The tall grasses in the field were dried brown and flattened with dug-out paths crisscrossing from the different buildings. A wider path, dotted with mounds of horse poo, circled the field like a riding ring. I walked along it toward the barn.

I didn't see anyone, but sensed I wasn't alone. I was pretty sure an ex-con wouldn't like me wandering around her property, but I couldn't stop myself. I only hoped no one decided to shoot me now and ask questions later.

The barn door was open. Inside was dark and spacious. The air heavy with a dried, smoky smell.

"Hello," I called. "Anyone home?"

A small rusted tractor was parked against one wall. Rakes, hoes, pick axes rested against it. At the back, hay bales were stacked three deep and as high as the roof.

"Hello," I called again.

"The Kahills are out of town," said a voice, startling me.

I flipped around to find a petite woman standing behind me. Dressed in stained jeans, riding boots, and a plaid shirt with the sleeves cut off, she wasn't an inch over five feet. A red bandana bound her thick curly hair into a ponytail. In one hand, she held a bridle and looked as if she intended to use it as a weapon.

"I'm looking for Peppi..." I started to say Rodriguez, but if she was this well off I figured she might have changed her name.

"You a cop?"

"No." I shook my head. "No. Not at all."

"Once was enough."

"Right. I'm a journalist."

She lowered the bridle to her side. "What would a journalist want with Peppi?"

"It's about her old...friend, Jean Newman."

"She's dead."

"You're Peppi?"

Her nod was given by a slow blink of the eyelids. Then, she stared straight at me as if challenging me.

"You and her lawyer seemed to be the only people who knew her well."

"Who cares?"

"It's kind of complicated."

"Make it simple." She shook the bridle in the air. "I got work to do."

Something was nagging at the back of my brain, but I didn't have time to stand around and think about it. Peppi was rushing me out the door and I had to get what I came for.

"Friday morning an article about Jean was placed in a daily out of San Francisco. I'm trying to locate the person who wanted Jean's story told."

"Wasn't me."

She was five feet and maybe a hundred pounds. I was sure she hadn't kidnapped Dusty. "Yes, but you and Mr. Underwood are the only two people I know that were close to her. Can you think of someone else who may have felt Jean was wrongly accused?"

"On our cell block almost every woman in there was a victim of some prick. Love makes a woman stupid. Take me. I robbed convenience stores while my old man drove the getaway car. Guess which one did time?" She slapped the side of her leg with the bridle as if to punish herself. "Some of the women had been messed with as kids, some by their own mammas and daddies. Others were forced into prostitution by their fathers or lovers or both. Everyone in there applauded Jean for shooting the bastard. Wished we'd had the guts."

So the killer was possibly a cellmate, but killing abusers to avenge felt more personal. "Anyone else? A friend or family member that she had regular contact with?"

She walked past me. "Can't think of anyone."

She dropped the bridle on the ground and picked up a pitchfork. I followed her to the back of the barn, where she started to break apart a bale of hay. Her biceps bulged as she jabbed at it.

"What can you tell me about Arlette Kerns?"

"The guard? She's the one who deserved to burn in hell. Bully bitch. Had the run of the block because she was supposed to be protecting Jean."

Hay lay at her feet; the bale demolished. She started stabbing another one. "Jean was way too nice to her. Probably that cop thing, you know? But I was the one who protected Jean from her." She stabbed the hay as if she were tearing Arlette apart. "Woman was built like a cinderblock, too. Took some convincing, but Jean learned pretty quick she had to buff up or she'd be at Arlette's mercy once I was sprung."

Peppi tossed the pitchfork like a javelin into the stacked bales. She grabbed a wheelbarrow and rolled it over to the hay. Yanking the pitchfork free, she loaded the loose hay into the wheelbarrow.

I sneezed.

"You got hay fever?"

"Not that I know of."

She pitched another load. "Anything else? You've pissed my day bringing all this back up."

"Do you think Arlette would have wanted Jean's story published?"

"No."

Short and sweet. "How can you be so sure? Maybe after all these years she feels remorseful."

"Think what you want and I'll think what I want. You need to go. I've stuff to do." She grabbed the wheelbarrow of hay. Its single wheel squeaked as she started pushing it toward the door. When she reached the bridle, she stopped and picked it up. "You coming?" she asked and threw the bridle on top of the hay.

I felt like I was forgetting something, but I couldn't pull it out of my head. I was pretty sure Peppi wouldn't be so talkative in the future. What was it?

"Do you know where I can find Arlette?"

Peppi's cold stare let me know my time was up. With a jerk of her head, she gestured me out of the barn. "You can find your way out of here?" she asked and turned the squeaking wheelbarrow toward the stables.

The Stall

As I walked down the driveway to my car, I lit a cigarette and picked at my brain trying to figure out what was bothering me. Yes, Peppi hated men and yes, Peppi would want Jean's story told. But no matter which scenario I imagined, I couldn't see Peppi kidnapping Dusty. Even if he was knocked out cold, her miniature, buff biceps couldn't have dragged him from the car. I doubt she could lift me.

Dusty's car had held no trace of blood or signs of a struggle so maybe she had walked him out at gunpoint. Maybe. But knowing Dusty, I figured he'd think he could disarm her. And he'd be right.

What about Underwood? He was big enough to lift Dusty. He would want Jean's story told. Or would he? He'd failed in her defense. Not something he'd want to advertise unless in some sort of twisted logic, he put the fault solely on society. Even if he desperately wanted Jean's story told, I couldn't see him murdering abusers. That would take more hate than I'd seen in the man.

That left Arlette. Would Arlette help Peppi? Peppi clearly hated the woman and blamed her for Jean's death. I couldn't see Arlette approaching Peppi without getting shot. Peppi said that in prison she'd protected Jean from Arlette. What kind of protection did Jean need?

I stubbed out the cigarette in the car's ashtray and thought through everything I'd learned so far. Nothing was making sense. I was missing an important part of the puzzle and I hoped the FBI was smarter.

Fat chance. They hadn't even found me yet. Maybe they were too busy trying to find Dusty. I could only hope.

I pulled the laptop across the seat to see if I had wi-fi here in the driveway. If the house had it, maybe the signal was strong enough for me to hook to it while no one was looking. A weak signal popped up, but it was password protected.

I wanted to call the Sheriff's Department again, but I didn't dare turn on my phone. Instead, I brought up the photo of Dusty once more. It was two days old. For all I knew he was dead.

The space around my heart tightened. I gripped the laptop hard and harder until my fingers felt like they might snap. I wanted to scream from the bottom of my lungs.

Instead, I gritted my teeth until my jaws screamed in pain. I exhaled and looked through the windshield at the green branches and the blooming daylilies. I had to calm myself. I had to stay focused. *I-can-not-fail.*

I couldn't lose it now; not before I knew Dusty's fate. If the roles were reversed, he wouldn't give up either. I knew that as sure as I knew my name.

I wouldn't let him down.

I stared at the photo. What made it significant? What clues did it hold? I felt the desire for another cigarette, but I stayed focused on the image.

The afternoon sun was beating down on the roof and inside the car I was starting to sweat. I should lower the windows, but I was reluctant to take my eyes off the photo. I chewed my fingernails while trying to be objective, scanning inch by inch. Dusty's clothes. The wall. The ground. Five minutes must have passed before I saw it, but once I did, I began to notice other things.

Dusty was propped up in a corner in what I'd assumed were two joining walls. But one wall was made of stacked six-by-one boards. The joints between the boards were now obvious.

I'd seen a partition in Peppi's barn built exactly the same way. For all I knew this wasn't a wall but another partition like in a barn or…a stable.

The thick brown rope, which held Dusty's hands to an iron ring on the back wall, might not be rope but the same type of leather I'd seen on Peppi's bridle. That was what had bothered me during our discussion. The minute I saw the bridle my subconscious had made the connection, but it had taken my consciousness longer to play catch up.

Now what?

Nothing in Mr. Underwood's garden or greenhouse looked like anything I saw in the picture. But Dusty hadn't been in Peppi's barn and there was no sign that he'd ever been in the barn. I hadn't seen any iron rings like the one Dusty was tied to in the photo.

What about Peppi's stables? I looked at the photo again. No hay. Didn't stables have hay? Wasn't that where Peppi was carting the wheelbarrow? Also, there was that other building across from the barn. The flat one-story building with windows across the front. That was all I remembered. But, if the owners were out of town, there was also the house.

A shiver rolled down my spine. The hair on my arms stood at attention. What if the owners weren't out of town? What if they were dead?

Whoa, horse.

My thoughts were running their own race. I'd discounted Peppi as the kidnapper because of her size, but if she'd had help… I still didn't have any proof Dusty was here or had ever been here. But the similarities of the barn and image of Dusty were too coincidental. I knew.

I just knew.

I was starting to trust that weird feeling more and more. I was beginning to know the difference between when something was true and when I *wanted* it to be true. My dad and his cop buddies called it a gut feeling, but it didn't feel like it was in my gut. It was effervescent and prickly and just below my skin. And the surer I became, the brighter the feeling grew. Warmer.

I lowered the car window to let a cooling breeze in.

Who was helping Peppi? Underwood? The mechanical voice on the calls sounded male, but that might have been the distortion software that gave it that quality. Did it matter who was helping her? What counted was that she wasn't working alone.

Peppi had been a little too friendly for an ex-con. I'd brushed it off, thinking she was talking to me because it was a subject she was passionate about, but now, I saw her cooperation in a different light. She didn't want me coming back.

I glanced up at the house, quiet and still. It was two stories, half brick and half shingled. Quite ugly really. Old-fashioned and starting to fade. The garage, which was all shingles, looked cleaner and more modern.

I had to get a better look at the place. Had to verify that the corner in Dusty's photo was around here somewhere. If it was in the house or the other out-buildings, Peppi would be on her guard. And the others. How many were helping her?

I started the car and backed down the driveway. Once the house was out of sight, I pulled to the side of the road and turned off the engine. My heart was racing. This was a solid lead. Should I contact Wagner? Yes. What if I was wrong? But I wasn't. But I might be.

I could be. I hadn't seen anything in the barn that resembled the ring Dusty was tied to in the photo. I didn't see any hay in Dusty's photo, either. Hay was all over the barn and piles of it outside the stables, indicating that there was probably hay in the stables, too.

So far all I had was coincidences.

I went back and forth with this. If I was right, but was caught by Peppi, Wagner wouldn't get the information I now had. If I was wrong, I'd give the Feds my position and wouldn't be able to look for Arlette, my next suspect.

TJ's backpack lay in the floor on the passenger's side. I snatched it up and pulled out my phone, the SIM card, and the battery. I shoved all three into my pants' pocket. Next, I grabbed the directions that I'd jotted down from the map search. At the bottom of the page, I'd sketched a rough drawing of the area. I'd marked an intersection farther down the street to let me know that if I saw it, I'd passed Peppi's address. The street that intersected eventually curved until it was almost parallel to Peppi's street, but behind the ranch.

With adrenalin pumping through me and my muscles so tight I was shaking, I restarted the car and counted the miles to the intersection. Three. After making a left turn, I drove back three miles and found a place to park. On the side where I parked was a barbed wire fence and behind it were rows upon rows of grapevines. Across the street, woods stretched for as far as I could see. These had to connect with the woods I'd seen behind the stables. Now, I had to figure if I was too far up or too far down from the ranch, and adjust.

It was only two in the afternoon. I should probably give Peppi enough time to think I'd left for good. If I was smart, I'd wait until almost dark, when the lights would help me see where people were gathered.

The Prayer

I lit another cigarette and waited.

And waited.

Nature. Who knew it could be so loud? Squawks and yaks. Cracks and thumps. When the wind rolled through the grapevines, it made an eerie rattling sound.

I walked around the car to the passenger's side and opened the glove compartment. No gun. I pulled out the rental agreement and ran my hand over the bottom of the glove compartment to be sure my eyes weren't fooling me.

I squished the cigarette out in the ashtray and grabbed TJ's backpack. I unzipped it and dumped the contents on the passenger seat. I fished through everything.

No gun.

I bent and slapped around under the seat, panic rising in my chest.

"TJ, what have you done?"

I popped the trunk and checked every space and corner. I slammed the trunk hard. I lunged across it, my head in my hands. "Oh, TJ!"

I wondered how righteous he'd feel when I turned up dead.

I rolled off the trunk and popped it open again. Under the spare, I found a good old-fashioned tire iron, solid and lethal. Shoving it into my belt loop, I kept looking for anything else I could use as a weapon. A can of flat tire fix looked promising. The spray might be toxic to the eyes if I were close enough to use it, but the bulky can wouldn't be easy to carry without a pack, and I didn't see an advantage to taking the backpack.

I crawled into the passenger seat and left the door hanging open. I checked the laptop for a wi-fi signal, but nothing was available. I relit my cigarette and picked at my fingernail polish. Once again, I thought about calling Wagner. I was pretty sure I'd programmed his number into my phone, but to be sure, I used a ballpoint pen to ink it on my palm.

I smoked another cigarette and hummed a few bars of Queen's *We Are the Champions*. The song was to bolster my courage. I couldn't think of a time when I needed it bolstered more. Not only was I without a gun, but I might be walking into a lair without backup. If the horses didn't kill me, Peppi might.

I checked the time. Twenty-seven minutes had passed. I climbed out of the car and walked around it a few times. Dusk was at what? Eight p.m.? Did I really think I could wait six hours? Also, if Dusty was in there, Peppi might be freaked by my showing up. She might want to get rid of him A.S.A.P.

I slammed the car door shut and locked it. I ran across the street and into the woods. Growing up in Boston, I'd had little chance to commune with nature. What little I knew came from the time I'd spent in Vermont. Aunt Eileen had taught me how to tell time by following the sun across the sky, a trick I'd practiced since. She'd also taught me how to—as she called it—"walk like an Indian." How to creep across a terrain without making much noise. As I ran through the trees, my feet crunching the dead leaves and dried twigs, I thought about her training.

She'd been a devout Catholic, yet practiced some of the old rituals, honoring the Earth Goddess. She grew herbs for healing and danced beneath a harvest moon, always explaining how both belief systems wove together in God's universe. In later years, my dad tried to have her committed, and that was about the time I started to see her as a crazy old lady, and not the caring aunt who had taken me in when I needed a woman's care.

Peppi had said all the women on her cell block were victims of a man in some way. Aunt Eileen had been a victim of my dad's pragmatic beliefs. He turned not only me away from her, but also the rest of the family. He trusted something as visceral as gut instinct, yet he assumed that her belief in the old ways were insanity.

My lungs burned from the running. A coughing spasm overtook me and I stopped to wheeze in some air. I coughed some more and waited until I could breath normally. I had to slow down. I listened. Birds chirped and flitted in the branches overhead. My father had put down Eileen's beliefs as I had put down Dusty's Buddhism. I teased him about his idols, joked about his meditation. Maybe Buddha was the one true God.

Yeah, right.

But my Catholic education had taught me to be mindful of each man's journey to God. Even Jesus told his disciples that they were to bless those who had yet to see his divinity and who had yet to believe in him.

"Dear God, our father in heaven," I said in a low voice. I pressed my palms together for effect. "If you return Dusty safe, I promise I'll never mock his or anyone's beliefs ever again. No matter how crazy they sound."

As the burning sensation faded from my lungs, I started walking. I listened to the sound my steps made. I was quieter.

Walk like an Indian.

I stopped and looked up. I could have sworn I'd heard Aunt Eileen's voice. I glanced around. My stress was causing me to hear things. I started off again, watching my steps, looking for solid footholds so as not to make a sound. The game made me feel safer. More in control.

A break appeared in the trees ahead.

Peppi, cell phone pressed to her ear, was walking a big brown horse around the path that circled the field. Her shoulders and head were moving in a way that made me think she was arguing with whomever she was speaking with. Would she walk a horse if she was only hiding out? No, she really worked there. Okay, so maybe the owners *were* out of town, but she could still have Dusty tied up somewhere.

I stood behind a tree until I was sure she was out of sight. That gut feeling had withered. Was I wasting my time? Was this another dead-end? Should I be hunting down Arlette?

The building across from the barn was in front of me. I crept over to the back window and peered in. A kitchen. Long and narrow with a good-sized coffeemaker on the cabinet. The pot was half full. Oh, oh, oh.

Through a doorway I saw several beds lined up. A bunkhouse. The ranch workers lived here. Peppi lived here. I pressed my ear against the windowpane. The silence made me think the building was empty, but I wasn't going to take a chance. If Peppi had taken Dusty, she'd had help. I ducked and inched along below the window line. When I reached the edge of the building, I saw the first stable.

A wide grassy clearing separated the bunkhouse from the stable. If I tried to cross it, Peppi would surely see me. She was across the field just passing in front of the barn. She slipped the phone into her back pocket. The horse whinnied and lifted its head as if it knew I was there. Peppi tightened her grip on the bridle and petted the horse's neck. She looked as if she knew what she was doing.

My doubts were returning. The first victim, Mr. Schuss, was killed when Peppi was still incarcerated. Why hadn't I realized that? She couldn't be the kidnapper unless she was helping someone else. Someone from the cellblock? Arlette?

I had to find out what happened to Arlette. But I was here now and I wasn't leaving until I had a look inside those stables. I glanced across the clearing. The stable doors were open and the smell of horses was strong.

Peppi was out of sight again.

If she made another turn with the horse, at one point her back would be to me. That was when I would run across the clearing. If she didn't make another turn, she might enter the stable by the doors across from me. Then I'd need to get out of sight.

I waited.

I heard the horse before I saw it. Peppi held the bridle below the horse's mouth. Still on the path, they passed the bunkhouse and headed toward the stable. Luck was with me; it looked as if she was going to make another pass. I inched into position and got ready to run.

As soon as her back was to me I took off. My lungs burned, but I reached the stable doors. I pressed my back against the wood, holding down the cough eager to burst forth. The stable might not be empty. I covered my mouth with my hands and swallowed several times, waiting for my lungs to quiet. I breathed deeply through my nose and exhaled through my mouth. One day, I had to quit smoking.

My lungs were still on fire when Peppi came into view again. I couldn't wait. I ducked around the doorway and into the stable. Several horses snorted. I counted seven. They were separated by the same type of partition that I'd seen in the photo and in the barn. My heart thudded.

I rushed the length of the building checking all twelve stalls. Many were empty. No Dusty. Peppi didn't appear the least bit bothered either. Except for the phone call, she was going about her work as usual.

At the end of the building, I looked across another clearing to the second stable. The doors were open, but it looked darker. Empty.

"Come on, Misty, let's get you brushed," Peppi said, her voice carrying.

She was bringing the horse back to the stable by the same doors I'd come in. I didn't hesitate. I ran across the next clearing to the second stable. Once inside, I peeked around to see if Peppi had seen me. She was tying the horse's bridle to something out of my line of sight. She was facing the rear of the first stable and couldn't see me.

I exhaled and glanced around. This stable smelled of leather but not horses. The stalls looked as if they hadn't been used in a long time. Near the doors was a shelf lined with several saddles. Bridles hung on several stalls, but as I walked along, looking inside they were all empty. As I neared the opposite end, I heard uneven footsteps approaching. But Peppi was in the other direction.

I slipped into a stall and squatted behind its gate.

A metal latch slid open and another stall gate creaked. I heard some shuffling and the ringing that tin makes when it's hit.

"Okay, cowboy. Open wide. This is the last dose."

The voice was female.

A grunt. A moan. Deep and male. And… The hairs on the back of my neck stood up. Was it possible? I hadn't heard his voice, but I was sure it was Dusty. From just a grunt? It was Dusty.

Relief rained down on me. He was alive. I shot up and saw the top of a head in the last stall on the left. I dropped down before she looked up. I reached for the tire iron, gripping it tightly. This meant there were at least two of them working together, if not more, and one of me. Dusty didn't sound as if he'd be much help. What was she dosing him with?

I put down the tire iron and pulled the cell phone from my back pocket. I snapped in the battery and SIM card. When I pressed the ON button, a high-pitched jingle played.

Oh, hell.

I'd been made. No doubt about it. The woman, whoever she was, had to have heard that.

With trembling fingers, I keyed in the number written on my palm and hit call. I slid the phone to the stall's corner and grabbed the tire iron. The stall's gate swung open, hitting me in the shoulder. I leaped away and stood to face my attacker. Despite the angry red burn on her neck, I recognized her from her last photo.

"The fire," I said, but as the words left my mouth I remembered she'd been identified by her dental records. Records could easily be switched. "Arlette didn't kill you, you killed Arlette."

I didn't wait for confirmation. I swung the tire iron at her face. Jean ducked and it connected with the top edge of the stall. She tucked her head and charged me, catching me in the midsection and shoving me back against the wall. I felt as if I'd been hit by a tractor.

My knees gave way and I crumpled to the ground. Jean stood over me, hands on her hips. "Nice to finally meet you," she said. "I liked the article you wrote."

From behind, she cupped me under the arms. She half-lifted, half-dragged me out of the stall. "You should have stayed out of this."

She pulled me down the aisle and into the last stall. When I saw Dusty, I tore free of her grasp and lunged for him.

"Dusty!" I patted his cheeks. His skin was chalky white, his lips cracked and bleeding. He smelled as rank as the homeless men who hang out by his boat. His brown eyes flickered open for an instant, but didn't seem to focus.

"Dusty!" I shook his shoulders. Turning to Jean, I screamed, "What did you give him?"

A tin bowl filled with a blue liquid sat on the floor about a foot away. I kicked out and knocked it over, the liquid soaking into the earthen floor.

"Why'd you do that? Now I have to make another batch. Enough for two." Her fist connected with the side of my face. For an instant, tiny points of white light danced in my vision. I slumped against Dusty, his stink sinking into my nostrils.

Where the leather bound his wrists, the skin was broken and bloody. At some point he'd struggled hard against the restraints. I closed my eyes and felt his pain.

"Peppi!" Jean called. "Need some help in here."

I was fading, but I had to stay alert. I forced my eyes to open and fought my way back from the brink of unconsciousness. Light boot steps approached.

I rose up to my knees and landed a punch on Jean's rock hard stomach. She looked more stunned than hurt. She swung her fist, catching me in the throat. I fell back gasping for breath.

"Aw, hell," Peppi said, stepping into the stall.

"Yep." Jean said, picking up the overturned bowl from the ground. "Can you tie her up while I go make another cocktail?"

Peppi knelt and grabbed my hands.

"This is a law officer, not some abuser," I said to her.

"They're all abusers some way, some how." She wrapped the leather strip from Dusty's wrists around mine so that my hands were next to his.

"Not Dusty. He's here because he was protecting me. He's one of the good ones. Please, let him go."

She tightened the knots, and left.

My head lay against Dusty's chest, listening to the weak beat of his heart. Tears welled in my eyes. Why had I waited so long to call Wagner? Stupid, stupid, stupid. Even if the agent acted immediately on the call signal, Sonoma was an hour's drive from San Francisco. We'd be dead before he got here.

"Knew you couldn't stay away," Dusty said in a dry, raspy voice that didn't sound like him.

I cocked my head around so that we were nose to nose. "I'm so sorry. I should have—"

He pressed his cracked lips against mine. I started to pull away, but suddenly there was nothing I wanted more than his touch. I leaned into his kiss. The warmth of his skin made my fear dissolve. My passion, like a jackhammer, chipped away at the safety wall I'd stuck between us. When his lips parted, I arched, wanting more, but he went slack, his mouth fell away.

My eyes popped open as his chin fell. "Dusty. Wake up. Dusty!"

I shook our joined hands, trying to move him or loosen the straps. Fact was I didn't know what I was doing, except panicking.

"Don't you die!"

The Argument

Dusty didn't move.

I jostled him. I screamed at him. I even managed to shift to my knees and try and lift him, but he didn't open his eyes again. I didn't know whether Jean had managed to get any of that blue liquid down his throat. If he was this much out of it, he couldn't have swallowed.

"Wagner," I yelled. "If you can hear this, we don't have much time." For all I knew the call I'd made had gone to voicemail, but surely, he had someone monitoring my phone's signal in case it went back online. If he didn't, he was as much use as a back pocket in a shirt.

Right. And how much use was I?

Had I really thought I could catch the killer alone? In my stupidity, hadn't I wanted to show up Wagner? Hadn't I wanted to be the one to save Dusty? The Irish had a saying: If you dig a grave for others, you might fall in it yourself. Right now I was looking up from six feet under.

The short but so sweet kiss made me realize how I'd been running on raw emotional power since Dusty disappeared. Logic be damned.

Rule number one in an investigation: Don't get emotionally involved. I hadn't taken time to think things through, hadn't fully trusted my "gut" feeling. I'd sensed something was going on here, but I'd wanted proof so I wouldn't look like an amateur. At some point my ego took over and I'd broken the golden rule. I hadn't waited for backup.

Dusty was dying because of my impulsiveness. My recklessness. And I was going to have to live with that. Luckily, I wasn't going to have to live with it for long.

My vision spun. A feeling of vertigo rolled through my head while the ground shifted beneath me. My exertion at trying to lift Dusty up had taken its toll. If I'd been smart, I'd have eaten more and kept my strength up. Clearly, I should stick to journalism because I made one miserable detective.

"I'm sorry Dusty."

I pressed my head against his chest. Numbness filled my head. Then Star's cliché danced through what was left of my gray matter. *He who laughs last, laughs best.*

Jean.

Star had nailed it. Jean was getting the last laugh, all around. She'd escaped an unjust life sentence. She was getting paid for the pleasure of wreaking revenge on men like her husband. Cathartic. And now, she was going to kill the only person who'd figured out her secret.

Hot, angry voices drew near. Jean and Peppi were arguing. Good. I needed time. As much as I could get. Maybe Wagner had a helicopter.

A few minutes later, footsteps, strong but uneven ones, stomped through the stable. Jean.

The stall's gate swung open. Her jaw was set fiercely, her facial muscles taut as she stooped to put down the tin bowl.

"You'll be happy to know, I'm retiring," she said, sliding the bowl far from my reach. "If a stupid journalist can find me, I'm getting sloppy."

"Stupid. I'll tell you who's stupid," I said then shut my mouth. I wasn't going to tell her the FBI was only a few steps behind me. Dusty and I might die, but she wasn't getting away. My one solace. Once Wagner linked this place to

Peppi, he'd have the same information I had. The FBI would figure it all out.

Too bad I wouldn't be around when she realized how brilliant I really was. Okay, I'd be dead, so maybe I wasn't that brilliant.

"Look, I know who you are, but Dusty here doesn't. You can let him go. You kill a detective, hell will rain down on you a lot faster than if you just kill me."

"A male detective, too."

"Oh, please. Take some responsibility."

No sooner had the words left my mouth than a knife blade pressed to my throat.

"Want to go faster? I'll take responsibility for that."

I choked back my words and waited to see if this was the moment heaven opened its gates and I joined Haylee and my daughter, Siobhan, and my mother and father. My chest tightened as it occurred to me that I might have veered off the path to heaven a few years back. The Lord knew I had lots of regrets and much to atone for.

Jean removed the knife, wiped the blade on her pants, and put it on the ground.

I shifted around so that I could kick the bowl if it came anywhere near Dusty. "Why did you take him? He's not an abuser."

She took two syringes out of her pocket and laid them on the ground near the bowl. She reached for the bowl. "It was a way to keep you in line. I saw the two of you laughing while you were walking the dog. I saw the way he looked at you when you went up the stairs. Then he goes and sits in his car and waits. Guess he wanted to see if you were meeting anyone else." She snickered.

"It's not like that."

"I figured that out once I saw the badge. He was watching over you. You told him about my call."

"I didn't. I swear."

Jean filled one of the syringes with the blue liquid from the bowl. She wasn't taking any chances that I might kick it over again. I had to buy Dusty more time.

My head shot up.

Something had changed. The air in the stable almost crackled. Jean felt it too; she dropped the bowl and grabbed the knife.

A flurry of feet, stomping, shuffling, sliding.

Before I knew what was happening, the cold steel blade pressed my throat again.

"Drop the knife." Wagner's voice. "Put it on the ground."

With the blade against my jugular and Jean behind me, my head was angled so that all I saw was the bottom of Jean's chin. From the sound of his voice, Wagner must have been on Jean's right side, and hopefully, had a gun to her head. She could still yank the blade across my throat, but hopefully, Wagner's shot would take her out before she could do too much damage.

But Dusty was safe. She couldn't kill both of us.

"Drop the knife," Wagner said again.

The world stood still as we waited. Me, especially.

From a distance, Peppi's high voice broke the silence. My heart was pounding in my ears. I couldn't make out what she was saying. Spanish maybe.

Time for one last prayer. *Dear God...*

The pressure against my neck disappeared. I dropped my head as Jean leaned over to place the knife on the ground.

"Hands in the air," Wagner said. "You know the drill."

Jean stood and Wagner led her out of the stall.

"I love you, Peppi, now and for always," Jean said.

"Mi amor, stay strong," Peppi said.

Agent Clark dropped to her knees beside me and cut the leather binding my hands to Dusty's. Free from his restraints, Dusty slumped to the side.

I pointed to the tin bowl. "She was trying to make Dusty drink that when I arrived."

A male agent who I didn't recognize bent and picked up the bowl. He sniffed the liquid, then disappeared into the group of agents crowding the stall gate.

"Do you know if he drank any?" Agent Clark asked.

"I don't know," I said, watching her gently lay Dusty out on the ground. A twinge of jealousy surprised me. "She said it was the last dose though, so maybe," I added.

Two men with a stretcher inched into the stall.

"Can you stand?" Clark asked me.

"Yes, but I'm not leaving Dusty." I rose up, my legs cramping from the damp ground. When I faltered, Clark caught me.

"Let's give these guys room to work," she said, directing me to the other side of the stall. She turned back to the two men. "Don't give him any fluids until we know what that liquid is."

The man with his fingers on Dusty's neck pulse nodded.

The Kiss

The blue liquid turned out to be a mixture of several drugs and anti-freeze. Although Dusty's blood contained a lot of different drugs, he hadn't ingested any of the anti-freeze.

Jean had saved something special for her last dose.

Later that night, I sat beside his hospital bed as a nurse finished taking his vitals and started a new intravenous bag.

Besides being drugged for five days, Dusty was severely dehydrated.

"How'd you pull it off?" he asked, his voice weak and raspy from his dry throat.

"Let's just say Wagner isn't all that dumb."

"It was Wagner? Really? I was sure it would be you. I know how stubborn you can be."

If a heart could smile, mine had. "I sent the signal, Wagner followed it. I hear even a hound dog can do that much." I knew Wagner wasn't an idiot, but I wasn't about to be modest. I wanted Dusty to know I didn't give up on him. Mostly, I wanted him to remember that he'd kissed me, but I'd shoot myself in the foot before I'd ever mentioned it.

Dusty didn't remember how Jean had kidnapped him. Because of the drugs, he didn't remember much. "How does this tie to the Bolinas case?" he asked.

"The woman who kidnapped you was a killer-for-hire. She specialized in abusive spouses."

"She's an ex-cop," he said. "I could tell from the way she spoke."

"She was. Her name is Jean Newman. Her abusive husband broke her leg so badly that she had to leave the force. During their next argument, she killed him and went to prison for what should have been a case of self-defense. She and the little one, Peppi, must have tricked a guard into thinking that Jean was in love with the guard. When the prison caught fire, Jean and the guard were probably planning Jean's escape, but Jean had other plans. She killed the guard instead and somehow had the dental records changed. Laetitia, the woman I interviewed at the prison, said that Jean spent a lot of time in sickbay with sports injuries."

"More likely," Dusty said and took a deep breath, "she paid someone to switch the records."

Wagner bound into the room. "We've finished with this," he said, offering me my phone.

"How did you get to the stables so quickly?" I asked.

"Your rental car had been flagged at a service station in the area. We were on our way. I also had an agent on the way to Ms. Rodriguez's address. When your call came through, we corralled local authorities and drove faster. Figured you wouldn't call unless you were in trouble."

Dusty chuckled then cleared his throat.

He was allowed to make fun. My stupidity almost got him killed. "Is Jean cooperating?"

"We've made a deal. She knows she's going back in for life, but we've agreed to put the two of them in the same prison. Different floors though." He looked at Dusty. "She pulled up next to your car and got out with a bag of groceries. Said she walked over to your car and you rolled down the window. She pretended to be a resident and asked you why you were parked there. When you reached for your badge, she shoved a hypodermic in your neck. You went out quickly because she'd misjudged the dosage. She almost killed you then."

"How did she get Dusty out of his car?" I asked. "She's strong, but not that strong."

"The other one, the girlfriend, was helping her." He looked at Dusty. "What were you doing in your car?"

Dusty's gaze shifted to me. "What *was* I doing in my car? You know, don't you?"

Now both men were focused on me. Why hide the truth? Jean had probably told Wagner everything anyway. "Jean called in a disguised voice and warned me to back off. When I didn't, a black rose was delivered to my door. Dusty found it when he came for dinner."

"Right, the rose. I remember that."

Wagner shook a finger at me. "We need to talk," he said sternly. "I want to hear everything, and we'll see if you can get off without charges."

"How much did she make killing the three husbands?"

"Four. There was one that didn't come up in our search because Jean didn't start removing parts until Mr. Schuss. Looks like half a mil is the going rate to off an abusive husband. In two cases, though, the women didn't have access to the money until the husband was dead, which means Jean was working on credit, if you can believe that."

"I can," I said. "Jean's one angry woman. Was that ranch really theirs?"

"No. They worked there, but Ms. Rodriguez had put an offer on another piece of property not far from the ranch. Her accounts were being investigated. That's when the flag went up for us."

I sighed, thinking how close we came. "Glad it did." I started to pat Dusty's arm, but remembering Wagner, I jerked my hand back to my lap. "What will happen to the widows?"

"They've been rounded up and charged with a couple of things, including capital murder," Wagner said.

"Capital murder?"

"Same as first degree in California," Dusty said.

"But they were abused."

Wagner shook his head. "They all have enough money to tie up the justice system for years and negotiate down to justifiable homicide." Then he gestured to me. "Come on, we need to go talk."

"It's late. I'll come by tomorrow. Tonight, I'm staying right here."

Wagner surprised me.

He didn't argue or threaten me, but turned to Dusty. "You better talk to her," he said. "This is serious and she may do time." Then he left.

I shrugged. "I may have broken a law or two."

"Only two? You should have told me about that threatening call."

"I wanted the story. I was afraid you'd take it away from me. Then the scary call caught me off-guard."

"We almost died for a story. Are you kidding me?"

"Not just a story. A serial killer. A big story. Acropolis big. Great Wall of China big."

Dusty tried to raise a hand to shut me up, but the gesture was weak. My chest tightened at his struggle.

Still clasped in my hand, my phone rang. The ID showed an unrecognized caller. It rang again.

"Aren't you going to answer that?" Dusty asked.

Wagner had already put up a roadblock between us. I wasn't ready for another. The phone rang again. I had to remember to put it on silent after this call.

"Go ahead," Dusty said. "It might be important."

"Hello," I said and shook my head at Dusty.

"Hey, Hon, Conor here. I just hit town."

"Wrong number." I hit the end button before I could process what I'd done. I switched the phone off. "See not important."

Great! My soon-to-be ex-husband. Any other time I'd ream him out, but all I cared about now was this man lying before me. "Do you remember anything of those days you were tied up?"

Dusty shifted his shoulders. His discomfort with not remembering was bothering him. "I remember meditating. I remember preparing for death."

"Whoa, what? Preparing to die?"

"It's a Buddhist thing. I tried to change my perspective to see things in a more positive, compassionate way."

"Two killers had you tied up and drugged. What's positive about that?"

"It wasn't about them. It was about dying with a calmness of mind. Death is eventual. Buddhists believe it's better to embrace it and go into it with loving mindfulness."

"Poppycock."

Dusty laughed, deep and loud. Then he started coughing. I got up and gave him an ice cube. He still wasn't allowed water.

"Where did that word come from?" he asked when he'd settled down.

"It's something Haylee's mom says."

I was just glad to hear him laugh. If the kiss had come from his heart, and I felt it had, he'd remember. Maybe not today, maybe not tomorrow, but soon.

The End
©2013

About the Author

Nicola Trwst has a gypsy heart. She currently
resides in California, but has lived in Virginia,
Georgia, France, and Canada. She loves languages
and speaks several, including Pig Latin. Due to an
overactive imagination, her stories thread many
genres such as mystery, thriller, paranormal, and
contemporary. Her short stories have appeared in
several anthologies.

Discover more of Nicola's work at www.nicolatrwst.com

Also by Nicola Trwst
Bayou Nights (2013)

Briana Kaleigh Mysteries
The Belvedere Club (2012)
Bolinas Bongo (2013)

Continue reading for the opening of Nicola's
suspense thriller *Bayou Nights*

Bayou Nights
Prologue

He'd pinned her to the soft earth. Caught her unawares. She squirmed, turning her head inch by inch. Her hair, wedged beneath his hand, pulled at the roots. She bit into his fat wrist like a snapping turtle, tearing and holding until he rolled off.

"Filthy whore."

She sat up and sucked in a breath. Ah, sweet summer air. "You two bricks shy or what? That ain't no way to treat a lady. Now, get me up."

Baring his teeth, he turned away. "I'm sorry."

"You should be."

The blow came fast, knocking the breath from her lungs. Something deep inside cracked. She gasped. Gulped. Searing pain shot across her chest. Tears bubbled up. His other fist caught her upside the head. A flash of white lightning behind her eyelids and then everything went dark.

Her eyes burned. That was the first thing she noticed. They wouldn't open. For a second or two, she struggled to figure out where she was. Then, she remembered.

Panic squirmed like mud worms in her chest, but she lay still, listening, and taking in every noise. She must have passed out. Now, she felt like she was floating on a lily pad. The moon was gone or maybe it wasn't. With her eyes stuck shut, she couldn't much tell.

The night's cooling breeze raked her raw skin. The air was thick with the scent of night-blooming flowers.

The Cadillac's door slammed, its heavy sound carrying across the empty field. She stiffened. Bit her lip to keep from crying. The motor roared to life. She listened as it faded with the distance. She listened until the hum sounded as if it was coming from inside her head.

She'd liked the car. Flashy. She liked flashy. Before tonight, she'd liked him, too. Hell, everyone did. Was high in the cotton, but could hold his own. Always left decent tips.

Damn, she knew how to pick 'em.

Weeping sounds pulsed up from her throat, but she couldn't feel the tears. Her face was wet, sticky wet. But where were the tears? Why weren't there tears?

She caught her breath. No time to panic. She had to hightail it out of there. But her chest really, really hurt. He had fists like cinderblocks. Just lifting her arm felt like someone shoving a knife down between her ribs.

She lay still again, smelling the night gladiolus. Drifting.

"What was that?" Her twitch sent a ripple of hurt through her chest. A bullfrog croaked. Not close, but close enough. She must have fallen asleep again.

He was gone. He'd driven away. Hadn't he? Her thoughts were jumbled tighter than a ball of yarn.

She was cold. Too cold for this time of year. And her stomach felt queasy. She just wanted to lie a spell, but she'd best get over to the road. Her eyelids felt swollen to the touch, the left worse than the right.

"Ouch!" She couldn't find her left cheekbone. Was like it wasn't there. Weird. Maybe her face was just too swollen.

That jerk. Wait till she told Clyde what he'd done. He'd go after Mr. Fancy Pants with a stick.

Was that another car? She listened, her limbs tensing.

Her dress was bunched up around her breasts. Thank God she wasn't naked. Probably couldn't make it all the way home, but if she wanted to get help, she'd have to get over to the road. No one would find her back here.

Let's go back in the field, away from the road. It's more romantic.

And she'd followed like a giggling school girl. When would she learn? Why the hell did men always have to hit! Was she wearing a sign that said "*punch here*"?

And this guy was the champ. Hit harder than her ex on a good day.

More tears that had no place to go welled beneath the lids. Was that footsteps? Was it her imagination? She was breathing too fast. She needed to calm down and get out of here. Fast. She pushed up with her hands, but lightning bolts of pain shot through her chest. Oh, hell.

That wasn't going to work. Hurt too bad. She'd have to roll over and crawl. It was the only way.

"God, I'm done with men. Done, I said." Her voice sounded strange, garbled. She rolled over and pushed up to her hands and knees. "I know I said that just a few weeks ago, but this time I mean it. Lord, if you can see fit to get me home, I will never so much as look at another man."

"I can help you with that," said a familiar voice.

She swung her head toward the sound, her eyelids still glued shut. Her trembling arms risked giving out. She hunched back, rested on her knees.

"Thought you could help me relax, but you let me down, Sweetheart."

Her lower body still throbbed. He'd torn her up down there. "I done what I could. Please, don't hit me again."

"No, you didn't. You kept passing out. And I'm still in need."

"Okay, okay, well…" It'd hurt worse, but she couldn't take another fist. "I can do it better. Let's try again. Just don't hit me."

"Heard you're through with men."

"Not you." She gulped in a breath, the words frozen on her lips.

"That's good, Sugar, but I can't have you telling tales, can I?"

"I won't tell nobody. Promise, please Mr.—"

The kick caught her between her ribs and her stomach. She was flying, weightless. And for an instant, pain free. Then, thunk. She crashed.

Facedown. Arms splayed.

She spit away the grass. Coughed. She coughed again, but couldn't clear her throat. Couldn't catch a breath. She struggled to her knees, fighting for air.

There was none.

www.ingramcontent.com/pod-product-compliance
Lightning Source LLC
Chambersburg PA
CBHW050021180626
46810CB00002B/526